LIES & Seduction

ALLISON CASSATTA

Dreamspinner Press

Published by
Dreamspinner Press
5032 Capital Circle SW
Ste 2, PMB# 279
Tallahassee, FL 32305-7886
USA
http://www.dreamspinnerpress.com/

ISBN: 978-1-62380-144-1

Printed in the United States of America
First Edition
November 2012

eBook edition available
eBook ISBN: 978-1-62380-145-8

This book is dedicated
to the friends and fans who
have continuously supported me.

Thank you for helping me make
my dreams come true.

ACKNOWLEDGMENTS

Thank you to the amazing staff and editors at Dreamspinner Press. Huge thanks to everyone who continues to follow my work and support me no matter what. As always, a huge thank you to Jessica Murchie for proofreading all my work and giving me constructive feedback.

AUTHOR'S NOTE

Dear Readers,

In this book I've created a fictional club—just outside the French Quarter in New Orleans—where a lot of questionable activity takes place. That's not to say I've seen this type of behavior in any of the New Orleans nightclubs or gay clubs I've visited. I'm not trying to stereotype or assume this kind of lifestyle comes with being gay. It may for some, but certainly not all. It is important to remember this is purely a work of fiction.

When selecting this series of books, please keep in mind that they are meant to be gritty and you as a reader may not agree with the decisions the characters have made. I assure you they're made for a reason and not just put in there for shock factor. Please remember you might absolutely despise the characters for the things they've done, but *everyone* deserves to find true love. Everyone deserves a happily ever after, even the bad guys.

Thank you,
Allison Cassatta
www.allisoncassatta.com

1

"LOOK at that man standing to the side of the stage, the one with the dark blazer." Lance's arm perched on Jason's shoulder, finger extended, pointing out an exceptionally gorgeous man with perfect sandy-blond hair and perfect pink lips, hiding in the dark beside the main stage. "Is that who I think it is?"

Jason narrowed his green eyes on the mass of darkened forms surrounding the main stage. He sifted through his ecstasy high until he could almost see the guy Lance pointed out. "Where do I know his face from?"

"I think that's Bradley Britt. You know, the news guy?" Lance offered, still peering over Jason's shoulder, though now he had his arm wrapped around Jason's chest.

The warmth from Lance's flesh radiated through the thin tank top covering Jason's firm chest. His sense of touch had spiraled into hypersensitive just after dropping the X less than half an hour ago, and having Lance pressed so tight against his backside had his cock coming to life. He would ignore it for now because he had a job to do, and honestly, he had a rule about getting involved with people at work. Just seemed like a really bad business practice, especially when he had to play the bad guy because one of the dancers had gotten out of line.

He gave a little shrug and shimmy to back Lance off, then took a step forward and said, "What the hell is he doing in here?"

"Maybe...." Lance stopped and thought about it for a moment. "Well, this isn't officially a gay club. Maybe he's meeting a friend or something."

Jason rolled his eyes. Straight men didn't go to Sin & Seduction to "meet friends." Sure, it wasn't a gay club, he'd give Lance that, but straight men didn't darken the doors of that place, not unless they had a dirty little secret hiding in the darkest corner of a forbidden closet. And even then, the club was way too popular to risk an unintended coming out.

Arching his brow, Jason tapped his forefinger against his chin as he devoured Mr. Newsman with his stare.

"He's fucking hot, you know?" Lance said as he closed the distance between them. His hand caressed Jason's side, fingers gingerly patting the hard edge of his hip, chin now lying on his shoulder. Those gentle touches made Jason's nerves tingle a bit more.

"Don't you have a show to get ready for, Golden Boy?"

"You're no fun, you know?"

"No. I know it's my job to make sure your pretty ass is on stage and looking as good as you can before your music starts. Now, get over there and get your costume on, pronto."

Jason snapped his fingers and as soon as Lance turned to march away, he gave the dancer's firm little buttocks a quick swat. Lance leapt, whimpering as he reached back to rub away the sting.

The kid padded toward the rack of costumes. Jason's eyes shifted back to the man in the black blazer. Bradley Britt stood there with his arms crossed and his hair perfectly styled in some cocky, conservative coif that begged to be tousled. He watched anything and everything around him, though he never turned his head. The look was nothing more than a façade of confidence, and possibly arrogance, hiding a bottomless pit of fear and nervousness. No, Bradley Britt hadn't come to Sin & Seduction to meet a friend. He'd come to sate a hunger he hid from his wife and kids.

Mr. All-American Beauty watched as the next dancer took the stage. Music flared, bass pounding out some type of tribal club mix. "Amante Quente," better known as Davi to his coworkers, was the club's newest import. For reasons he'd failed to truly explain to the curious ears of the Sin & Seduction staff, he'd left Portugal in search of more open-minded freedom. How the hell he'd landed in New Orleans was anyone's guess. Didn't really matter; everyone loved the Latino beauty with the body of Adonis and hair like black silk, and Bradley Britt appeared to be no exception to the rule.

Jason smiled and shook his head as he stared. Apparently, Mr. Britt had a thing for phallic splendor. His eyes locked on Davi's muscled thighs, then wound up to the bulge of black satin at his crotch, then further up his body. Jason couldn't help being amused by the sight of that not-so-straight man drinking in a piece of art like Amante Quente.

He loved being so right about the newcomers.

"Is this okay?" Lance asked. The sound of his voice pulled Jason's attention back to the dressing room. Golden Boy stood there holding a police uniform, the same uniform Sweet Heat had worn almost a year and a half ago.

"Whatever." Jason shook his head and rolled his eyes. *The new ones always go after the corniest outfits,* he thought, but actually said, "It'll work out fine. People seem to have a hard-on for cop fantasies around here. Now, go get your ass ready. You have to be on stage in ten minutes."

As soon as Lance ducked around the corner to change, Jason looked back down at his clipboard. The dancers' schedule lay on top of the pile of paper clipped to the board. He hated not seeing his name there. What he wouldn't give to shake his shit all over that stage again... and right in front of Bradley Britt. But since Jason had hurt his back, he hadn't been able to dance. He was such an asset to the club, though, they'd kept him around to help with stuff like managing the stage and the dancers. He guessed they considered him a house mother—or father—of sorts.

He flipped the pages back, knowing the one thing he'd been so strategically avoiding would be waiting to glare in his face from the very bottom of the stack and remind him of what might be the biggest regret of his life. He'd gotten the RSVP card in the mail a few days ago, but couldn't bring himself to respond to it. Every time he read the words, he cringed. It made his jaw tick with aggravation.

"A commitment ceremony, really, Jansen?"

According to the card, Dorian and Jansen planned to take the plunge and commit themselves to each other. *What a ridiculous notion.* Jason had no trouble convincing himself the terrible two were doomed because he'd been against that relationship—train wreck—from the start. Not without good reason, though. Dorian had been a complete prick to Jansen, and the silly boy had been so blinded by lust, he never really saw it.

Jason sighed and shook his head as he let the pages flop back down to cover the card. In all honesty, he wanted to be happy for Jansen. God, if anyone deserved to be loved, it was him, but he couldn't help worrying, and maybe being a little jealous. That man, that thug—Dorian Grant—had stolen away the only person Jason had ever really cared about. Now he felt all lonely and empty inside. The club became his only real escape, and yet, the place still reminded him of his best friend.

At first, Jansen made sure to come around every so often. They might've met for lunch or dinner, maybe spent a night partying in the French Quarter while Dorian handled the affairs of his businesses, but even those trips became few and far between. Jason hated that. They were supposed to be best friends, and now, just because Jansen had found his true love, Jason was supposed to be alone?

Bullshit!

"Jason, are you coming to help me or not?" Lance whined.

"Oh, for fuck's sake. Didn't your mommy teach you how to get dressed, little boy?"

As soon as Jason rounded the corner into the backstage dressing room, his angry footsteps came to a dead stop. Kneeling down on the filthy concrete floor was Lance, completely naked and half-hard. The fluorescent lights above rained white light down over his bronze muscles, accenting every glorious mound and sinew. It made his blond hair a pale shade of gold. Slowly, his stark blue eyes traveled up Jason's body until their gazes met. Golden Boy's lips curled in a devious smirk.

The sight made Jason's cock twitch. It'd been a long damn time since he'd done anything more than jerk off, and Jansen had been the last boy he'd fucked. It was a pity lay and he knew it, but that hadn't made it any less amazing, hadn't kept him from getting off.

Lance reached down and wrapped his fingers around his hardened shaft. His tongue slowly slid out between his parted lips. He seductively licked a moist sheen across his mouth as he eyed Jason's crotch. The view of Golden Boy was damn appealing, kneeling on the floor in all his naked glory like a waiting and well-trained slave, and for a moment, Jason became lost in the idea of that tongue sweeping around his holiest of holies.

"You gonna stand there all night or let me blow you while you're still high?" Lance asked. "I have to be on stage in"—his eyes turned toward the wall clock as the "in" purred from his plump, pursed lips—"eight minutes." He looked back at Jason, at the blatant bulge threatening to burst through his zipper. Lance smiled. "I can make you come in four."

Without a second thought, Jason's fingers went straight to his zipper, and he pounded right up to Lance's kneeling body. His hard-on sprang free, slapping against Lance's open mouth. "You have three minutes," he growled as his hand locked behind Golden Boy's head.

He drilled hard into the kid's mouth, so hard the tip of his cock pushed against Lance's throat. Fuck. He didn't gag. *Screw it*, Jason thought. *Just go with it. You need this.*

Jason rolled his hips, keeping his hand locked around the nape of Lance's neck. He closed his eyes and went with it, pushing harder and faster with each thrust. All that beautiful warm heat sheathed his shaft, and every time Lance took a breath, the brush of hot air made Jason's cock throb a little harder.

One hand suddenly cupped his sac, giving Jason's twin jewels a soft squeeze, while the other reached around his outer thigh. Not that he really cared about what a set of hands were up to—he was too taken by the tongue swirling over his swollen shaft—but then he felt one finger slip inside of him and he gasped.

Jason wasn't a bottom, not by a damn sight, and this kid had just made an assumption he wasn't too fond of, until Lance's finger grazed that special spot inside a man's body that could bring him to his knees with a mind-blowing release. Jason gripped Lance's shoulder with his free hand while the other stayed locked around the back of Lance's neck. His knees started to weaken. His thighs began quaking, and the new sensation was enough to send him over the edge quickly.

Lance took him to the hilt as he eased his finger in and out of Jason's ass. A hard moan rumbled up through Jason's chest. His hand fisted Lance's long golden hair, pulling his head back before slamming his cock down the kid's throat again. With each thrust, his sac bounced against Lance's chin.

"I'm about to come," Jason rasped as his head rolled back.

Lance's finger brushed the buried nub again as his head bobbed up and down, up and down. Jason could feel the pulsing of his shaft growing thicker against Lance's tongue. And with a thunderous roar, he shot his load straight down Golden Boy's throat. The kid swallowed every single damn drop.

Between the ecstasy high and the orgasm, Jason's mood would probably be on the warmer side of sunny for the rest of the night. Hell, he might even join the crowd and enjoy the show for a moment. Who knew? At this point, the possibilities were endless.

With a pop, Jason's flaccid dick fell out of Lance's mouth. He stumbled back, sank down in the dressing-room chair, and fought to even his breathing. "Holy shit," he croaked, hand rubbing back and forth across his chest. "That was surprisingly amazing."

"Glad I could be of service, baby," Lance said with a smirk as he pulled his royal-blue G-string into place.

"Don't gloat. I'm not going to take it easy on you or give you special treatment just because you got me off." Jason's lazy eyes slowly lifted to the clock. He said, "Get dressed. You have two minutes."

Lance laughed as he pulled his tear-away pants up over his slender, yet toned, thighs. He kept his triumphant blue stare locked on Jason. "You know, I would bet my earnings tonight that you would make a perfect dom."

"And you'll never find out."

Lance feigned a disappointed pout. "Why not?"

"Because, I don't get involved with co-workers. It never works out. A rule you might want to learn." Jason stood from the chair. "You have one minute. Get your ass in place."

He stalked back to the edge of the stage just in time to catch the last of Davi's number. Bradley Britt still hadn't moved from his spot, though he looked a little more comfortable now. His arms still crossed his chest, but his shoulders rounded slightly. His lips held a hint of a smile. His eyes stayed glued to Amante Quente.

Jason scoured the crowd. Most people were too involved with the gyrating body on stage, but a few had taken notice of one of New Orleans' most notable reporters. They whispered and pointed, obviously gossiping about Britt. So, Jason had a choice: sit there and watch them make assumptions, or do the man a solid and get him out of the limelight.

2

IF ANYONE asked, Jason walked out into the club's main floor simply to work the room, not to scope out the hottie newsguy. The excuse worked. The managers had asked him to take care of their club, make it the one place everyone wanted to be. He was supposed to go down to the floor and watch the show, then up to the VIP booths to do the same. Management wanted the dancers to look good from every angle and Jason took pride in bringing the show to life.

That attention to detail was one of the myriad reasons Sin & Seduction sat at the peak of social nightlife in New Orleans. The VIP booths, the ambience, the booze, and the stunning view were but a few of the others. Everyone wanted their chance to see if the rumors were true, if people really did sneak off for a quick fuck with one of the dancers, if drugs floated around like candy. They wanted their slice, but thankfully for the old-school regulars, management didn't let just anyone in the door.

Jason floated out to the dance floor. A mob of people rushed the stage just as Golden Boy pranced out to the pole. Sirens blared. Bass pounded. The lights flashed in blue, red, and green. The dancer gyrated, ground his crotch against the pole, and the crowd went wild. Very good. Just what Jason wanted to see.

His eyes cut toward the mysterious newsman, who still stood at the edge of the stage. From down there, no one would've been able to make out his identity, not with any degree of certainty. Darkness cloaked his face and drenched his solid form. That explained why only a few people had been chattering about him.

Licking his lips, Jason took a few steps closer, acting as if he was simply doing his job, but he wanted a better view of Bradley Britt. He stood next to the man, kept his stare on the stage. It wasn't until Britt turned his head that their gazes met. His powerful hazel eyes ripped the breath right from Jason's body. They stopped his heart midbeat.

"I…." Jason's mouth opened but his mind failed to keep up. He held out his hand for a shake. Britt took it. "Is it safe for you to be seen here?" he somehow managed to choke out.

"What do you mean?" Britt asked. His voice sounded so rich and velvety, like smooth milk chocolate or a martini made to perfection. It made Jason's body tingle in all the right places.

"You don't want a scandal, do you? This place isn't exactly known for its moral fortitude, ya know?"

"Right. What would you suggest? I'm rather enjoying the show here."

Jason turned, pointed his long skinny finger up to the balconies in the back. Fluorescent blue bar lights haloed black silhouettes. Even the faces leaning all the way forward were completely indistinguishable. He said, "That's the best view, but you obviously won't be able to touch the dancers." He turned back and gave Mr. Newsman a lascivious, eye-twinkling grin, and with a seductive purr he said, "Though, if you wanted to touch something or someone, I'm sure we could arrange something for you."

His fingers carefully wove around Britt's hand. Jason took a step back, keeping his bright green eyes on Bradley Britt's gaze. He waited, wondered if the man would follow him up to the private VIP booth. He wondered if Britt would let him cross the line, or if he was just another straight reporter checking out the lewdness of another New Orleans nightclub. God, he hoped the latter wasn't true.

"You say it's safe up there, huh?" Britt's thick voice whispered against Jason's ear, hot breath brushing across his flesh in a way that made the fine hairs at the nape of his neck stand on end.

"Um—" Jason cleared his throat. "—yeah. It's completely private, guarded and everything."

They took the steps slowly, Jason walking in front but still holding Britt's hand. They passed the bouncer, then the first booth, but kept walking. That booth still belonged to Dorian Grant, and he sometimes brought Jansen back to the club to relive the early days of their relationship. The last thing Jason wanted was to be hilt deep in the reporter just to have Jansen and his fiancé catch them in the act.

That might be wishful thinking, being buried in Britt's body and whatnot.

Jason walked him down to the very last booth, farthest away from the few occupied ones. Not that it mattered. The seats were high enough even someone standing would have a hard time stealing a peek. The kind of shit that went down in those booths wasn't usually safe for public consumption, Jason knew. Not only had he pulled cleanup duty a time or two, but he'd been part of the party on more than one occasion.

"Is this okay?" he asked.

Britt nodded as he slid in around the table. He sat back at the farthest edge, close to the balcony so he could see the stage. Jason slid in beside him, watching as the reporter glued his stare on Golden Boy's performance.

For whatever stupid reason, he felt a pang of jealousy. Britt wasn't his and would never be his, but the fact he paid attention to a man more than fifty feet away instead of the one right beside him really tweaked Jason out. Not to mention, it confused the hell out of him. That made Jason believe the man actually came to the club for a story and not a good time, and if that were the case, then Jason needed to figure out a way to get the newsguy out of there ASAP.

"So what brought you here tonight?" Jason asked carefully.

"Just wanted to see the show," Britt said, barely pulling his eyes away from the stage.

"Then you're doing a story on Sin & Seduction?"

"What?" Britt's head whipped back. "What? No. God, no. I was um… curious."

"Curious?"

"Yes, curious. Why? Do you ask all your clientele why they're here?"

"No. Only the straight reporters."

"What makes you think I'm straight?"

Jason reached over and slowly stroked Britt's ring finger. A white band of flesh circled that very important finger just below the knuckle. He could tell a wedding ring normally hid the pale skin. Jason stared down as he said, "Have a picture of your wife and kids in your wallet too?"

Britt lowered his head. His Adam's apple bobbed against the flashing lights blazing from the stage. "You don't understand," he said with defeat as he pulled his finger away from Jason's touch.

"And it's not my business to understand."

"Don't judge me."

"Why would you think I'm judging you?"

"Because everyone judges me." Britt's hard hazel eyes seemed to darken as he met Jason's deep green gaze. An uncomfortable moment of silence fell between them as they stared at each other. "I can't open my mouth without someone judging me. They look at the clothes I wear, the music I listen to, the food I eat, the people I'm with. My home life isn't even my own. Privacy is a foreign thought in my world. You want to know why I came here?" Jason nodded. "I came here to escape."

The sad desperation in his voice was almost astonishing. Though Jason couldn't relate, he could damn sure sympathize. He touched Britt's hand one more time, hoping to give the man a little comfort and reassurance. "Look, anything that happens here will stay here. Up here, you'll have all the privacy you want, okay?"

"But how do I…?"

"I'll give you a VIP card. You can use the private entrance with it." Jason fished a golden card from the back pocket of his jeans. He laid it down on the table right beside the reporter's hand. He looked down, then back up at Britt and said, "No one will ever see you, Mr. Britt. You're completely safe, I promise."

Letting his breath go, the reporter looked down at the card. He said, "You're sure?" Jason nodded. Britt picked up the little golden plastic card then slid it into his jacket pocket. He didn't say anything, though; he didn't have to. The "thank you" was written all over his stare, the gratitude evident in his obvious relief.

He turned his eyes back to the stage, back to Golden Boy. Jason's jaw clenched. He couldn't take this anymore. It was one thing not to be able to dance, but another thing to be so blatantly dismissed. He slid to the edge of the booth and started to stand when a hand on his wrist stopped him from moving.

"Don't go," Britt said in an almost pleading voice.

"I…." Jason frowned. "I need to check the stage. I need to make sure the next dancer is ready. I, um… can come right back."

"Please?"

"Sure thing, Mr. Britt."

"Call me Brad, okay? Just Brad."

Jason nodded slowly, eyes lingering on that beautiful hazel stare and those perfect pink lips. He imagined those lips pressing kisses all over his body, surrounding his cock and milking his release. He imagined their mouths locked as their hands explored every inch of each other's flesh.

"Brad it is then," Jason said in a hoarse voice. He shifted his hips to relieve the sudden pressure in his groin. No way could he explain away his sudden hard-on. He kicked his thumb over his shoulder, nervously clearing his throat. "I have to go, but I'll be back."

Brad gave him the most marvelous smile he'd ever seen, and Jason had to go because he knew if he didn't, he would never make it to that stage.

3

FASTER than he'd ever run before, Jason went back to the stage. He made it in time to catch the third number coming off. Everything still moved like fluid. Everyone was still on time.

He huffed and puffed, doubled over, and gripped his knees to catch his breath. Golden Boy's laughter made Jason raise his head. "What's so funny?" he panted.

"You. Why are you breathing so hard?"

Jason's brow quirked, lips pinched together as he scowled up at Lance's half-naked body. Not that it was Lance's business, but Jason explained, leaving out a few unimportant details. "I got tied up in the VIP section. I ran back because I'd missed too much already."

"Tied up in VIP, huh?" Lance smirked, arms crossed over his chest.

"Don't, okay? What I do is none of your business."

"Was he good?"

"Who?"

"Bradley Britt. I saw you at the front of the stage with him. Then, he disappeared the same time you did. Now, you tell me you've been busy in VIP. I'm not that damn stupid."

"He's straight," Jason said flatly. "He's married."

"Then why in the fuck is he hanging out here? Is he doing a story?"

"He was curious, just wanted to check the place out."

"Curious, huh?" A devious grin spread across Golden Boy's face. A twinkle appeared in his rich blue eyes. "Maybe I can settle his curiosity for him."

Lance grabbed a robe to cover himself and his blue G-string. He glanced in the mirror, fixed his slightly tousled, slightly dampened hair, then started to saunter right past Jason as if he were going to go up to the balcony and have his way with Brad.

"I don't think so," Jason said as he reached out and grabbed Lance's arm. "You're going to stay the hell away from him. You have to be back on stage in twenty minutes." Lance huffed, shoulders rounding with disappointment. He glared at Jason like he hated him, not that Jason cared. "And you're not going to say shit to anyone about seeing Britt here. If you do, tonight will be the last time your feet ever touch that stage."

"You wouldn't."

"Wouldn't I?"

Lance rolled his eyes. An exaggerated sigh escaped his pursed lips as he stomped back over to the vanities where the other dancers had gathered. They all huddled around Davi, the import from Portugal everyone had fallen in love with the moment he'd stepped through the door. They fawned over him in an almost sickening display. Whatever. Jason didn't mind as long as the dancers got their asses on stage when they were supposed to.

Grabbing the schedule, Jason walked toward the huddle and said, "Listen up, girls. Right now, we're on time. Can we please keep it that way?"

"Yes, mommy," sarcastically sang from all their lips.

"Good. I'll be out on the floor, watching the show."

"You mean up on the balcony, putting on a show of your own?" Lance teased.

Jason narrowed his glare on Lance, jaw clenched. He didn't have to say a word. His look alone threatened enough, and Lance wasn't so blind he didn't see it. Golden Boy lowered his head submissively. "Like I said, I'll be roaming the club. I have my phone if any of you need me."

He slammed the clipboard down on the vanity so hard the clap echoed off the cinderblock walls of the backstage area. Every single dancer jumped. Their eyes widened, watching an otherwise mild-mannered man storm away. Little things like that kept the fear of God in those poor boys, kept them behaving like they had some sense.

Club lights flashed. The music changed again. The MC's booming voice churned and whirled through the air as he announced yet another name the crowd seemed all too excited to see. Their persistent yelling and screaming pierced Jason's eardrums. His eye twitched, body cringing as one overly enthusiastic patron screamed the dancer's name right in his ear.

At least upstairs he could escape most of the noise.

He headed straight for the booth where he'd left Bradley Britt sitting alone. Two empty martini glasses in the center of the table immediately caught his eye. Then he saw Brad tipping back another one while yet another sat on a cocktail napkin where Jason had been sitting before he'd left. Brad gave him a wickedly handsome grin.

"I ordered drinks," the reporter said as he patted the empty spot beside him. "I tried to wait for you, but you took too long."

"Sorry. Those boys can be a bunch of rowdy children sometimes." Jason sat down and Brad slid the cocktail toward him. "I probably shouldn't."

"It's one drink."

"And one drink leads to another, then another, maybe a hit of X or a line or two, then…."

"I don't do drugs."

"Oh," Jason said flatly, though he knew he had complete shock written all over his face. It had always been safe to assume most of the patrons of Sin & Seduction didn't hesitate to partake in any variety of mind-altering cocktails. He sure as hell didn't expect a local celebrity to be the exception to the rule. "One drink."

"One drink." Brad held up his martini. They clanked glasses and he said, "Cheers."

"Cheers." Jason smiled. They both tipped their glasses to the air, apple martini spilling down their throats. "Delicious." Jason sat his glass down and turned back toward Britt. He totally lusted over the reporter and probably didn't hide it worth a shit, but Jason rarely tucked his feelings away. He normally didn't give a damn who knew what. He normally put it all out there... unless Jansen was involved. And now, apparently, Bradley Britt would get the same treatment.

"So, where were we?" Jason asked, propping his arm against the table.

"Talking. But... I would rather not talk about me."

"Then what would you rather do?"

"This." Brad's strong, slender hands clamped down on Jason's cheeks. He pressed his lips to Jason's mouth, tongue licking across the seam and begging for entrance.

Jason barely had time to gasp before the reporter stole his lips. The surprise of it made his heart leap and his breath hitch. He sure as hell never expected Brad to make a move on him. He honestly thought he would have to take the first step if he wanted to get up close and personal in a downright dirty way with the guy. But damned if Bradley Britt hadn't come on to him, hadn't stolen his lips like they belonged to only him.

Brad's tongue slipped between Jason's slightly parted lips and licked at the roof of his mouth. It swirled and twirled and danced, tasting the furthest depths and the darkest corners. If Jason were to be completely honest, he would admit how good it felt to be kissed again. He would admit to himself that the surprise and the passion made things low in his body stir with excitement. He would've given himself to the moment and just let it happen, but he couldn't. He couldn't deny that something wasn't right, and he'd made damn good practice of avoiding sticky situations in the past. No need to stop now.

The kiss broke with a mutual gasp. Jason stared, absolutely shocked speechless. A ragged breath somehow managed to wind its way up through his body. Fingers shaking, he wiped the edges of his mouth then said, "What the hell was that?"

"I'm sorry. I assumed...."

"What are you trying to do here?"

"I don't know. I thought maybe we could...." Brad shrugged his shoulders, enough innuendo to lead Jason straight down the path of carnal knowledge, or the promise of it anyway.

"But you're married. Does your wife know about your—"

"Curiosity?"

"If that's what you want to call it."

"She knows I occasionally like to go out for drinks after work. She knows I come in late sometimes."

"So, you've been living a lie? You've been cheating on her?"

"I've never had sex outside of our marriage."

If Jason's eyes could've widened more, they would have. Mr. Britt had just become twice as confusing as he was before, and probably ten times more complicated. For a long moment, Jason sat speechless, only staring at the other man because he couldn't manage anything more. He knew if he opened his mouth, something stupid and possibly cruel would come out. He knew if he tried to make sense of the puzzle sitting beside him, it would completely screw up everything he thought he knew about people.

"Are you going to say something?" Brad asked.

"I don't know what to say. I thought…. You kissed me. Why would you kiss me if you didn't want to fuck me? Do you even know if you like sex with men?"

"Yeah, I like sex with men." Brad suddenly had a droll expression on his face. "You think I would've made an advance if I didn't?"

"Honestly, I have no clue," Jason said as he sank down against the leather seating. He raked his hands through his hair, but a long auburn tendril managed to escape. Brad leaned over and pushed the fallen hair back behind Jason's ear. "What are you doing, Brad? What exactly are you looking for?"

"Honestly?" Brad mimicked. Jason nodded. "I miss having sex with a man. Melody and I haven't had sex since our daughter was born. She'll be two in May. I thought I could do it. I thought I could forget about this part of me and be a family man, but I…."

"Why are you telling me this?"

"I have no clue." Brad half laughed. A beautifully crooked smile raised the corner of his perfect pink lips. The smile gave away just how nervous the newsman really was. He obviously didn't make a routine of going out in search of men to play with for a night. Sex aside, Jason wondered if Brad got out as much as he claimed to. "But now that it's out there, I think I feel better about even coming here tonight."

"And when you kissed your wife good-bye, when you climbed in your car and drove out here, what did you expect to happen?"

"I have no clue."

The waiter passed by the table, and Brad called him back for another round.

Brad licked the apple-flavored vodka from his lips, and Jason couldn't help but stare. The man did have amazingly gorgeous lips, high cheekbones, and eyes so deep he thought he would drown in them. Brad didn't even have a hint a facial hair, no five o'clock shadow or anything. He was the epitome of everything Jason deemed to be beautiful. Perfect.

Exactly what he liked in a man.

The waiter came back. He sat one of the green cocktails in front of Jason and one in front of Brad. Jason locked his hand around the stem of the glass and tipped it to the air, drinking down every drop of the martini. It tasted delicious but didn't make the haze of what was going on between them any easier to see through. He took a deep breath and let it out in a ragged gust of apple-scented air. Could he really allow himself to be used just to quench some lurid sexual curiosity? Could he be a dark, dirty secret, a hidden affair? Could he be the one thing that could end a marriage?

"So what now?" he asked in a low voice.

Brad reached beneath the table. His strong hands wrapped over Jason's crotch. He gave it a firm rub, back and forth, back and forth, until Jason's eyes rolled back and his head lolled against the seat. A low moan rumbled up through his body. His sac tightened. His shaft thickened, straining against the thick denim of his suddenly too tight blue jeans. Brad's rich, velvety voice whispered against his ear, "Let me fuck you."

4

"NO," JASON declared in a low, firm voice as he clamped his hand down on Britt's. The sudden pressure only made the reporter squeeze a little harder, which in turn made Jason's cock throb a little more. "You're not going to fuck me."

"What do you mean 'no'?" the reporter asked as he pulled his hand away from Jason's crotch. The expression on Brad's face instantly changed from lust-filled delight to astonishment, like he wasn't used to people telling him no or something. He almost looked offended. Jason opened his mouth to say something, but Brad immediately cut off whatever thought was about to spill from this lips. "You're not seriously turning me down, are you?"

"No, but if anyone here is getting fucked, baby, it's you. Sorry, but that's the way this is going to work."

"Wait. You're not a…?"

"Bottom? No. Not even close."

"Shit. I would've sworn…."

"And why is that?" Jason quirked one thick auburn brow, crossing his arms over his chest. "What, because I'm a little less manly than you are? Because I dance? Because I don't walk around pretending to be straight?"

"No, I—"

"Stop."

Brad's lips sealed tight. His gaze stayed glued to Jason's.

"Fine," Brad finally said. "Fuck me then."

Jesus Christ, the guy kept throwing Jason curveballs. He thought not being a bottom was going to be his out, but then Brad flipped the script on him. He changed the whole damn scenario with three little words.

"Fine," Jason said as he reached in his back pocket for a condom. He tossed it up on the table then went to relieving the pressure on his groin. He unzipped his pants and his cock burst free, completely erect and completely ready to drill deep into Bradley Britt's body.

It didn't matter that Lance had gotten him off less than an hour ago. He was full again and ready to go. Hard as a rock and aching to feel the reporter's tight ass sheathing his shaft. He tore open the little foil square, took the tip of the condom in one hand, and with his thumb and forefinger, rolled the rest of the white rubber down to the base as far as it would go.

"Kneel on the seat," he demanded and Brad immediately lifted to his knees.

Jason reached around his waist, unbuckled his pants then pulled down the zipper of the reporter's high-dollar dress slacks. They pooled at the bend of Brad's knees. That worked just fine. Jason aimed for one spot only and that warm, welcoming opening was well within his sight and haloed by one glorious ass.

He plunged his finger into his mouth, lubed it up good, then slipped his digit inside of Brad's tight opening. Brad hissed, but instantly relaxed. He may've claimed to be a top, but old boy sure seemed damn comfortable being a bottom. Jason eased his finger back and forth, whispering sweet but naughty nothings into the reporter's ear.

As he eased another finger in, he reached his free hand around and gripped Brad's shaft. He slowly stroked up and down, making the rhythm match the scissoring motion of his fingers. Brad's muscle loosened, opening him almost wide enough to take Jason's cock. He wanted to make this as painless as possible, because for some fucked-up reason, Jason wanted him to come back. He wanted to have another rendezvous beneath the cover of darkness and club lights with this gorgeous, forbidden man.

"Ready?" Jason asked.

Brad nodded, trying to subdue his hisses and moans.

Jason lowered his lips to the back of Brad's shoulder as he pressed the tip of his cock to the newsman's puckered opening. The head slipped in, easing through the ring of muscle, and as soon as he was inside, Brad clenched.

"Don't do that," Jason whispered. "Relax."

"I'm trying. I swear, I'm trying."

"Breathe, okay? Relax and breathe. It'll get easier, I promise."

"I know. It's been a while though."

As Jason pushed a little deeper, he said a soft "I know" against the side of Brad's neck. When he felt him finally relax, he pushed a little deeper, and the feel of that muscle gripping his shaft nearly made him come undone. It had been far too long for him as well, and while Lance's blowjob had been pretty fucking amazing, it just didn't compare to being hilt deep inside another man's body like that.

The kisses Jason lavished at the back and side of Brad's neck became more ferocious as the glide in and out of his body became easier. Jason closed his eyes and rolled his hips, not quite meeting the rapid pounding of the club music below, but just as fluid, like the music and the sex had entranced him and fucking had become another form of dance.

He fisted his fingers around Britt's shaft as it thickened against Jason's palm. Stroke. Stroke. Stroke. Up and down. Faster. Faster. The more he tugged at the reporter's cock, the louder Brad moaned. And the louder Brad moaned, the more excited Jason became. They were both on the verge of carnal explosion, both on the verge of release. He felt Brad's sac tighten.

Jason whispered against the back of his ear, "That's it, baby. Let go. Come for me."

And with that, Jason plunged deeper. His hips slapped against Brad's tight, round ass. His cock grazed Brad's sensitive nub, and the reporter cried out to God.

Brad's hands white-knuckled the seat and his head ripped back. He screamed Jason's name as lips and teeth toyed at the side of his jaw. Jason worked over his cock until it was soft and his sac was empty. He growled against Brad's skin as the muscles undulated around his shaft, milking one hell of an orgasm from Jason's body.

He eased out, then gently slipped the condom off his spent dick. The rubber pulling away from his sensitive skin ripped a hard hiss from his parted lips. Brad laid his head against the back of the leather seat, eyes closed as he obviously tried to regain normal breathing. The sight of it put a generous smile on Jason's face.

He tossed the condom onto a cocktail napkin before pulling his pants back up to his hips. "Wait here," he said. "I'll get a wet towel so you can clean up. Would hate for your wife to find any evidence of your indiscretions."

"Thanks," Brad muttered, but Jason was already out of the booth and halfway to the bar.

A few minutes later, Jason came back with a warm cloth. He reached around Brad's body, gripping the reporter's soft cock with his toweled hand

"You want to take care of this?" Jason asked. "I really need to get back to the stage."

"Sure," Brad said in a disappointed voice. The wet cloth switched from Jason's hand to the reporter's, but as soon as Jason started to walk away, Brad called him back. Their eyes met, and for a moment, Jason didn't know what the hell was going on behind that gaze. Though it didn't look like the satisfied internal musings of a man who'd just gotten his dark, dirty fantasy. He asked, "Will I see you again?"

Jason licked his lips then swallowed down an emotion he didn't want to think about. He didn't want another interlude with the reporter. What he wanted was his best friend back. He wanted the confidence to finally tell Jansen how he felt so the kid didn't run off and marry the first goon to act like he cared. Too bad for Brad. He would end up being the victim of Jason's confusion and sadness. He would pay the price for Jason's jealousy.

"Bradley, why don't you do yourself a favor? Go back home to your family. Kiss your kid goodnight. Tell your wife you love her, then have the most sensual, amazing sex you've ever had with her. Forget about this place. Forget about what we did and live your life."

"What if I don't want to?"

"Then, I feel really fucking sorry for you."

"Why?"

"Because, this isn't your life. You have the American Dream. Go home and live it."

Jason didn't give him a chance for rebuttal, didn't wait for another silly question or thought. He didn't run, but he speed-walked away from that booth and away from Bradley Britt—family man and local superstar and brutal reminder that some things just weren't meant to be. He got the hell away from that train wreck before that man's delicious lips and piercing hazel eyes convinced him to buy another ticket.

5

WITH a hard sigh, Jason sank down on the old, ratty couch hidden backstage. He felt like shit, guilty and curious and a little lusty for the reporter. What the fuck had he just done? Seriously. The dude was married. The one rule Jason had always had just flew straight out the window for what? A pair of eyes that could've lit up the sky and a set of lips dreams were made of? Sure wasn't the prestige of screwing someone famous, because that little secret would *never* get out.

He scrubbed his hands over his face, silently cursing himself for what he'd done. His palms hid his expression so no one could possibly overanalyze the shit tumbling around in his brain. He just needed a moment to himself. If he could just have a second to compose himself, then maybe he could carry on with his job like nothing had ever happened.

The seat beside him dipped down. Lance's cologne enveloped him. The scent drowned out everything around him. He didn't bother looking up, but said with a muffled growl, "What?"

"Jesus, what's up your ass?"

Jason's jaw clenched. He turned his head only enough for Lance to see the absolute seriousness and anger in his eyes. "Now's not the time."

"What's wrong?"

"Did you not hear me?" Jason sat up, leaning against the back of the couch. There was still a hard tick in his jaw. He stared up at the rafters. "I don't feel like being fucked with right now."

"What did he do to you?" Lance demanded, brow quirked as his baby blues bored holes in Jason's face. "What did that cock-sucking reporter do to you, Jason?"

"He didn't do anything, okay?" Jason shoved up from the couch and started to storm away, but Lance grabbed his arm. "I swear to God, if you don't leave me alone...."

"I won't, so deal with it." Lance took a deep breath. He turned Jason around to face him. Their gazes met again and Lance's expression pleaded for Jason to talk to him. Yeah, Jason knew that look all too well, had used it on Jansen more than once. "Just tell me he didn't hurt you. Just tell me he didn't do anything to you," Lance begged.

"He didn't do shit. This isn't about him. It's about me. Just drop it, okay?"

"Fine."

"And he never went up there with me. I took him to the VIP booth then came back down to the floor. Okay?"

"Whatever."

"No." Jason gripped Lance's shoulders, eyes narrowing with authority. "Not 'whatever'. We weren't together."

"Fine. You weren't together." Lance pulled away from Jason's grip. They stared at each other for a long moment before Lance finally said, "I hope you're not going to get yourself wrapped up with him. You said it yourself, he's married. He's straight."

"What makes you think I'd get wrapped up with him?"

"Because I know you." Lance lightly thumped Jason's chest, right over his heart. "Sometimes, you let this get in the way and you don't think clearly. Just look at Jansen."

"That shit is none of your business. Jansen is my best friend."

"Tell me it doesn't hurt. Tell me you aren't waiting for him to come running back."

"Fuck off," Jason growled, shoving Lance away.

"Tell me you aren't waiting for Dorian Grant to screw up so you can tell Jansen the truth about your feelings," Lance yelled. Half the faces in the dressing area turned their way, curious eyes and ears paying full attention.

Jason flipped his middle finger up over his shoulder and kept walking. If he didn't get the hell out of there, he'd lose his temper for sure, and he couldn't guarantee he wouldn't knock the shit out of Lance.

He made his way to that back door, far from the club music and prying ears, far from the dancers and patrons. Then he reached in his pocket and fished out his phone. No way in hell could he stay the rest of the night. He couldn't keep doing his job if he tried, not after everything he'd been through already.

"Daniel," he said as soon as he heard his boss's voice on the other end. "This is Jason. I'm taking the rest of the night off. The stage is on schedule, so there's nothing to worry about."

"You okay?" Daniel's deep voice made the tiny speaker in Jason's phone crackle.

"Yeah. I'm fine. Just... I gotta get out of here. I'm not feeling so hot."

"Okay then. You'll be here tomorrow, yeah?"

"Yes, sir. I'll be in early to make up for leaving tonight."

"Don't worry about it, son. Get some rest. We'll see you tomorrow."

"Thanks," Jason said before hanging up the phone. He slipped it back in his pocket then pulled his keys out.

A thought stopped the shuffle of his feet. Where would he go? What would he do? Home still reminded him of Jansen. His thoughts were already winding down that gravelly road, and tonight, they'd reached the downhill slope. He was stuck there and about to tumble down uncontrollably thanks to Golden Boy.

And when he did somehow manage to push Jansen out of his thought process, Bradley Britt popped up. That was two major life fuckups and he hadn't even hit thirty yet.

"Dammit," Jason muttered as he pulled his cell phone back out of his pocket and sank down to the curb. A streetlight hung over him, bathing his body in a copper glow. As Jason absently kicked the back of his boot against the curb, the heel of his boot scraped back and forth along the moist, filthy pavement. He was actually considering calling Jansen.

What the hell?

His finger hovered over his best friend's name. It was well after midnight already. Would Jansen be asleep? Would he be in bed... with Dorian? Would the barbarian Jansen fell in love with get pissed if Jason called? He pulled up a new text message. Typed out a quick "You up?" Then hit the send button.

Jason stared down at the phone, waiting for a response. The display would darken, and every time it did, he brushed his thumb across the screen to wake it up again. Not that it would make Jansen respond any faster. All that stupid, weak, hopeful action did was manage to drain his battery quicker.

He hefted himself up from the curb then started toward the back parking lot, back toward where he'd left his little red beater parked. He'd all but given up on Jansen when the phone blared his best friend's ringtone. Jason was a closet Adam Lambert fan, and Jansen had always given him hell about that, but that didn't stop him from setting "If I Had You" as Jansen's ringtone. In the truest part of the chorus, Lambert sang "If I had you, that would be the only thing I'd ever need."

"God, I need to change that," he mumbled right before he answered the phone. "Hello?"

"Hey," Jansen said, his voice hoarse like he'd been asleep or had just gotten laid.

"Sorry for bothering you so late."

"No, it's cool. Dorian and I were just watching a movie. I think I fell asleep on him."

"You, um... feel like getting out for a bit? Maybe get some breakfast or something?"

"Yeah, let me see what Dorian wants to do."

"Can you come by yourself?"

"Sure. Why? Is everything okay?"

"Yeah," Jason swallowed as he leaned against his car. He raked his fingers through his sweat-moistened auburn hair. "I just need... I miss my best friend, okay? Can we meet somewhere to talk?"

"Sure. Wanna meet at the Clover on Bourbon?"

"You know it."

"Alright. I'll be there in thirty."

"See you in thirty," Jason said before ending the call.

Technically, the Clover Grill was walking distance from Sin & Seduction. Though no one in their right mind would make that walk alone in the middle of the night, and Jason wasn't stupid or brave enough to give it a try.

He hopped in his car and swung around in the parking lot, pulled out and headed back toward the French Quarter. It took a while, but eventually he found a well-lit place to park not too far from the hip little corner diner hidden in the French Quarter's rainbow district.

At most hours, it was nearly impossible to get a table, but the wait was always worth it. The food tasted like something right out of mamma's oven. The music always blared just like it did at the club, and every personality in the place was just as colorful as the rainbows they garnered.

"Hey, Marcus," Jason said in passing to the man behind the counter, shaking his ass in front of the grill as he flipped an omelet. He gave Jason a little nod then went back to cooking.

Along the line of windows was the only row of tables, and directly across from that, a counter separated the world from the kitchen. Stools lined the bar for extra seating. Jason went straight to the back, thanking God he'd managed to snag the one open table. He sat down and took a deep breath of bacon and fresh coffee.

Not too many minutes passed before Jansen's face peeked in the open doors. His soft brown eyes wound down the single row of tables. Jason raised his hand and gave a little wave. And when Jansen saw him, the most magical smile curled the edges of his utterly kissable pink lips. His face almost had a glow to it.

The sight tugged Jason's heart. He'd never seen Jansen so happy in all the years they'd known each other. It would've been cruel and selfish to put a damper on that happiness by admitting feelings that could never blossom into something tangible. So he kept them hidden in the deepest place in his heart, where he hid things normal people really didn't want to talk about.

He stood and greeted Jansen with a hug. "You look good."

"I wish I could say the same for you," Jansen said, giving his best friend a quick kiss on the cheek. "You look like you've been through hell."

"Close. I've definitely sinned." Jason laughed.

They both took their seats. The waiter came and went. He took their order, which hadn't changed in three years: ham-and-cheese omelet, hash browns, coffee, and water.

"I fucked a married man," Jason blurted after he felt safe that the coast was clear.

Jansen choked on his water. "You did what?"

"Look." Jason's eyes combed the room. He leaned forward and Jansen leaned with him. In a whisper, he said, "Bradley Britt. I fucked him in a VIP booth at Sins. He's married... to a woman."

Jansen stared with wide eyes, didn't say a damn word, and the way his lips kept fluttering, Jason knew he wanted to say something but didn't know where to begin.

He waited on pins and needles for his best friend to say something... anything. Uncomfortable silence filled the space between them. Jason furiously tapped his foot under the table. He started to fidget with the flatware. "Will you say something, please?"

"Bradley Britt, huh? At least he's gorgeous."

"Yeah. That doesn't help," Jason said with a sigh as he sat back in the little metal chair, arms folded behind his head. "I feel like shit for it."

"So, he's not straight then, huh? Who knew?"

"Don't say anything, okay? I don't want this getting out. Bradley is...."

Jason shut his trap as soon as the waiter returned with their food. The guy asked them if they needed anything else, and they both shook their heads, giving him nervous smiles. He grinned in return before moving on to the next table. Jason didn't open his mouth again until he was satisfied no one could hear them.

"He likes screwing men." Jason shrugged. "Said he hadn't had sex with his wife in two years. He wanted to top me."

"Did you let him?"

"Hell no!"

"Wow."

"Is that all you can say?"

"Are you going to see him again?" Jansen asked before cramming a huge bite of omelet into his mouth.

"No. I told him to go home and forget about Sin & Seduction. I told him to make love to his wife and live his American dream."

"But?"

"But nothing."

"Oh, there's a 'but'. If there wasn't, we wouldn't be here talking about it right now." Jansen's eyes narrowed, head slightly tilted. The fork in his hand clanked against the plate. He crossed his arms over his chest, gave Jason a knowing look, and said, "You want to see him again, don't you?"

Jason nearly choked on his food. "No," he barked, wiping a napkin across his lips as he swallowed down the rest of his food. "He was fun, but that was it. He's married, and you know I am not the type to break up a happy home."

"But it isn't a happy home, is it?"

"He has too much baggage. Plus, he's a local celeb. Could you imagine the scandal?"

"So."

"So nothing. It's not happening."

"You wouldn't even give it a chance? Even if he came to you and told you he only wanted to be with you, you wouldn't consider it?"

"No. Not for a second. He needs to stay with his family."

"What if you're the one person who can make him happy? What if you're the one person who can give him everything he really wants?"

Jason's hard green eyes fixed on Jansen's rich brown gaze. He immediately opened his mouth to argue, but words failed him. They failed him so epically all he could do was sit there and stare at the man who was—at one time—supposed to be *his* everything.

Those questions made him truly realize what it meant to walk away from someone who meant the world to him. He knew what it felt like to be lost without the hope of finding home. "I can't be his everything. I can't make him happy," Jason mumbled, lowering his head so he didn't have to look his lost happiness in the eyes.

Jansen reached across the table and gripped his chin, raising his head so Jason would have no choice but to face him. "Why not?"

"Because my one chance at happiness is about to commit himself to someone else."

6

"WAIT," Jansen called out, chasing behind Jason as he hiked down Bourbon Street. He had to get out of that restaurant and away from Jansen before the kid decided he wanted to talk about things, because inevitably, Jansen always wanted to talk things out. So Jason bolted. It wasn't that he'd been running or even speed-walking. Jansen had just been too stunned to move from his seat, and Jason wasn't dumb enough not to use it as a chance to bail on the convo.

"Jason, stop!" his best friend called out again, feet clapping against the pavement.

"What?" Jason spun on his heels. He could feel his aggravation flaring up like a blazing fire and filling his eyes with an undeniable amount of heat. Had he not just said all that needed to be said? Had he not just come clean about all the bullshit he'd been penning up over the weeks, months... hell, the last few years? "Do you need me to spell it out for you?"

"No. I got it, but... why didn't you ever say anything?"

"Why would I have said anything? By the time I'd realized I wanted you, you already had your head too far up Dorian's ass." Jason shook his head, turned his back, and started walking away again. "Just let it go. You're happy and I'm happy for you."

"Fine. But you're going to have to face me again, and we're *going* to talk about this."

"Sure, okay." What the fuck ever....

Jason left him standing there alone, yelling down Bourbon Street at two in the morning. It might not have been safe for Jason to be out alone at that hour, but Jansen was protected now. Word spread through the criminal element fast after someone had tried to kill the kid. His Mafioso-style lover had turned the perpetrator into alligator food. No one messed with Jansen after that. Maybe it was better for Jansen that he'd ended up being Dorian Grant's one true love. At least now, Jason knew no one would ever hurt him again.

He climbed into his little red beater and headed back to his shitty two-bedroom apartment in Gretna, thankful he didn't have to fight traffic clogged with idiots to get home. That might've been the only upside to working late nights.

The ride wasn't half as bad as he thought it would be. He cranked the music up until his speakers started to rattle just so he didn't have to hear his brain rambling about shit he couldn't change. He wouldn't have to wonder what life could've been like had he just owned his feelings and come clean to Jansen. He wouldn't have to wonder if Bradley Britt had gone home to his wife and fucked her properly like he'd suggested. With the noise of the music and the car and the road, he was finally free to not think at all and just... be.

Gravel kicked up as he hauled ass into the apartment's shitty, unlit parking area. The neighborhood wasn't the safest, and ever since Jansen had quit the club and moved away, he no longer had the safety in numbers thing going for him. But hey, at least the rent was cheap and the place wasn't falling apart. He climbed the rusty stairs as fast as he could, fumbled with his keys, but finally made it inside. Jason locked two deadbolts, the doorknob, and latched the chain behind him.

The room was dark and for the most part, still pretty empty. Jansen had always given him hell for his lack of interior design skills, but the place should've only been temporary. Something better should've come along by now. So why bother decorating?

Three years and nothing had changed. Maybe it was time to consider buying furniture and stupid little dust-collecting tchotchkes just to make the place feel more like a home.

The door to Jansen's old bedroom was slightly ajar. The edge of his unmade bed peeked through the crack, and for whatever dumb reason, Jason felt a compulsion to go in there. It had to be curiosity. A small part of him wondered if the room still felt like Jansen's, if it still smelled like him. He wondered if he pulled the pillow under his head, would it feel like Jansen was still there. Would it still smell like him?

Jason went into the tiny unlit room, flopped down on the mattress, and pulled the pillow to the back of his head. The scent of his best friend's cologne had faded away. His presence had left long ago.

He stared up at the ceiling, wishing he could turn back time and actually tell Jansen everything he felt before Dorian Grant had a chance to step in and ruin everything. And the more he thought about it, the more he hated how cowardly he'd been.

He hated dealing with regret.

Regret. Yeah, there it was again, nagging him about the man he'd fucked at the club. The *very* married man he'd had sex with on the leather-covered booth of a sleazy nightclub. It would be a damn lie to say he hadn't been attracted to Bradley Britt. Everything about the reporter was attractive in the best kind of way: the strong features and chiseled jawline, the kissable lips, the hazel eyes that looked more green than brown, and God, the man had an amazing cock. Not that Jason had seen it in the light, but he'd felt every glorious, hardened inch against his palm.

Brad was perfect, even more perfect than Jansen.

Okay, so maybe he did want to go another round with the reporter. Maybe he did want to do it proper and see what the hell came out of it. Maybe the same kind of curiosity that had brought Bradley Britt to Sin & Seduction now controlled Jason's libido.

But even if all that were true, wasn't it too late now? He'd sent Brad packing, told him to go back home to his wife and kid, right after he'd screwed him in the VIP booth. Men didn't take that kind of rejection well. They didn't easily recover from being turned away like that. So, Jason had probably ruined any chance he might've had at getting to know Bradley Britt on any kind of intimate level.

Big freakin' deal, right?

Jason rolled onto his side, tucking the pillow against the curve of his neck so the only thing he could smell was the down and the fading scent of a man who had his heart in knots. He closed his eyes, took one slow breath then another. Before too long, he fell asleep. He'd try not to dream about Jansen, try not dream about the reporter. But the events of the night made him seriously doubt he would be so lucky.

7

BRAD didn't go directly home after leaving the club. Instead, he walked around the French Quarter, trying to blend in with the tourists and escape the few hours he'd spent at Sin & Seduction. He wasn't ready to face his wife, face what he'd done to her. Not that she knew about it, and thankfully, his guilty conscience had a voice only he could hear.

His designer loafers slapped against the cobblestones as he wove in and out of the drunken bodies. The myriad scents of New Orleans night beat against his nostrils with each ragged breath he took. Booze and Cajun spices. Different colognes and perfumes. Sewage and the Mississippi River. It was all better than smelling his wife's floral body wash or her coconut shampoo. At least, at the moment it was.

His gut started to churn, knotting as though his guilt had been a meal that didn't sit well. He'd really just cheated on her. He couldn't quite wrap his mind around the idea. In the six years they'd been together, he'd managed not to break that one vow. He'd managed to keep that one desire in check without having to cheat on her, but one weak moment in a nightclub with a hot man had soiled the sanctity of that solemn promise to her.

What was he supposed to do now?

It wasn't like he could run back to Jason. The guy had told him to get lost, to go home to his wife and live the American dream. Obviously, the dancer wasn't ready for the sort of emotional baggage Brad would come with. Not to mention a possible divorce and taking turns sharing custody of his kid with a scorned ex-wife.

"What the hell did I do?" he mumbled, leaning against the brick outer wall of some random Bourbon Street bar. "How the hell do I fix this?"

Maybe he could just forget about it, pretend it never happened and go about living his lie. He could forget about Jason and the club, forget about the need to have a little playtime with balls and shaft. But what good would that do? Would he come to resent the woman he honestly loved, who gave him a beautiful daughter? Would she grow to hate him, hate his coldness?

Brad shoved up from the wall, tightened his jacket around his body, and then started back toward the dark end of Bourbon. He thought about catching a cab back to Sin & Seduction just so he could get a feel for where Jason's head was as far as their interlude in the VIP booth was concerned. The place didn't close for another hour. Maybe he could see him before he got off work.

"Yeah, that's what I'll do."

He thrust his arm into the air, waved his hand like a madman until a yellow car pulled up to the four-way. "Sin & Seduction, in the warehouse district," he said as he climbed into the back. The cabby nodded his head, set his meter, and headed away from Bourbon.

And that's where Brad's beautiful plan ended. That's as far as he'd thought it out. When he actually had a chance to see Jason face-to-face again, he had no clue what he would say, how he would act. He wasn't sure what he would be willing to give up to be with Jason again, if Jason would even consider spending more time with him.

Throw six years of his life and his family away but keep living a lie?

Be truthful to himself and take a chance on being truly happy?

The need to see the guy again became almost as compulsive as the need to eat when you've starved for days. Something about Jason, about his strength and unyielding personality, his honesty and straightforwardness, caught Brad right in the gut and pulled, and nagged, and twisted until he had no choice but to act on it.

Brad's palms started to sweat. His fingers started to tremble. The closer they got to the club, the more his heart started to race. He didn't know if he could do this, didn't know if he could approach Jason after everything the guy had said. It would be a ballsy move for sure, and Brad had never done anything brave in his life.

The cab pulled to a stop just outside the front door. A line of people still rounded the corner, praying for their chance to see the inside of the club. His heart sank down to his toes. How the hell would he get in that place? Then he remembered the little gold card Jason had given him.

He tossed the cabby two twenties and told him to keep the change before tearing out of the backseat. The racing rhythm of his heart hadn't slowed. In fact, it pounded so hard he wondered if it would rip right out of his chest. Each footfall came down faster and heavier, and when he reached the side entrance of the club, all he had left in him was a hard pant. His hands clamped down on his knees as he sucked wind.

"Trying. To get. Inside."

The bouncer arched a brow. Brad held up one finger while he searched his back pocket for the card. He flashed the gold plastic and the bouncer raised the red velvet rope with a smile. Brad charged up the stairs, full steam ahead.

Inside the club, he noticed most of the crowd from earlier had dwindled down. One of the dancers he'd seen the first time was back on stage, kneeling down at the edge and thrusting his cock out for the few excited hands to cop one last feel. He didn't see his auburn-haired friend roaming about, and for whatever reason, that felt like the biggest disappointment of his life.

"Hey," he said to the bouncer standing at the top of the inside stairs. "Jason, the stage manager, is he around?" The big guy shrugged his massive shoulders but kept his lips sealed. "Well, can I go down there and look?"

The man nodded his huge head and Brad squeezed past him, flying down the stairs like his ass was on fire. He hit the bottom floor, both feet planted firmly. His eyes scoured the crowd and he still didn't see Jason, but he did see the dancer they'd called "Golden Boy." Brad charged toward him, reached out, and touched the guy's back.

Golden Boy yelped, grabbing his chest as he gave a little jump. "You!"

"I'm sorry. I didn't mean to startle you. I'm looking for Jason. Is he here?"

"Hell no he's not here, and you got a lot a nerve coming back here."

Brad's head jerked back, his features curling into a frown. "Why? What did I do?"

"Jason left here all pissed off right after he came down from the VIP booth. What did you do to him?"

"Nothing."

Golden Boy stabbed his finger at Brad's chest. "I swear to God." His baby-blue eyes narrowed as he stepped in and invaded Brad's space. "If you did something to him, I'll fuck you up, celebrity or not."

"Really?" Brad said, trying to subdue a laugh. The kid was half his size and there wasn't a damn thing threatening about him. "Look, I'm not trying to start anything with anyone. Just…." He reached in his suit pocket and pulled out a little silver card holder. With two fingers pressed together, he flicked a business card out for Golden Boy to take. "Will you please just tell him I came by?"

The dancer took the card with a casual nod. "Yeah, I'll tell him." He smirked. "But I can't promise he'll call you. Baby, you were just a lay."

Brad's throat knotted. He imagined Jason taking random men up to that booth and doing to them exactly what had been done to him. It hurt, made his heart thump against his chest. He suddenly felt clammy, like his whole body had paled. He choked out, "That's a shitty thing to say to someone."

"Truth hurts," Golden Boy said coldly, shrugging his shoulders. He slipped Brad's card in the front of his blue G-string. "Don't worry, he'll find it here." He gave his own crotch a gentle tap just to add insult to injury.

Brad didn't know what to say to that. So instead of standing around and getting into a battle of wits, he turned and walked away. It wasn't like he trusted his voice or his temper anyway. He didn't trust his eyes not to shed tears, as ridiculous as that was. Why did he even care?

He left the club, hailed a cab, and went back to his car. He'd only muttered enough words to get him back to Bourbon and St. Ann, close to where he'd left his fun gray family-mobile. His head and heart hurt, both warring with each other. Maybe he should've just listened to Jason in the first place. Maybe he should've just gone back home to his wife.

By the time he pulled into his driveway in Marrero, it was almost four in the morning, and he knew if his wife had waited up, he would be in deep shit as soon as she saw him walk through the door. But when he made it inside, she wasn't sitting on the couch with her arms crossed and steam pouring out of her ears. The house was actually silent, frighteningly silent. Had he not seen her car in the garage, he would've thought she'd taken his kid and left him.

He shirked off his jacket, tossed it onto the recliner, kicked off his shoes and shoved them under the coffee table, then curled up on a cold, leather couch. One of those throw pillows that wasn't really comfortable because it wasn't meant to lie on supported his heavy head. His eyes closed, but as soon as he stared at the back of his lids, all he could picture was Jason at his backside. He remembered the dancer's strong finger sliding inside his body with a gentleness he didn't know a man could be capable of. He felt ghost kisses at the back of his neck and his cock began to stir.

"Not now," he mumbled as his reached down and gripped his crotch. Just a little pressure to ease the pain. His eyes fluttered shut. Images of Jason wrapped around his body slowly faded away. Finally, sleep came.

8

THE alarm on Jason's phone blared out a spine-wrenching noise that shattered the serene silence once coddling and caressing him as he'd enjoyed his dreams. The sound made him shoot straight up in the bed. His palms slapped down against the bare mattress as his eyes slammed wide open. The sun pierced his retinas. He threw an arm over his face to block out the morning light spilling in through the window beside the bed. "Damn it!"

Something wasn't right though. His bed wasn't this high. *His* bed had sheets—nice, soft, high-dollar sheets. And that damn window, totally off the mark. He'd blacked out his bedroom windows almost a year ago, right after Jansen had moved out, back when he'd had trouble falling asleep every night.

Things slowly started coming into focus. The walls were the wrong color. The door wasn't where it was supposed to be. Shit, this wasn't his room. He'd passed out on Jansen's old bed last night.

With an aggravated groan, Jason pushed himself off the bed and padded out to the one bathroom he had. He looked in the mirror and what he saw disgusted him. His eyes were worn and dark, chin littered with stubble like he hadn't shaved in weeks. Hair tousled. Cheeks hollow. He reeked of sex and nightclub, a special combination of booze and sweat and God only knew what, powerful enough to make any empty stomach stir with repulsion.

But the worst thing of all was the guilt he saw when he stared at his haggard reflection. It was almost painful looking into his own eyes. He wondered for a brief moment if Bradley had the same problem, or if he'd already forgotten what had happened between them. Did Mr. Hotshot Reporter go home and make sweet, gentle love to his wife like Jason had told him to? As he plunged his hard cock into her body, did he think about how hard Jason had made him come?

Doubtful. And guilt was a dish best served in solitude.

He blindly reached back and fumbled for the shower knobs. He had maybe an hour before he had to be at the deli for his morning shift, then it was back to Sin & Seduction for his night job. Hell of a life he had, but he lived it the best way he could.

Hot water sprayed down from the showerhead. The cool overspray hit his chest and made him hiss. If nothing else, it woke him up and made him a little more aware of the world around him. Though his head was still clouded with images of Jansen and Brad and things he knew he should've never done. He stepped inside the shower, leaned his body against the cool tile, and let the heat soothe his muscles.

But the longer he stood there and thought about how good it had felt to be inside Brad, stretching him and fucking him until they both came, the harder and thicker his cock became. It was one thing to wake up with a semi, but the sights and sounds from the night before—Brad's luscious ass and those low, primordial growls he'd let out—pushed him over the edge to fully hard, and the sudden pain of it was almost too much to endure.

He wrapped his fingers around his shaft, gripping with the same tightness he remembered the reporter having. "Amazing," he groaned, hot water warming his skin.

One palm pressed against the shower wall, just like he'd gripped the back of the booth as he drilled deep into Brad's puckered opening. If he kept his eyes closed, he could be back in that moment, but this time, there would be nothing to feel guilty about. He wouldn't be fucking a married man, and his conscience could take enough solace in that to enjoy the feel of something warm and tight riding over every sensitive ridge and wrinkle.

A pearly bead spilled from the head of his cock as he started to stroke. He imagined the touch of Brad's body and not his own hand, and that alone had his pulse racing a little faster. A purr rumbled up Jason's throat. He bit down on his bottom lip, rolling his hips, pulling and pushing his shaft across his warm palm and through his tight fingers. He could almost smell Brad's cologne again, could almost taste his sweet, salty skin. He could almost feel the firm length of the reporter's body against his chest.

In the back of his mind, he prayed for Brad to come back, to ignore the bullshit Jason had said to him last night and give it all another go. Jason had honestly started to believe that Brad was the man who would finally take his mind off Jansen. Because he was the only one Jason had been with who stayed in Jason's mind. Not Lance with his impressive blowjob. Not the dancer whose name escaped him, who'd given him a hand job on the couch in the back. No other man stayed with him like Britt did. And maybe Bradley Britt was the one meant to give his heart a kick in the right direction.

Pressure built low in his body. His sac pulled tight. His thighs quivered. His cock throbbed as it thickened against his palm. He could almost feel the curve of Brad's firm, round ass against his hips as he drilled deeper and faster. He could almost hear the subtle slapping of flesh against flesh despite the hard pounding of bass-filled club music.

"Ah shit," he hissed, gripping the shower tile as the pressure worked its way down his rock-hard shaft. He lowered his head, panting and moaning, working his hand faster and faster. "Fuck!"

With a growl, he shot his load all over the shower wall. The sudden release nearly took him to his knees. He slid down the opposite wall, ass-planted in the bottom of the shower, trying to steady his breathing and slow his racing heart. His legs were bent at the knees. Water that had been cooling by the minute rained down against his body.

"All for you, baby," he muttered, wishing Brad had really been there to see it.

God, he couldn't believe it; he really did want to see the reporter again. Have sex with him. Hold him. Breathe in air filled with nothing but Brad's cologne and the mingled scent of their bodies after Jason had hot, passionate sex with him. He wanted to be with Brad again, even though the guy had a wife and kids at home. Jason was almost willing to be the reporter's dirty little secret just for a chance to be close to him again.

"I can't do this," he said as he pushed up from the shower floor. "This" being the pining day in and day out, the nights filled with loneliness, days filled with regret. He couldn't quietly sit back and pretend he didn't feel something. He could keep telling himself he only wanted Brad because he couldn't have him, just like he couldn't have Jansen, but there had to be more there. There had to be something making his libido go all haywire every time he thought about the reporter. Surely, there had to be a better reason for the insistent chirping of Brad's name in his brain.

He killed the water and grabbed a towel, dragging it across his back and chest, down his legs and arms. He stormed out of the bathroom and straight to his closet, ripped down a pair of jeans and a blue T-shirt with the deli's logo in bright yellow all over the back. His mind ran ninety to nothing.

Things were *going* to change. He'd kept his feelings secret from Jansen and look how that'd turned out. Jansen wasn't with him. Asshole even wanted to commit himself to someone else. He'd left Jason fighting to keep his crumbling heart intact. But Jason didn't blame him. Jason had been the one who hid his feelings, who kept everything secret because he was scared.

Yeah, well not this time. This time, he would do the right thing... or maybe it was the wrong thing, but that didn't matter. He would tell Bradley Britt that he hadn't stopped thinking about him, and he wanted to be with him again. Even if it meant keeping their relationship—or whatever the hell they would call it—a secret, he didn't care. He *would* be Brad's dirty little secret.

He had a new zeal, a new reason to be excited about facing the world. He wasn't going to be mopey, lovesick Jason anymore. He was going to be a doer instead of a dreamer. Somehow, he would find Bradley Britt and make things right. He would apologize for being an asshole. He would ask for another shot. And if the reporter turned him down, at least he could say he tried.

At least this time around, he would've been honest.

9

THE best part about working at the deli was being able to get a good parking spot in the middle of the French Quarter long before the hungover tourists rolled out of bed for beignets and chicory coffee from Café du Monde. Jason parked right beside the deli, grabbed his messenger bag, and then hauled himself to the front door. Thankfully, he had a little over an hour to screw off before he had to unlock the restaurant for the world.

Thoughts of Brad still tap danced all over his cranium. There was so much he wanted to say and do, so many different ways to show how sorry he was for being such a pompous ass. One problem still remained though. He had no clue how to get in touch with Bradley Britt, and frankly, he didn't think the guy would want to have anything to do with him. But that was the bed he made for himself. Time to lie in it, right?

Jason grabbed the remote from the bookshelf by the door and flipped on the flat screen hanging in the corner. It had become a routine of his. The noise kept him company until his coworkers arrived and the insanity started. He would listen to the television as he mindlessly shuffled through the store, taking care of all the menial, monotonous chores that came with being the manager.

Background noise. Sweet bliss.

But this time, when he turned the TV on, Bradley Britt's velvety voice filled the void of the empty store. Jason sank down in one of the little metal chairs, arms propped up on the table as he stared at the screen.

Brad's lips moved with precision. The subject didn't matter. That's not what caught Jason's attention and reeled it so far in he refused to move. Bradley Britt could've babbled on about anything and Jason would've happily listened to every damn pointless word without complaint… just so he could stare into those magnetic eyes and watch that warm, kissable mouth go to work.

He sighed, shoulders rounding as he slumped down in the chair. This was so wrong, so very, very wrong. He sat there half pining, half lusting over a man he couldn't really have. Well, he could, but God it would be so damn wrong. And sadly, that only seemed to make Jason want him more.

Eyes glued to the TV screen, Jason followed along without blinking as Brad walked through a crowd of people, talking about the farmers' market on Magazine Street. It started that morning, only an hour or so ago, and apparently, it was the big news of the day. The reporter stopped and talked with a few older women, knelt down beside the kids and let them talk in the microphone. He even had a moment with the mayor. Everyone seemed to love him. No surprise there. Jason had never met someone so utterly adorable and easy to talk to in all his life. And heaven help him, that smile was the most engaging smile he'd ever seen.

Damn, what he wouldn't give to see Brad in person right now, just to talk and apologize for being such an asshole. If God would only give him that, he might actually consider spending some serious one-on-one time with the big guy upstairs.

The words "Live from Magazine Street" flashed across the bottom of the screen, and Jason's heart stopped beating. It was like time instantly froze and the miracle he'd asked for had been given to him. If he hauled ass, he could be there in fifteen minutes, probably less, and the news van would be easy as hell to spot. Surely Brad would have to go there before leaving.

Perfect!

Miraculous!

A sign of fate!

That settled it. Jason would go to the farmers' market and hunt the reporter down. Sure it might make him look like a stalker, but desperate times called for desperate measures.

Heart now racing, he tore out of the store, locking the door behind him, then hopped in his little red beater, flipped a U-turn, and booked it out of the French Quarter. He zigzagged in and out of traffic, speeding through amber lights while praying he didn't get caught. He didn't want to miss his chance of seeing Brad. If something happened and the guy left before Jason got there, then he might never see the man he'd been obsessing over again.

When he rounded the corner onto Magazine, he swore his car almost got up on two wheels, but that didn't slow him down. The news van was parked at the entrance. Its huge antenna reached up toward the sky. A parade of cars filled the parking lot and the street and even some private driveways. He parked as close as he could, but the place was too damn crowded. Even the people looked like an endless sea of blurry faces.

He jumped from the car and ran straight toward the van. His tennis shoes pounded against the pavement, thumping and flopping until his feet finally stopped. Jason doubled over, grabbing his knees and panting for breath.

"Bradley… Britt?" he rasped, sucking in air that might as well have been razorblades.

The camera guy shook his head. "He's out in the crowd somewhere. Probably shaking hands and shit. That's what he does."

That wasn't surprising at all.

Jason stood straight up, hands gripping his hips. Finally, he could breathe again. "Do you mind if I wait here?"

"Hang on. I'll call him."

"That would be great. Thanks."

The guy fished his cell phone out of the green camo-looking tack vest covering his rotund chest. He paced a small circle, running his fingers through his shiny black hair as he held the phone to his ear. It took a whole lot of willpower not to follow him and listen in as he spoke to Brad.

"Hey, there's this guy here for you." The cameraman slipped his hand between his mouth and the phone. "What's your name, buddy?"

"Jason. It's Jason. He met me last night."

The guy's brow quirked, eyes traveling up and down Jason's body. He removed his hand and said, "Jason. Says you met him last night." He was silent for a moment before mumbling some noises that must've been coherent language between the two of them. Hanging up the phone, he looked back at Jason and said, "He'll be here in a minute."

"Thanks," Jason muttered again.

He started pacing his own small circle. Voices and a million different conversations floated through the air. Birds chirped from the tree beside him. Morning sun beat down on his face. It was almost blinding. He rarely saw sun so bright. Not for any real length of time anyway. But at least it was cool outside. At least the breeze eased the heat.

Something made him turn around. Maybe it'd been a sound or a smell, he didn't know, but when he turned on his heels, the first person he saw was Brad. In that infinite sea of people, Bradley Britt stood out like a shining star. His sandy-blond hair caught the sun in such a way his face seemed haloed by golden light. His eyes sparkled and his lips, dear God, his lips were just as perfect as they had been the first night Jason had laid eyes on him.

Brad smiled and the sight made the breath hitch in Jason's throat.

The man was absolutely walking perfection. From his sleek gray suit and the viridian dress shirt that really brought out the green in his hazel eyes, all the way down to his designer loafers, he was beautiful. Mouthwateringly beautiful.

"Hey," Brad said, his winning smile never fading as he offered Jason a hand to shake.

"Hey," Jason mumbled, taking the offer. "Do you have a minute to talk in private?"

Brad looked around. Privacy was slim pickings around there, but Jason trusted the reporter would find a way to make it happen. Brad nodded his head as they released each other's hands. "Let's go over there."

They started walking back toward the street, close to where Jason had parked his piece-of-shit car. Neither one of them said a word, not until they'd reached the edge of the crowd, far away from prying ears. Jason spoke up first. "Look, I'm sorry for being such a dick last night. I...."

"It's okay. I get it." Brad shrugged.

Jason frowned. He turned to face Brad and said, "You get what?"

"I was only a fuck. You don't have to explain it to me."

"Who the hell told you that?"

"Does it matter?"

"Yeah. It matters. Who told you that you were just a fuck?"

"That guy they call 'Golden Boy'."

"Mother fu—" Jason bit down on his bottom lip, jaw clenching, fists tightening. He was going to kick Lance's ass when he saw him again. "I never said that," he gritted through pinched lips and a tightened jaw. "I left the club without really talking to anyone. I was upset with myself."

"Hey," Brad said, hands clamping down on Jason's shoulders, forcing the guy to look at him. "You were right. What I did was wrong. Maybe it's best that we just forget it ever happened."

Jason's heart sank and his gut twisted. "Is that what you want?"

"Yeah, I... I think it's for the best. Don't you?"

Hell no! "Sure. Whatever. I guess coming here was a mistake. Sorry for bothering you at work. I'll um...." Jason swallowed hard. He could feel his throat tightening like he was about to start bawling his eyes out. No way in hell would he do that in front of Brad. "I should go."

He started to stalk away when Brad's velvety voice called him back. Jason stopped, but didn't turn around. His vision had already started to burn. The ache in his temples meant he was trying really damn hard not to fall apart.

"You okay?" Brad asked.

Jason only nodded. Then he felt Brad's hand at his shoulder. He smelled Brad's cologne embracing him, and the scent brought back memories of what they'd done at the club, the way he'd stretched the reporter with so much care, care he'd never really taken with anyone else because there'd never been a need or desire before. When Brad spoke again, his warm breath grazed the side of Jason's neck and made every inch of his flesh tingle.

"You're not okay," Brad whispered. "Talk to me."

"I'd hoped," Jason choked. He closed his eyes, lowered his head, and took a shallow breath because he couldn't manage much more. He let it go slowly and said in a low voice, "I hoped we could see each other again. I hoped apologizing would.... Fuck. I don't know what I thought. I don't know why I came here."

"I doubt you're the kind of man that goes into anything unprepared. Talk to me."

Jason finally turned around. His green eyes met Brad's heavy hazel gaze. The seriousness, the hope and desire in the reporter's eyes, nearly knocked Jason on his ass. He had to look away just so he didn't forget how to breathe. "I want to be with you again, but I want to do it right this time," Jason whispered. "I want to take you somewhere nice. I want to be in a bed with you. I want to be able to hold you after we fu… have sex. I want to shower with you and be close to you."

"Why?"

"I don't fucking know," Jason growled. "Sorry. Sorry, I just…." Jason shook his head, scrubbed his hands over his face. "I don't know. I just do."

"What are you doing tonight?"

"Working at Sin & Seduction."

"What time do you get off?"

"Around three."

"I'll meet you in the back parking lot."

Jason's eyes widened. He stared in disbelief, unable to utter the first word. He licked his lips and absently nodded his head. The thoughts slamming against his brain made everything around him blur into nothing. What had once made his mouth water now made it dry. "You sure?" he somehow managed to choke out.

"I'm sure."

"What about your wife."

"Don't worry about that. I'll be there. Don't stand me up, okay?"

"Never."

10

THE rest of the day crawled by so damn slow Jason thought he would go insane. Every few minutes he would check the clock. It felt like hours should've passed, but they hadn't. He even tooled around and made up stupid chores, hoping that being busy would make the seconds fly by. It didn't. It only made him sweat a little harder and made his body ache a little more.

His relief showed up thirty minutes early, enough time that he could watch the sun setting on the Mississippi river through the pane glass windows in the front of the shop. As the sky shifted from light blue to soft shades of pink and gold to a darker blue, almost purple color, Jason thought about Brad and Jansen and slapping the shit out of Lance as soon as he saw him.

"I'm out of here," he yelled back to his coworkers.

They all said their good-byes just as he hit the front door. He started down Decatur, toward Jackson square. The scent of Chicory and powdered sugar from Café du Monde filled the cool night air. Booze and Cajun seasoning fought against the stench of the Mississippi and the cars racing by. The contradiction almost burned the nostrils, but damn, if Jason didn't love every bit of it. That hell was his perfect home.

About halfway between the deli and the club, nestled in the backside of the French Quarter, was his favorite coffee shop. They all knew him by name, by drink, and they all knew what time to expect him. Every Saturday, when he worked both the club and the deli, he stopped in for a vanilla latte to finish off his walk.

Thirty minutes later, Jason ducked into the club's back entrance. Black walls and low lights made it almost impossible to see anything, and anyone could've been waiting in the shadows. Not that Jason really worried. Sin & Seduction had more security than any place he'd ever worked before. But the walk still sucked, still drained the happy right out of him. It felt like walking the last mile of his life because he knew he would run into Lance and boy, the pissed-off he felt for that guy right now....

His hands locked around the strap of his messenger bag. Maybe if he reminded himself that he would see Brad at the end of the night, he'd be able to get through this day without wanting to beat the hell out of someone. Maybe if the boys kept the show rocking along, he could keep his head in his job and avoid the inevitable verbal smackdown he had planned for a certain blond-haired, blue-eyed dancer who couldn't keep his damn mouth shut.

Then *that* dancer met him in the dark hall. Fate couldn't just leave well enough alone, huh? Had to throw the kitten into the lion's den.

"Hey, sexy," Lance said, reaching out to pull Jason into a hug. Jason kept walking. "What the hell?"

"Don't say a word to me," Jason growled.

"What's wrong with you?"

"You really need to learn to mind your own business."

Jason charged through the dressing room door, pitched his empty coffee cup into the trash, then dropped his messenger bag on his desk. He grabbed the clipboard with the night's schedule and silently read it over. The five dancers, including Lance, all stared with their mouths agape.

It wasn't like Jason to charge through the group without speaking to anyone. It wasn't like him to come in wearing an angry face. Even when something bothered him, he didn't make a show of it, never had. But there he stood, rocking a heavy dose of pissed-off and scowl that would make an old west outlaw cower in his boots.

And Lance—the guy who'd pissed him off almost as much as he'd pissed himself off—had to be the one to step forward and ask him if he needed to talk. Thankfully, Lance had kept it to a whisper. But that didn't change the fact he was the very last person Jason needed or wanted to have any one-on-one time with.

"Back. Off," Jason growled under his breath, hoping if he put a little of that temporarily harnessed rage into his voice, it would put the fear in Lance, but it didn't. Dude didn't back off, didn't try to get out of his way.

"No. We apparently need to talk." Lance pressed his palm to Jason's chest.

The touch made Jason's eyes drop. He glared at the hand then back up at its owner. Silently, he counted backward from ten, hoping the seconds would put enough intelligence in Lance to make him remove his palm. It didn't. Jason's nostrils flared.

"Not a good idea. And I suggest you get your hand off of me."

Lance removed his hand. Smart move. But he didn't step back, didn't look away. Not so smart.

Jason looked down at the clipboard then back to the dancers. He called one of the first acts forward to make sure the kid had gotten himself ready for the stage. Everything looked good... except for the fact Lance still consumed a good chunk of his personal space. The guy stood there glaring with his arms crossed over his chest like he was some kind of badass who could break Jason down and make him talk when he didn't want to. Yeah. No. Shit didn't work that way. If he knew what was best for him, he'd give Jason some space and let him calm down before they even broached the subject of why he'd stormed into work tonight with an attitude.

Jason slammed the clipboard down hard enough it made them all jump. A few dancers were smart enough to turn away and find something to make themselves look busy. Some were too shocked to even move or look away. Lance was the only one stupid enough to keep up the cocky pose.

"You really want to fucking talk?" Jason yelled, nearly chomping off Lance's head. Lance nodded. Jason took a step closer. "Fine." Jason daggered Lance's chest with his stiff forefinger, pounding out each word against Golden Boy's sternum as he said, "Stay. The. Fuck. Out. Of. My. Life."

"What did I do to you?"

"Bradley. Britt. Ring any bells with you?"

Lance's eyes shifted away. His chest deflated like he knew exactly what he'd done without Jason having to recall the whole scenario. "Yeah," he said in a low voice as he took a step back. Jason closed the distance. "Look, I'm sorry. I… have no excuse."

"You really don't. You'd better stay away from him like I told you to."

"I thought he hurt you."

"I don't really give a shit. It's none of your business."

"Yeah, it kinda is." Lance reached out to touch Jason's hand, but Jason pulled back immediately. He sure the hell didn't want any physical contact with the dancer unless it involved punching his lights out. Lance leaned in close and whispered low enough so the other dancers couldn't hear him say "I care about you." There was a long pause. Lance's blue eyes met Jason's glare. "More than I should."

11

"WHAT the hell are you trying to say?" Jason asked, wrapping his hand around Lance's bicep. He pulled the guy to a far corner of the backstage area, away from the other dancers, away from curious ears and gossiping lips and anyone who didn't need to hear this conversation. By Jason's best guess, that meant everyone. "What do you mean you care 'more than you should'?"

"Forget I said anything," Golden Boy mumbled as he *tried* to jerk away from Jason's hold, but Jason's strong fingers kept the kid's arm pressed hard against his palm. "Please, let go of me."

"No." Jason pulled him closer, eyes so stern they probably pierced right through Lance's heart, but he couldn't just let it go. He couldn't let some young dancer walk around the club with a hard-on for him, especially not with all the other shit happening in his life. "What the fuck?"

Lance spun on his heels, glared up at Jason like he wanted to kick the dude's keister all over the backstage. *Whoa. Take a step back. What the hell just happened here?*

"Look," Lance finally said. "I know you're like… completely unavailable or whatever. I know you have a hard-on for Britt and God only knows what's going on with—"

"Don't you dare say his name."

"I didn't plan on it. I'm just saying. I know you don't want me or anything like that. I know you have rules and shit. But I mean, don't we always want the ones we can't have?"

With a hard sigh, Jason leaned against the black-painted cinder-block wall behind him, brushed back his chin-length auburn hair, and stared down at the floor. This is exactly why he didn't do his coworkers. After the bliss wore off, things always became more difficult than what they were worth.

And then there was the reporter. More complications. If the insanity didn't kill him....

"Lance," he said, still staring down at the floor, waiting for a gaping hole to open up and swallow his body down into the bowels of the earth. "You're a nice guy...."

"Don't give me the 'nice guy' speech please. I can't take it from you."

That made Jason raise his head. Lance swallowed so hard, Jason could see the Adam's apple bob up and down in the dancer's slender throat. The kid started pacing a small circle, eyes trained on the floor. Jason opened his mouth to say something, but thought better of it. Last thing he wanted to do was taste his own toes because his discombobulated ass said the wrong thing. So he stood there in utter silence, watching the kid fall apart and feeling twice as guilty about his existence as he had before this startling revelation.

"Jason?" Lance's voice finally broke the silence.

"Yeah, man?"

Their eyes met and something about Lance's stare made Jason regret the fact he couldn't give the kid what he wanted and needed. He just couldn't do it. His heart wouldn't be in it. His heart was already torn between two other men. It couldn't handle another one.

"I don't want shit to be awkward between us," Lance said in the most defeated voice Jason had ever heard. Too late. Shit was already awkward. "I don't want my big stupid mouth to cause problems at work. I like it here and I really want to keep this job. So I'll um... I'll back off, okay? We can pretend I never said anything, okay?"

"Come here."

Jason held out his arms, eyes softening as Lance closed the distance between them. He pulled the kid into a tight hug, almost enveloping the smaller guy completely. Lance tucked his face in the curve of Jason's neck. They didn't say anything to each other for a long moment. It wasn't about careful words to ease unintended pain. It was more about a mutual understanding, an acceptance of what had been said and not said. Jason needed to let him know everything would be okay as long as the feelings didn't go any further than friendship.

"You okay?" Jason asked in a soft voice. Lance only nodded, didn't let go and didn't raise his head. Jason stroked his hand up and down the kid's back. He hated to sound so uncaring and God only knew he didn't want to be one of *those* kinds of assholes, but they both had a job to do. The show had to go on. "I have to get to work."

"I know," Lance mumbled.

Dropping his arms, Jason raised his body from the wall and the movement forced Lance to take a step back. The kid quickly swiped his hand across his face, like he'd nearly been in tears, or maybe he'd cried a few and didn't want Jason to see it.

For a long moment, they stood in awkward silence, trying like hell not to look at each other and not be obvious about it. So much for keeping things cool. Jason cleared his throat. Lance made an about-face and started back toward where the other dancers all gathered during the night.

Once Lance was no longer in his line of sight, Jason let out a deep breath. He could feel his heart skipping every other beat. More stress. Stress he damn sure didn't need. For God's sake, he needed to work on getting his head on straight, not help some kid who had a crush on him. Hell, he could barely help himself. How the hell was he supposed to help someone else?

Jason shook his head, following Lance's saddened footsteps.

When they both stepped into the bright white lights of the dressing area, heads turned away in unison, like they'd been listening to the entire conversation and just got their hands caught in the proverbial cookie jar. And here came daddy, ready to smack their little hands away.

"Okay," Jason said, grabbing the clipboard again. He cleared his throat, swallowed hard, and brushed back the tangled mess of his hair. No one said a word. They all sort of froze where they stood, stared like Jason had a third arm growing out of his forehead. "Davi, you're up first tonight. Then the twins. Lance you're third. You guys think you can handle this or do I need to stay and babysit?"

A unified chorus of grumbles rose from the group. Jason lifted his eyes from the page, one brow quirked. The boys fell into their normal routine almost immediately. Good little soldiers, they were. "Good. I have a call to make. Let's not be late getting to the stage."

He dropped the clipboard on the desk in passing, made his way back down the same dark corridor and out into the parking lot where he was sure no one would hear him. Damn sure didn't want Lance to hear him making arrangements to meet a man who had a better chance of making a permanent place in his heart than the dancer did. He needed to get a hotel room for when Brad came back. They needed a place to escape together, to be intimate without the club and hundreds of prying eyes watching them. More importantly, Jason wanted a place where he could treat Brad to a little TLC.

"I need a room for the night," he said into his cell phone as he fought to get his wallet out of his back pocket. He fished his one credit card from the leather folds. He only kept the one, just for emergencies. This classified as an emergency. "Yeah. I have a Mastercard." He read out the numbers to the receptionist, waited for what felt like an eternity. When she finally came back, she gave him the confirmation number and thanked him for his business. "Not a problem," he said with a satisfied grin.

He hung up the phone and shoved it back in his jeans. At least now he could go back into the club in a much better mood than he'd been in the first time he'd gone in. And a few hours closer to seeing that utterly gorgeous, utterly mesmerizing reporter he'd recently found himself so addicted to.

Shifting his eyes around the darkened parking lot, Jason smiled again. He pushed through the staff door, shuffled his feet down the hallway and into the backstage area. The dancers all scurried about, picking costumes or plain outfits for their numbers. So far, so good. He kept going out to the floor so he could get a glimpse of the show, or better yet, so he wouldn't have to face Lance and his little crush.

He hung to the far wall, away from the crowd so he could get the best view of the club's happenings. Everything looked great. Everyone looked happy, looked like they were having fun. He started toward the stairs leading up to the VIP section and that's when he spotted Bradley Britt sneaking in the side door.

A smile curled his lips. Man, did he like this unexpected surprise.

Brad looked like he'd just left work: pinstripe suit clinging to his perfect body, viridian dress shirt making the green in his eyes almost electric, and that perfect blond coif of his clinging to his head in beautiful honey waves like he'd just left the salon or some business like that. The sight alone made a jolt of excitement and lust push down into Jason's groin.

He let out a soft growl, rolling his hips only slightly to readjust and relieve the pressure pushing against his denim-covered crotch. In that moment of seeing Bradley Britt's gorgeous face, all the complications in the world seem to fall away into the ether. Even the complication of being with Britt, gone, like it'd never existed. Something primal and demanding, an insatiable hunger, blossomed inside him and took control of him. Somehow, some way, Bradley Britt would be his. Only his.

12

"WELL, if it isn't my favorite reporter," Jason said with a grin as he rounded the edge of the booth. He cleared the high leather back of the chair and slid in beside Britt. Their clothed thighs met at the seam of rough denim and soft dress slacks. At the sudden and unintended touch, a flurry of warmth tickled Jason's spine. "You're here early."

An enchanting smile spread across Brad's face as he looked over. Bright, perfect white teeth beamed from between two plump parted lips. God, Jason wanted to lean in and pull that delicious bottom lip between his teeth and suck the taste onto his tongue. His business twitched again, thumping harder against the zipper of his jeans. Heat rushed his cheeks as he shifted once more. Not too much longer and there would be no room left for his erection to grow.

"Yeah, we finished up and I went home to have dinner with the family." Brad lowered his head like he was suddenly ashamed of the sneaking around. "I wanted to tuck my daughter into her bed before I left for the night."

"And the wife?"

"Her book club is coming over tonight. They'll probably drink and rag on their husbands. She always kicks me out of the house when the girls come over. I told her I would probably be out late tonight."

This conversation, the lies and deception, it was all wrong on so many levels, but Jason couldn't help what he wanted. He couldn't help how he felt, but it wasn't all his fault. Hadn't he been perfectly fine with walking away from Brad and forgetting the whole thing had ever happened? And hadn't Brad called him back when he'd tried to leave the farmers' market? Jason wasn't the only one to blame here. He didn't start this immoral journey alone.

But didn't Jason tell himself he didn't mind being Brad's dirty little secret?

Shit.

"You okay?" Brad asked.

The sound of his voice made Jason raise his head. He hadn't even realized how low it'd been hanging. "Yeah. I'm...." Jason stopped, swallowed, and cleared his throat. "I'm good."

"If this is too much for you...."

"No. No, I'm fine. I'm okay."

"Good, because I really like seeing you. I would like to keep seeing you."

Awkward silence seemed to be the theme of the night. Jason really didn't know what to say to that. He liked seeing Brad too, even if they'd only been together once... intimately, that is. It didn't always have to be about sex though, right?

Then Jason remembered the way it felt to have Brad's body beneath his: the firm, muscled backside and the perfectly rounded, perfectly toned ass, the way Brad's warmth gripped his cock and pulled one righteous orgasm from his body. Maybe it was just about sex. After all, they didn't know each other at all, hadn't spent one second getting to know the men behind the bodies. And there was good reason for that: Brad's wife.

"Do you ever feel guilty?" Jason asked as he moved a little closer. The club music had gotten so loud they could barely talk without screaming at each other, and Jason didn't want another soul getting wind of this conversation. "Do you feel guilty for not being faithful?"

"Yeah." Brad's eyes turned back to the stage. "I feel very guilty for screwing around on her." He looked back over at Jason, reached out for Jason to take his hand.

Hesitation. Jason could feel his heart rush and his pulse starting to race. Fingers trembled. Sweat blossomed on his scalp. It took a moment of consideration, but Jason finally took Brad's hand. "Then why keep doing it?"

"I don't know." Brad shrugged. "When I went home the other night, I curled up on the couch and closed my eyes, but you're the only person I pictured. I tried to think about my wife. I tried picturing myself making love to her, hoping there was still something there to make me go up to the bedroom and climb into bed with her, but there wasn't. I only wanted to climb into your bed."

Flattering, but in the same thought, not so much. Home wrecker, a wonderful title for someone with a heart as big as Jason's to wear. Not. He licked his suddenly parched lips, turned his eyes to the stage so he wouldn't have a wall of sexy man clouding his judgment.

In an uneasy voice, he said, "You know, I thought I could be your dirty secret, but I honestly believe that was desperation talking. I think I needed and wanted you so badly, I was willing to do anything, but…."

"I know. You don't have to say anything." Brad reached up and touched his palm to Jason's cheek, pulling his head back until they looked into each other's eyes. They stayed locked in a stare for a long moment, neither one of them brave enough to trust their voices. Then Brad finally said, "If this feels like it's going to go somewhere, I'm going to tell her. I promise. I swear I'm not this guy. I don't cheat on the person I love. I don't sneak around having sex with whoever comes my way. I'm honorable and honest, but…."

"Heat of the moment. I know. Trust me. I'm not the guy who breaks up happy families."

"Right."

"Right."

Jason gave Brad's hand one last squeeze, eyes swinging the reporter's way, but he couldn't bring himself to meet that warm hazel gaze. "I need to get down to the stage. I'll be back up in a few hours, when my shift is over. I'm going to try to call it an early night, okay?"

"Okay. I'll be right here waiting."

Jason started to walk away, but remembering the room stopped him in his tracks. His jaw clenched, teeth grinding against teeth. This was the perfect opportunity to *try* to be the good guy in a very bad situation. This was his chance to give Brad a choice, completely uninfluenced by heat-of-the-moment feelings, completely uninfluenced by his own desire. He could give Brad an out and hope for the best, or at least, what was the best for Brad.

He turned back, leaned across the table, and said, "I reserved a room for the night at the Bourbon Orleans hotel. Go there... or not. Your choice. I'll be there when my shift ends. If you're there, we'll... whatever. If you're not, I'll understand, okay? This—" His hand waffled between the two of them. "—is your choice. I'm not going to pressure you into anything."

13

LEANING back against the booth, Brad gazed at Jason's body as the guy walked away. As soon as he disappeared from sight, Brad's stare turned toward the ceiling, tracing the steel forms of I-beams and exposed ductwork hidden in the darkness. It seemed a hell of a lot easier taking in the crude industrial architecture rather than face the ramblings of his brain or the pitter-patter of his heart.

Did Jason seriously just give him a choice to walk away? Why would he want that? Did Jason not want him? *Shut up, Brad. You're over-thinking this. The guy just wants to do the right thing.* That sounded so damn easy, doing the right thing. Too bad it wasn't.

Somehow, Brad managed to pass hours staring up at the rafters and considering his life from every possible angle. He thought about his little girl and how daddy not being around every night to tuck her in would hurt her little soul. Thinking of tears in her sparkling blue eyes and not feeling her swaddled against his chest as he sang lullabies to her broke his heart. He thought about how hurt his wife would be if he finally came out to her. How she would probably hate him no matter how much he would always love her. He thought about Jason and how much the guy seemed to care already. How Brad felt like he could finally be himself with someone who might actually make him happy, whom he didn't have to lie to and sneak around on.

Brad could already feel his blood pressure shooting through the roof.

But honestly, if there was anyone he could see spending time with him and his daughter, playing in the park and going to the zoo, it was Jason. For whatever reason, he could picture Jason being the guy to settle down and do the family thing with. He could see many happy, fulfilled nights in their long life together. He could finally see himself completely at peace in a relationship.

"God, where the hell is this crap coming from?" Brad groaned.

The waiter came over to his booth and asked him if he wanted his usual. Was he already a regular enough to have a "usual"? He shook his head. "Not tonight. I think I'm about to get out of here. Need a little air."

"But you're going to miss a great show."

"I didn't come here for the show."

Brad slid out of the booth. The waiter went on to the next table like he'd never actually been concerned with what Brad wanted anyway. But that was cool. The guy just wanted to make a buck.

His designer loafers pounded on the steps. Brad thought if he just got away from everything for a little while, let all the possible paths he could take play on through in a perfect preview of where his life could possibly go, then maybe he could make the right decision.

But no matter how the images played out, no matter how the roads and paths crossed, someone ended up hurting. Swear to God, if there was any way Brad could take any of their pain into himself and keep them safe from it, he would. This mess was his fault, and the people he cared about deserved so much better than this. Something had to give and soon. He had to make a decision to be faithful to his family or follow the pull of his heart.

After nearly an hour of aimless walking and thinking, he finally reached the crossroads, the corner of Orleans and Bourbon.

The hotel stood over him like a grand montage of the choices he'd made over the years of his short life. This had been the place where he and his wife had spent their wedding night, the place he'd brought her to relax when she found out she was pregnant with their daughter. The place he stayed for the one Mardi Gras he'd ever been to and the place he'd had sex with the first guy he'd ever fucked.

As he stood there staring up at the building, he scrubbed his hand over his face, like the friction could make anything clearer. Oh, if life could possibly be that easy. His eyes shifted left, toward the end of the French Quarter where Sin & Seduction hid amongst abandoned buildings, toward Jason and the promise of something new and possibly peaceful. His eyes shifted right, toward the bright and lively end of Bourbon, toward all the happy people who just wanted to have fun and be free. Then he looked down Orleans.

The street was empty for the most part, save for a few wandering tourists and a man in a pirate suit. The bellboys stood waiting to welcome guests to their grand hotel. Brad could go inside, then up to the room, or he could keep walking, hail a cab, and go home to his family.

He took the first step, took another and another. He passed the huge paned windows of the hotel's bar. Everyone inside looked thrilled to be there, like they didn't have a care in the world. For the first time in his life, no one seemed to notice him. No one cared about the lost, confused mini-celeb aimlessly walking down the street. None of them would ever know the mess in his head, and he liked that. At least they couldn't judge him for the not-so-great decisions he'd made.

The bellboys nodded and smiled as Brad reached for the worn, weathered brass handle. One of them beat him to it. The younger man grinned wider, holding the door for him to step inside. Would he do it? Would he take the plunge and walk through that door or would he turn and walk away?

14

"BEHAVE yourselves, kids," Jason called over his shoulder, arm waving in the air.

The dancers waved and yelled their good-byes. The club still had another hour, maybe more, before closing, but the numbers had been on time all night and Jason had a good feeling they would stay that way. Besides, with his mind on a certain golden-haired, hazel-eyed reporter, he'd been moving about like a zombie and hadn't been exactly useful to anyone.

He headed out of Sin & Seduction's back door and into the cool New Orleans night—or rather, early morning darkness. This was the one time he wanted to curse himself for not driving to the club. If he had his car, he could get to the hotel so much quicker. But maybe it wasn't a bad thing. At least a walk would give him time to think, to psych himself up just in case he got there and Bradley Britt wasn't lying naked on the bed, waiting to be completely claimed by him.

God, that sounded so pathetically romance novel, but damn, it was so true.

Feet shuffling down Bourbon, Jason passed through the rainbow district with all its bright, colorful flags hanging from buildings easily five times his age. People danced around in the street, laughed with their friends, and waited to get their eager feet in the door of a club, a bar, or Jason's favorite little diner.

He came to the four-way at Bourbon and Orleans, stopped, and took a deep breath. "This is it," he mumbled to himself. Brad would be there waiting and who knew where they could go from there. The possibilities were endless. Or he would get up to the room and it would be empty, and he would probably end up spending the night hugging a pillow tight against his body, pretending it was someone who actually cared about him.

One deep breath in, then slowly out. Brushing his hands over his clothes, he checked his reflection in the plate-glass window beside him, then ran his fingers through his long auburn hair. That's when he realized just how badly he'd started to shake. His nerves were a frazzled mess, and he knew, beyond a shadow of a doubt, things wouldn't go down as he'd pictured. Things almost never happened the way he imagined, and nothing in the stars made him believe this situation would be any different, especially now that he'd put his heart on the line.

Without rational thought and before he could stop them, his feet started carrying his body toward the hotel's front entrance. He wasn't ready for this, wasn't ready to face the music that he'd been a fun, quick lay for a man who had a wife and a kid, who had a proclivity for other men but not in a permanent relationship sort of way.

The bellboys greeted him with kind smiles, which he returned with a nervous half grin. His feet kept up the dirty work of moving his body forward because his mind had checked into a very different place the moment he'd reached the corner of Orleans. He went straight to the desk, gave them his name, and got his room number and keycard. No problems there. No indication that Brad had already checked in for him either.

He turned left, took the few steps away from the counter and toward the elevators. Something stopped him. Maybe it was the hesitation and uncertainty. Maybe it was fear. He looked to his right and saw the double doors leading out to the pool. If he sat out there for a moment, maybe he could settle his nerves before going up to the room.

Yeah, that's what he would do. Breathe in a little fresh air, compose himself so he didn't turn what he pictured being a beautiful moment between the two of them into an utter disaster. He pushed against the wooden doorframe, and as soon as it spilled him out onto the patio area, his eyes found the man he'd been so scared to see face-to-face again.

"Brad," he choked in a low whisper. His heart started racing harder. This was it, the moment of truth. At least the guy showed up.

That was a good sign, right? Now why wasn't that enough to settle his body and calm his nerves?

Then Brad looked up, and his serene gaze landed on Jason. The breath hitched in Jason's throat. A soft smile curled Brad's beautiful lips. Jason swallowed hard.

He watched each and every step the reporter took as he slowly approached him. Every footfall made Jason's heart push further and further up into his throat. The knot it formed made breathing hard to do.

"Hey," Brad said, and it took everything Jason had not to throw his arms around him right there in front of the few drunken people lounging around the pool. "You want to go up?"

"Please," Jason blurted.

As they walked back inside and over to the elevator, Jason silently beat himself up for acting like some silly, virginal, hormonal teenager who'd never had sex before. He was going to ruin this. He could see it now. Fumbling hands. Fumbling lips. Moment ruined. The end.

The elevator chimed. The doors opened and Jason waited for Brad to step inside. They rode in silence all the way up to the fourth floor, and when the doors opened again, they stepped out into the barely lit hall. Jason looked down at the paper with the room number then shuffled down the hall toward the row of doors.

"Is everything okay?" Brad asked.

"Yeah, um... why?"

"You're quiet tonight."

"I'm... nervous." Jason laughed softly. "It's stupid, but I am." He slipped the keycard in the door and it opened up to an amazing room with one giant bed covered in a plush white comforter right in the center of the room. Jason dropped his messenger bag on the couch, turned back and watched as Brad secured the door. He stood there, hands trembling, waiting for the inevitable. "I was so afraid you wouldn't be here."

Brad smiled again and Jason's heart stopped for a moment. But when the reporter's hands touched his cheeks and their lips met in a kiss, normal beating resumed. God, his lips tasted so good, and the way he held Jason to the kiss was almost magical—and ridiculous in a girlie crush sort of way. Since when did Jason sign up for this hopeless romantic bullshit?

That's right, when he let his heart start having a say in things.

The kiss broke and Brad said, "Don't be nervous. I'm here. We're together. Just let it happen, okay?"

"What's going to happen when you leave?"

"You mean what am I going to tell my wife?"

"Yeah." Jason's head lowered. "Are you going to tell her about us or… or is there an 'us' to tell her about?"

Brad's forehead pressed to his. They stared for a moment before Brad closed his eyes. "I think…." His hands slipped down Jason's throat, down further until his arms wrapped around Jason's waist. "I want to tell her. I think I want to be with you, but I'm really scared. I want to be able to see my daughter. I don't want my wife to hate me." Brad raised his head and opened his eyes. Those huge hazel orbs searched Jason's face. Jason took another calming breath. Brad said, "I want to make sure that I'm giving up everything I know and love for something genuine. Not for some fleeting feeling or someone who won't be there in the morning. I think that's the way I need to handle this."

"Diplomatic," Jason said as he took a step back. He sank down on the edge of the bed, leaned down and started untying his sneakers.

"That's all you have to say?"

"Yeah. I mean, no. It's a smart move." Jason's tennis shoe dropped to the floor then he started working on the other one. "Why risk being alone just to be true to yourself?" Brad sighed and the sound made Jason lift his head. "I didn't mean that as snarky as it sounded." He dropped the other shoe, stood from the bed, and proceeded to undress. "I think you need to be honest with her no matter what happens here. If you're not straight, if she's just a beard to make people believe you're straight, then she has a right to know. Don't you think?"

It was Brad's turn to sink down onto the bed. He ran his fingers through his perfectly styled hair as the rest of his body fell back on the mattress. And just like Jason imagined, the moment was ruined, but not by fumbling hands, more by clumsy words.

"You're right," Brad finally said. "She does, but I'm not the kind of guy who can be alone, even if the person I'm with doesn't complete me. I just... I can't do it."

The mattress dipped as Jason sat down beside him. He reached over and laid his hand high on Brad's thigh. Words failed him. He had so much to say, so much on his mind he wanted to share with Brad, but no matter how many different ways he arranged his thoughts, the words sounded coarse and grating. So he chose not to say a thing. Better safe than sorry.

Brad's hand touched his, fingers lacing as he eased their joined hands closer to the very sensitive, very ready organ between his thighs. The reporter said in a soft, husky voice, "We have tonight. Let's not waste it on what-ifs. Let's do what our bodies want us to do, and tomorrow we can face truths and consequences from a fresh perspective."

15

"I THINK I can deal with that plan," Jason said as he knelt down in front of Brad's body. He removed the reporter's loafers one at a time, then placed them side by side at the foot of the bed. Hands shaking, he reached up and met Brad's gentle touch. Together, they slid his dress slacks down his legs until they pooled at his ankles.

As Jason neatly folded the high-dollar pants over the back of a nearby chair, Brad began unbuttoning his shirt. The room remained quiet, air tense. Though words of concern and words of promise had been shared, nothing had really changed. Jason still felt guilty as hell about this, and nothing short of Brad making himself a free man would take that pain away. But Jason couldn't blame him for that. After all, he'd been the one to initiate this meeting.

The shifting of bare skin against fine linens made Jason finally turn back to the bed. Soft golden light from the nightstand threw shadows on Brad's perfectly tanned flesh and immaculately manicured muscles. The sight of him made Jason's mouth water and his cock jump. It started throbbing the moment his eyes landed on the stiffening shaft jutting out from Brad's thighs.

"You plan on getting in this bed or just standing there gaping at me?" Brad asked in a husky voice, making the nerves low in Jason's body twitch with enthusiasm. It made the pulsing of his sac more prominent, made him very aware of the erection pressed between his legs. Then Brad reached down and wrapped his hand around his own hardened shaft, gave it a little tug, and grinned.

Jason's heart nearly jumped out of his chest.

"No. I plan on getting in the bed," he said with a hard swallow and a quick lick of his lips.

"Good, I want you here. Now."

With that little command, Jason lifted his knee up to the mattress, climbed on all fours until he straddled Brad's body. He pressed his lips against Brad's muscled abs as the tip of his cock grazed the firm flesh of Brad's thigh. Heavenly. And God help him, the sound of his lover's moans: Jason's utter underdoing.

A silky bead spilled from the tip of his hardened shaft. He looked over the line of Brad's body, over the expanse of that amazing chest and up to his softly closed eyes. A grin curled Jason's lips.

So beautiful.

He moved back down, lowered his mouth over Brad's cock, tongue licking across the sensitive vein running the length of his lover's shaft. Brad moaned louder, legs spreading a little wider to accommodate the width of Jason's shoulders.

His head bobbed up and down, tongue sweeping back and forth, over the firm ridge of the head then back down again. He took Brad to the hilt, let the tip of that perfectly glorious cock tickle the back of his throat. His fingers stroked Brad's sac with the same attention, the same rhythm.

"Oh God," Brad rasped as his hand fisted Jason's hair. The sensation made tingles ripple down Jason's spine. "I'm about to come." But Jason already knew that by the feel of his lover's shaft thickening against his tongue. He could taste the bitter promise begging to explode all over his taste buds and down his throat.

He picked up the pace, slamming his mouth down a little harder, a little faster, taking more of his lover's erection in and out, in and out. His lips tightened with the right amount of pressure and in minutes, if not seconds, Jason milked an explosive release from Brad's body as the reporter cried his name into the air.

"Holy shit. Stop," Brad panted. His fingers uncurled from Jason's hair.

Jason raised his head, licked his lips, and smiled. "You okay?"

"Perfect."

"You taste… fucking delicious."

"I do?" Brad laughed.

"Yeah, you do." Jason grinned. "Now roll over. It's my turn."

Gripping Brad's hips, Jason rolled the other man's body until he lay on his stomach, beautifully rounded ass exposed and begging to be taken. He plunged two fingers into his mouth, coating them and making them slick enough to slip inside Brad's puckered opening. One entered first, eased in and out. He heard a satisfied moan against the pillow, and Brad raised his hips, lifting his ass a little higher, spreading his cheeks a little wider. Then he pressed the other finger inside.

"I'm not hurting you, am I?" Jason whispered, fluttering his lips over the base of Brad's spine.

"No. Not at all, baby."

"Good."

He pressed his mouth to the top of the valley between two of the firmest, most perfect ass cheeks he'd ever laid his hands on, gave a gentle squeeze as his palms caressed those beautiful mounds. Excited moans hung in the air, each one making him harder, thicker, ready to dive right in and never come up for air.

But this wasn't about what Jason wanted. The way he saw it, he needed to give Bradley Britt a reason to want more, to keep coming back, and a reason to be honest with his wife. Love wasn't a factor. Not yet. Maybe not ever. If sex was the only bait he had, he'd gladly use it to catch the only fish in the sea he had eyes for… make that, the only *available* fish in the sea.

Thumbs stroking back and forth against Brad's baby-soft skin, Jason opened his lover a little further and drew his tongue down the seam and over the warm, welcoming opening, then back again. A hiss broke the silence. Brad's body arched and Jason raised his head. "Is this okay for you?" he asked, thumbs still stroking back and forth.

"No one has ever done that to me."

"Do you want me to stop?"

"Hell no. Keep going."

With a smile, Jason lowered his head again, put his tongue back to work, gliding up down the valley between his lover's cheeks, circling around and only retreating so his lips could pay homage to Brad's resplendent body.

On nothing more than desire and instinct, Jason's hips started to pump, brushing his hardened shaft against Brad's leg. He didn't know how much longer he could hold out. Sure, he'd wanted to take it nice and slow, pay attention to every single satisfied sound his lover made, but his erection was starting to get a little too painful to keep holding out. And apparently, Brad was ready for the down and dirty, one-on-one too.

As Jason pushed himself up, the reporter made little whimpers of protest. The sound made Jason want to chuckle, but damn, wouldn't that ruin the moment? "I'm not done," he whispered. He pressed his lips to one cheek, then the other, moved up his lover's spine until they landed at Brad's shoulder blade and his cock brushed the surface of that plump ass.

He pressed the tip to Brad's warm opening, whispering calming words against his lover's flesh as he slowly pushed himself inside. He eased through the ring of muscle, listening as Brad kept his breathing even, waiting for the hiss of pain, feeling for the clench and release. "You okay?"

"Keep going," Brad rasped, voice filled with desperation.

"Oh, I plan to."

But Brad had said once before he wasn't used to being a bottom, a fact made very clear by the tightness around Jason's completely erect shaft. He sure the hell wasn't going to hurt him. So taking it slow was obviously the only way to go, despite the burning desire to plunge in and take him full steam ahead.

Fingers gently stroking Brad's ribcage, Jason pushed a little deeper, eased himself in a little farther. He paid careful attention to the hard ridge of Brad's shoulder, kissing and caressing, teeth nipping and toying, anything to keep his lover happy, excited, and ready for more.

With an unexpected thrust, Brad pushed his hips back and his body swallowed every inch of Jason's sex. The sensation was enough to make Jason gasp, coming up from the kisses for a breath of air. "Damn, Britt," he hissed as tight warmth completely sheathed his cock.

"I'm not made of glass."

"Yeah, but...." Jason wrapped his arm around Brad's waist, lifting him up so Jason could kneel and roll his hips as fluidly and uninhibitedly as he wanted to. He knew once he started really pumping, once he found his rhythm, it could get messy, or it could be an incredible, lust-filled dance between two naked bodies intimately joined. "I just didn't want to hurt you."

"Like I said...."

"Not made of glass. I got it."

Jason rolled his hips, pulled back then pushed in. As he kept up the rhythmic ins and outs, he imagined spending many nights inside this man's body, pleasing him to the point of orgasm, bringing him again and again. Then holding him and sleeping in his arms until life came along to pull them away from each other. He imagined waking up every morning to Brad's tousled blond hair, a soft smile on his delicious, kissable lips. He imagined hours wasted to laughter and intimacy. Jason sighed.

"Please, God, don't slow down," Brad begged.

He hadn't realized he had. "Sorry," he whispered, fighting to get his head back in the game. Obviously, that would be a little problem. For the first time in a long damn time, sex wasn't just about getting off; it was more about making his partner feel good and a show of something that started feeling a lot like love.

Okay, time to get this over with.

They had a lot of damn ground to cover and a lot of confessions to make before the big bad L word could ever come into the picture. That's not to say Jason didn't want it to; things just needed to move a little slower. For Christ's sake, Brad had a wife who didn't know about the skeletons in his closet, and who knew when he would man up enough to tell her.

Rolling his hips again, his cock glided across Brad's tender nub. His lover's body gripped his shaft and the faster he thrust, the more his sac tightened. Pressure built and warmth shot through him. He could feel it coming, feel the release winding down into the head of his cock and with one last thrust... heaven!

16

"HOLY shit!" Jason drawled as he rolled onto his back. Each breath came in a shallow pant. Every inch of his body tingled, heart racing, pulse thumping along to its own kind of tribal rhythm. He trained his stare on the ceiling, fighting to keep control of his urge to fall into hysterics. The orgasm had pretty much turned his brain to mush, and processing anything beyond the bliss he felt at the moment would've been impossible.

One deep breath in. One slow breath out.

Eyes closed, he brushed his palm up and down across his sweat-covered chest, over his firm pecs and pounding heart. It stopped there. The romantic buried deep inside him started knocking on his brain, demanding a little attention, demanding Jason finally listen to the grumblings of his heart.

It was like a transforming moment of clarity, like the moment reality hits you right between the eyes in a very cruel way. It made almost every muscle in his body stiffen, made his heart still long enough to give him a good scare. Sleeping alone didn't work for him anymore. His shitty, empty, nondescript apartment didn't work for him anymore. The time had come for him to settle on that one person who made him happy and gave him a reason to smile.

Bradley Britt was the one.

No doubt about it.

And damn if that didn't present more problems than Jason had the desire to deal with. How stupid could he have been? Falling in love with a married man? And after what? No dates and a couple of sexual encounters? Really? Albeit, the hours he'd just spent with the reporter had been pretty damn amazing. Eye-opening even. But still, Brad wasn't his and would probably never be his. The guy had a family, a family Jason didn't fit into.

Another hand covered his, fingers intertwining. Brad's warm breath flittered across his skin. He looked down and found his lover's body wrapped around his, an arm over his waist, a leg tucked between his thighs, a cheek pressed to his pec. Brad's eyes had closed, lids gently pressed together like he wasn't even trying to sleep. It just came to him, nice and easy. He looked as delicate and peaceful as a sleeping baby.

Taking a deep breath, Jason settled his chin against the crown of the reporter's head. God, the guy smelled so damn good. He felt so amazing nestled in beside him. For the first time in years, Jason honestly believed he wasn't destined to be alone. The warmth beside him, holding him, cuddling him, gave him an honest sense of hope. Everything waiting for them outside of this hotel room didn't matter, because in that moment, in the now, it was just the two of them, and they could be whatever the hell they wanted to be. They could hold each other and kiss each other, and make love to each other. They could be true to themselves and true to their hearts.

Jason made the horrible mistake of glancing over at the clock on the nightstand beside them. Five thirty. Soon the sun would rise and the horrible truth of their relationship would have to be faced. Jason would have to go back to his shitty life: his lonely apartment, his shitty jobs, his personal hell. Brad would go back to his loving family, back to his American dream, and maybe one day their paths would cross again. Maybe Jason could keep from pining over him in the meantime.

BRAD listened to every rushed, ragged breath Jason took. Let the rise and fall of the kid's chest lull him, but he couldn't fall asleep. His eyes might've closed, but he was more than aware of every sound, every movement Jason made. He wanted to imprint this moment, these spent hours, so deep into his brain he would never forget it, no matter what happened between them.

Leaving Jason would be hard, harder than anything he was prepared to do right now. Maybe if he stayed, lay there and held Jason while they slept for a few hours, he could leave satisfied. Maybe he wouldn't go home and crave to be close to Jason while he spent time with his wife and kid... maybe.

But he knew as soon as the thought crossed his mind it would never happen. He knew the hours of quality family time would be lost to thoughts of being with the man in his arms. Something had to give. He had to come clean to his wife. Jason was right. This wasn't fair to her and she'd never done anything to deserve being lied to and cheated on. Brad could only pray for the strength to tell her, to come clean about what he'd done and what he now felt. He could only pray the woman didn't hate him after it was all said and done, pray that she would still let him have a place in their family, time with his beautiful little girl.

A few hours passed. Early morning sun spilled in from the corner of the thick curtains. The vicious intrusion made Brad's eyes flutter. He scrubbed his hand over his face to wipe the sleep away.

During those few hours, neither one of them had moved. Brad was still nestled tight against Jason's side, leg tucked between the dancer's thighs, cheek pressed to his chest. Their hands still held each other's, fingers laced tight together. Brad didn't want to move, didn't want to leave his lover's side.

But it was Sunday, family day. The one day of the week he and his wife sat down together, ate their meal, and spent time with their daughter. It was the one day their careers and friends fell by the wayside and time was all about them, their little family, their happiness and togetherness.

"I have to go," Brad whispered, more to convince himself. He doubted Jason even heard him. The dancer seemed to be sleeping.

"I know," Jason said. The sound of his voice raised Brad's head.

"I thought you were asleep."

"Nope. Couldn't."

"Me either."

"Were you planning to sneak out of here without saying goodbye?"

"No. I…." Brad sat up beside him, still holding Jason's hand because, God help him, he couldn't bring himself to let go. "That wasn't my plan, but I didn't want to wake you if you were still sleeping."

He saw the rise of Jason's chest and his eyes wound up his lover's body until they landed on his slightly parted lips. Then Jason exhaled. The low sound of his frustration broke Brad's heart. Instinct made him want to wrap his arms around Jason's body and pull him into a never-ending embrace. It made him want to pull Jason into the deepest, most meaningful kiss and never let those perfect pink lips go. But that wasn't reality for them. That wasn't fate's design.

Leaning forward, Brad pressed his mouth to Jason's chest. His fingers fondled the hard, rounded edge of his lover's hip. He moved up further until their lips met. His eyes closed as his tongue licked across the seam. Jason opened his mouth only enough for a quick taste, but that was all Brad really needed. An aftertaste of the most amazing morning he'd had in years.

The kiss broke and Brad cleared his throat. "I really need to go."

"I'm not stopping you," Jason said in a flat, uncaring voice.

"Right." Brad sighed.

He stood from the bed, gathered his clothes, and started to dress. As his legs slipped inside his slacks, a million thoughts ran through his mind, and sadly, they all ended with Jason not wanting to have anything to do with him. It made his chest ache, made the sunlight spilling into the room turn dark and foreboding. There was nothing sweet about the sorrow of parting, not in this case.

"Will I see you again?" Brad finally asked.

"Guess that depends on you."

17

EIGHT thirty-five and counting, Brad drag assed into his suburban palace. No one greeted him at the door, not even the overpriced light fixture hung at the base of the stairs. The place looked like a ghost town. Not that he would complain. It gave him a minute to pull himself together and switch gears so he could properly pull off the family man routine without his nerves causing a catastrophe.

With the utmost care and lightest footfalls, he worked his way up the stairs. The landing creaked under the weight of his foot, and the surprise almost felt like a hand reaching into his body and fisting around his heart. He took a slow, easy breath, went straight to his daughter's bedroom door, and poked his head inside.

There she was, his little angel, all dressed in pastel pink, lying in her white, frilly crib. Her tiny hands balled into fists at the center of her chest. Blonde wisps of curls framed her plump face and rosy cheeks. He couldn't imagine anything in the world more beautiful or perfect than her. He couldn't imagine loving anyone more than that miraculous little angel.

He reached down, gently rubbed her belly. She cooed and squirmed, but never woke up. For a moment, he considered staying in there with her, where everything in the world was perfect and easy, and no matter how badly he screwed up, she would look at him with absolute adoration. He considered pulling the glider over to her crib and watching her sleep the day away just so he could share her sense of peace. But wouldn't that be cowardly of him?

One last look, he kissed the tip of his thumb and gently pressed it to her pouty, pursed lips. "I love you," he whispered, and she cooed again.

Leaving her room, his heart pushed up and knotted his throat, strangling his short, desperate breaths. Across the hall from her room, he stared at the door leading to the bedroom he and his wife had shared for the past six years. No doubt she would be curled in the fine linens and down comforter she'd picked out back when they'd been so excited about having their first real home together. She would probably be covered head to toe in those frumpy pajamas she'd started wearing after their daughter was born.

He never understood her need to cover herself like that. The woman had always been incredibly beautiful, even more so after he'd witnessed her bringing their child into the world.

He touched his palm to the surface of the door, head lowered as he tried to even his breathing. The first sting of tears hit his eyes and he knew he couldn't do it. He couldn't go through with telling her about the affair because he knew it would break her heart, and honestly, that was the very last thing he'd ever wanted for her. His back pressed against the wall and his body slid down until his ass planted on the soft beige carpet lining the hall.

Maybe if he just sat there for a little while and pulled himself together, he could do it. Maybe if he could somehow quench the tears and stifle the guilt, he could man up enough to be completely honest with her and not break her heart.

The bedroom door beside him creaked open. He smelled her perfume long before he saw her standing there. "Brad?" her soft, loving voice whispered from above him. He raised his head and saw only a watery, distorted vision of his wife standing over him. She knelt down in front of him and took his hands in hers. "What's wrong?"

"Melody, I…." His tear-filled stare met hers. His voice suddenly felt completely choked, like it refused to say anything that might hurt her. His brain started backpedaling and God only knew what the hell his heart was doing. One minute it felt like it wanted to give up the ghost and wave the white flags, the next it wanted to take charge since his brain didn't have the gusto to go for it. "Melody."

"Brad, stop. Get up and come in the bedroom. Let's get you out of this suit and we'll… talk, okay?"

"I don't deserve you."

"Will you stop talking like that? Come on. Get up and come to bed. Have you even slept?"

In the arms of another man....

"Not much, but I can't sleep right now. I need... to talk to you."

Melody held his hand as he pushed up from the floor. They stepped into the bedroom and he guided her over to the bed. She sat down and he kneeled in front of her. His hands trembled around hers. A worried frown curled her beautiful features, furrowed her brow, and tightened her lips.

"Melody, I...."

He hesitated long enough for her to interrupt. "Just say it, Brad. Tell me you're having an affair. I know that's...." Her voice wavered and her eyes turned glassy. She looked away and he lowered his head. "That's what this is about, isn't it?"

"I'm so sorry." She ripped her hands from his grip and crossed her arms over her chest. "Melody, it isn't...." He licked his suddenly parched lips. "You're the only woman I love."

"How can you say that?" She stood from the bed and started pacing the room. He sat back on the floor, head still lowered, chest still aching. "Who is it?"

"A man I met." Her feet stilled. He didn't look up to see the surprise on her face, couldn't bring himself to look into her heartbroken eyes. "I, um...." He took a deep breath. "I'm gay." Silence. He didn't even hear the shuffle of her clothing. "Please say something."

"What do you want me to say? Our entire relationship has been a lie. Is that what you're trying to tell me? Our life, our family, is a lie?"

"No." He finally stood from the floor so he could face her and just as he'd expected, she had the most tragic look on her face. Her cheeks glistened with shed tears, eyes red and puffy. "I love you. I love our daughter. I still want to be part of your life and hers, but I... I need to be with a man."

"How long have you known?"

"You don't want to know the details."

"Yes, I do."

"College." He sighed and sank down on the edge of the bed. Arms steepled, elbows digging into his knees, his fists tucked under his chin to support the weight of his heavy head. "I messed around with guys on occasion, but I thought it was a phase. When I met you and fell in love with you, I thought that part of my life was done. I thought I'd grown up and moved on. Then we had our daughter and I never thought my life would be so complete, but it.... I was still missing something, and when I met Jason, I realized what it was."

She stood in the center of the room, glaring at him like she hated him. Her face had paled, and he could tell from the way the pattern on her pajamas kept moving that she was trembling from head to toe. He held out a hand to her, hoping she would take it and let him hold her while she fell apart. After all, he caused the pain she felt right now.

"Do you love him?" she asked as she took his hand and sat down beside him.

He pulled her into his arms, held her tight against him. "I don't know. I haven't been seeing him long. Two nights. That's it, I promise."

"So you're throwing away six years and a family for two nights in the sack with some random guy?"

"It's not like that."

"Then what is it like?"

"I have to be with a man. I know that now. I never wanted to accept it before. Jason just made me realize how much I miss it."

"Is that why you never want to make love to me?"

"Mels...."

"No, don't answer that. I don't want to know."

"I won't."

"So what do we do now?"

"I guess," Brad choked. "I guess that's up to you."

18

HIS scent—the ambrosia of his body wash and cologne, his hair and skin, his sex—remained on the pillow long after Brad had left the room. Jason spent hours breathing in the heady mix of it all, reliving the sensual touches and the loving tenderness, the warmth and the feeling of being truly complete for the first time in his life. It almost made him forget Brad had left him alone there to wallow in his self-pity.

The clock blared 11:00 a.m. in horrid, stark red digital numbers against a black backdrop. An hour before checkout time. An hour before he had to be at the deli. An hour before he had no choice but to walk away from his perfect fantasy and rejoin the ranks of his empty, meaningless life. God, he hated feeling like this: so helpless, so alone. What happened to him? Jason had always been the strong one in the group, the leader, the one everyone looked up to and turned to. Had he really been reduced to a brooding shell of his former glory?

Apparently.

Pushing up from the bed, he left the scents of an amazing night to cling to blankets and pillows that would be washed clean of everything they'd been through. No one but him would appreciate what the mound of soft linen had witnessed during those glorious morning hours.

He padded over to the bathroom, grabbing the clothes he'd worn last night in passing. His well-laid plans weren't so well laid after all. In the rush to be with Brad, he hadn't thought about grabbing a spare change of clothes, and his deli shirt was a crumpled heap in his messenger bag. There wasn't enough time to go home and grab something else, so he did with what he had.

Water poured from the showerhead above. Steam filled the room almost instantly. He climbed under the spray, gripping the off-white tile, head hanging low. The heat would wash away every trace of the time he'd spent with Brad, maybe even ease his muscles. Fortunately, or maybe not so fortunately, the water couldn't take away the memory of him being inside Brad's warm body, stroking and pumping until they both orgasmed. He knew he would end up spending the rest of the day and on into the hours of night trying to recall every detail of the time they'd spent together, wondering if Brad would tell his wife and if they would ever see each other again.

"Pull it together, man," he grumbled as he rubbed his soapy palms over his tense body. "If it's meant to happen, it will."

With a sigh, Jason turned beneath the spray, water running over his back and down his ass, between his thighs and down his legs.

Reluctantly, he hauled himself out of the shower, grabbed a towel, and dried off as much as he could. Too much time had been wasted reliving those hours with Brad, and if he didn't get his ass in gear, he would be late for the only job he had actually keeping food in his gut. The club paid the bills... barely. But the deli one kept him fed.

He threw on his clothes, raked his fingers through his hair, and vacated that damn room before he sacrificed hours of pay just to stay in a world that felt more like home.

His Chuck Taylors slapped against the sidewalk, carrying him back toward Jackson Square. Thankfully, the walk wouldn't take too long, and it might even give him a chance to clear his mind. But when he finally rounded the corner at the edge of the deli, the first thing he saw was the very familiar figure of someone he really didn't need to see right now.

"We should talk," Jansen said as Jason marched right past him.

"Not right now."

"Why not?"

"I have to get my ass to work."

Jason unlocked the deli's front door, and of course, Jansen followed him right in. That guy never really understood what "not right now" meant, and his persistence damn sure didn't help Jason's mood.

He dropped his messenger bag on the counter, grabbed the first apron he saw, and tied it on. Jansen stood on the other side of the register, arms crossed, eyes following Jason's every move. He would stay there until Jason got the business up and going. Way back in the day, before Dorian Grant had ever come along, they'd opened the shop that way on many, many occasions.

"You're not leaving, are you?" Jason said flatly as he shuffled utensils around and stocked miscellaneous containers with this and that.

"Didn't plan on it."

"What do you want?"

"I told you, we need to talk."

"Now?" Jason's head shot up and he stared straight into his best friend's eyes.

"Yeah, now. I don't know when we'll get another chance. You've been... God knows where. I've been busy with the commitment ceremony. Can we just talk, please?"

"Fine. Talk." Jason made his way around the counter, holding boxes of straws and napkins in his arms. "I'm all ears, man."

"What's going on with you?"

"What do you mean?"

"You tell me you have feelings for me then bail? Why?"

Sighing, Jason crammed a stack of napkins in their caddy. He kept his head down, too embarrassed—or maybe too damn stubborn—to face the only person he considered a real friend. From the corner of his eye, he saw Jansen standing there waiting with his arms still crossed over his chest.

"Talk to me." Jansen laid his hand on Jason's forearm.

Jason finally raised his head. It only took one good look into his best friend's eyes for him to break down and bare his soul. "After I told you I had feelings for you, I realized how completely wrong it was for me to do that. I'm sorry I even brought it up."

"Don't be sorry. You were being honest." Jansen sat down at one of the many empty tables. Jason avoided the hell out of making direct eye contact with him again by cleaning already clean tables and stocking overstocked caddies. "How long have you… 'had feelings'?"

"A long time," Jason said with a sigh. He tossed the damp rag he'd picked up somewhere along the way onto the counter, then slumped down in a chair across from where Jansen had been sitting. His elbows hit the tabletop, arms steepled, holding up his head just to make it a little harder to look away. They stared at each other for a long moment before Jason finally confessed, "I've fallen in love with a married man."

"The guy from Sin?" Jason nodded. "Wow. So um… what are you going to do?"

"I don't know. He said he was going to tell his wife but…." He shrugged. "I'll be the evil gay home wrecker or some shit. Part of me wants to forget anything ever happened. But, I… fuck me… I love him."

"Are you sure, Jason? I mean, and please don't take this wrong, but maybe he's just the first person you've felt something for since—"

"You?" Jason interrupted. Jansen lowered his head. "No, it's much more than that."

"You sure?"

"Yeah, I'm fucking sure. Now can we change the subject, please?"

"Alright." Jansen's eyes widened and he pressed his palms to the air. "Calm down."

"I'm calm. I promise," Jason said in a much cooler tone of voice. He sat back in his chair, crossed his arms over his chest, and sighed. Awkward silence made everything feel tense, strained even. Time to change the subject. "So how is the wedding planning going?"

"Commitment ceremony."

"What's the difference?"

Jansen shrugged. "I'm not sure, but gay marriage isn't legal here, so I'm guessing that's what the deal is. I don't know. It was Dorian's idea."

"Wait, you're telling me Dorian suggested you two making it official?"

"Yeah, are you surprised?"

"Very."

"Why?"

"Never thought of him as a family man. He's always been... loose."

"Yeah, I can't lie and say it didn't surprise me." Jansen paused. He lost his cocky, guarded composure and dropped his hands to his lap. "You're still going to be my... man of... whatever it is? I mean, you're going to be there, right?"

"I planned on it, unless something's changed."

"No. I want you there." Jansen stood from the chair, leaned across the little Formica-topped table, and pressed a chaste kiss to Jason's cheek. In a whisper, he said, "You'll always be my best friend. Okay?"

Jason's jaw flexed. He didn't say a word, only gave a slight nod and looked away. Both the men he had any sort of feelings for were unavailable, and what the hell did that say about his character?

19

LOAFER tapping a steady rhythm against the carpet, Brad sat on the edge of the couch with his clenched fists pressed to his forehead. He wasn't really aware of praying, though maybe he had been the entire time. He'd just told his wife of six years that sex with her didn't do it for him anymore. Not just her, but any woman. Brad finally came out of the closet. He finally managed to put a label to what he felt was true about himself.

Bradley Britt is gay.

It sounded so easy. Why the hell couldn't it be as uncomplicated as three little letters? Those three little letters came with so much implication, so many assumptions and stereotypes. God only knew what his wife thought now.

Damn it, if she would just talk to him.

He shoved up from the leather sofa and started to pace a circle around the coffee table. He just needed her to tell him to stay or go, if he still had a family or if he was going to be kicked out on his ass. Not that he would blame her for the latter. He deserved it.

"Calm down, Britt," he mumbled to himself. "She needs time to process."

The stairs behind him creaked and his head whipped back. There she stood, holding their daughter in her arms. Brad took a deep breath. He just knew this was the end, that he'd never get to hold his baby girl and lay her down to sleep. "Melody, I—"

"Don't. Please."

"I'm sorry."

"I know you are."

"I…." He frowned. "What are you…?"

"I'm trying not to be mad about this," Melody said as she took another step down. "I'm hurt, really hurt, but I'm trying to understand. I think the biggest problem I have is the fact you still married me, even though you knew you liked men."

She started toward the kitchen and he followed behind her, keeping his distance just so he wouldn't accidentally crowd her. If she decided to keep talking, he didn't want to miss a word.

After putting their daughter in her highchair, she went over to the cabinet and grabbed a few jars of baby food. "Would you like me to do that?" he asked. She handed the jar of carrot mush and a jar of applesauce to him. He grabbed a spoon and Melody sat down at the kitchen table.

"I don't understand why you would date and marry and… and God, Brad, you made love to me. Why would you do all of that if you knew you liked men?"

"I knew I loved you. I do love you." He pulled a seat over to the highchair and sat down in front of his daughter. For the first time in hours, he had a genuine smile on his face. "I love both of you."

"I still don't understand."

He spooned out a little applesauce and a little carrot, then held it to his little girl's begging pink lips. She sucked at the spoon until half the food was gone, and he repeated the process.

"Mels, I can only tell you I thought it was a phase. Or maybe I hoped it was a phase. When you came along, I thought I'd found my soul mate. You were perfect in every possible way, and I always had so much fun with you. You made me happy."

"And the sex?"

"Do you really want to talk about that?"

"Yes."

"I don't know." He shook his head. "It wasn't the same, but I could close my eyes and make love to you and…. I don't know."

"What, you imagined being with a man?"

Sometimes. "No. I tried not to think about anything other than making you happy." Tears formed in her big blue eyes, clung to her thick lashes, then dripped onto her rosy cheeks. The sight of it broke his heart, and he wished like hell he could take it all back, make things right for her. "If you want me out of here, I'll understand and I'll go. I just ask that you don't cut me off from my daughter."

"I wouldn't do that to you or her." Melody sniffled back her tears, looked up at the ceiling, and drew in a deep, ragged breath. "You don't have to go until you're ready. You can sleep in the guest room and we'll… keep up appearances, I guess."

"Are you sure?"

"Yeah, I'm sure. Just… please don't bring him around the house. I don't think I could handle seeing the two of you together."

"I would never."

"We haven't fixed anything."

"I know."

"This is in the best interest of our daughter."

"I know. But Melody, you need to know that I never set out to hurt you. I love you and I always will love you."

"I know, Brad." She gave him a weak smile. "There's never been a mean bone in your body. Don't worry. We'll figure this out, okay?"

"Okay."

20

THE deli's lights died down. Jason gave a last glance before locking the store up and leaving for the night. He stood out on the edge of the road and looked over at Jackson Square, looked up at the sun setting on the horizon, looked at all the happy people passing by. He didn't have anywhere in particular to be. The club wasn't open on Sunday nights, and normally, back in the day of the inseparable Jason and Jansen, he would've hooked up with his best friend to go for a walk or watch a movie or something. But now he didn't even have that.

"Shit." He rubbed the back of his neck, looked both ways, then crossed over Decatur toward Café du Monde and the French Market. He sort of just ambled about, feet dragging him through the crowd like they had something in mind for him. Whatever. As long as he didn't have to go home. He just didn't want to be alone right now, even if he had to be surrounded by hundreds of strangers.

He passed a booth of masquerade masks, and normally, he would've stopped to check them out, maybe buy a few for the dancers at the club. But this time, he just kept walking, letting the trail of color and feathers and glitter pass him by. He walked right by the jewelry stands and the people selling their own blends of Cajun spices. He just didn't care to stop. And honestly, he didn't know what the hell he was doing there or where he would end up. He just needed to keep himself busy so he didn't have the urge to call Brad.

As soon as Brad tap danced across his brain, his cellphone vibrated in his pocket. For a moment, he debated ignoring it. But what if was important. What if….

"Hello?"

"It's loud. Where are you?"

"I'm around. Why?"

"I need to see you."

"Brad, I don't think…."

"No, I really need to see you. Just to talk."

"Talk?"

"Yes. Can I meet you somewhere?"

"In private or does it matter?"

"Someplace quiet, but it doesn't have to be private."

"Fine. There's a sports pub down by the Riverwalk. I'll be waiting outside."

"I'll be there in about twenty minutes."

Jason hung up the phone and slipped it back into his pocket. He made an about face and started back down Decatur, away from the sea of shoppers meandering through the crowded French Market, past the sugar and chicory smells wafting out of Café Du Monde, then further down toward the Riverwalk.

The hike didn't last very long. Though he wasn't really paying attention to the clock. It felt like he had a darkened, hazy cloud surrounding him, and its thickness smothered everything else, like it meant to keep the world away from him. It even blocked out the beautiful purple evening sky. Everything felt gray and overcast, though the day had been warm. The world seemed dreary, though everyone else would've seen bright blue skies.

He finally made it to the sports pub and stopped without going inside. He would lean against the railing and wait. God knew, those places never let people just come in and have a seat. Not without ordering *something,* and right now, there was absolutely nothing on the menu to pique his interest. Right now, he only wanted to know what the hell Bradley Britt wanted to see him about.

BRAD'S loafers slapped against the pavement as he ran in the direction of the Riverwalk. The hand on his watch passed the half hour, and he just knew Jason would think he'd been stood up. It'd taken five forevers to find a damn parking spot, which was weird for a Sunday, even in the French Quarter.

He sucked wind, running as fast as he could. His lungs burned and his side ached. All that time in the gym didn't seem to be helping now that it was important. He could run five miles a day without getting winded, but right now, he felt like he was about to die.

As soon as he rounded the edge of the Riverwalk museum, he saw his sexy dancer leaning against the railing of the sports pub. Jason had his head lowered. A blanket of chin-length auburn hair cloaked his face. His strong arms crossed his chest. One foot tapped against the pavement like something bothered him, like he'd grown impatient.

He ran quickly, feet galloping, then slowed down to a brisk walk. Brad approached with caution. He couldn't—wouldn't—do anything to jeopardize this thing he had with the dancer. For God's sake, he'd just ruined his marriage for this man. Okay, maybe it wasn't entirely for Jason, but Brad would've never.... Would he have come out to his wife had he not met Jason? Would he have accepted his hidden truth in the first place?

Less than ten feet of concrete filled the space between him and the man who consumed his every waking thought, who roused his desire and excited him in ways he thought didn't exist anymore. The longer he stared at the ripples of that firm chest pressing against the thin fabric of a T-shirt a size too small and the bulge of strong thighs in faded jeans, the more he wanted to pull Jason into his arms and claim his lips. He wanted to take him back to their hotel room and fulfill every last carnal desire with him.

Then Jason raised his head.

Bright green eyes met his stare. It stopped Brad midstep, made his heart thump hard one last time, and then it seemed to stop completely. Jason's mouth opened like he wanted to say something, but he didn't. They both stepped forward, closing the remaining feet of empty air between them. Brad had to clench his fists at his side so he wouldn't give in to his urge to touch the dancer. He couldn't do that there, not in public, not where someone might see them.

"Hey," he said in a winded, almost hoarse, voice.

"Hey," Jason returned. Brad could hear the nervousness in that one little word.

"Can we um…?"

"Go somewhere to talk?"

"Yeah."

"Sure."

Jason nodded his head toward the water, away from the boat dock where people waited to board the Creole Queen. They could sit on the benches facing the water and talk, and no one would hear a word they shared. As long as people left him alone long enough to have a meaningful conversation with the man he'd come to… care for.

Brad extended his arm and Jason took a seat first, then Brad sat down beside him. Neither one of them dared to look at the other. It almost felt like sharing an enduring gaze right now would spiral into something the public didn't need to see and didn't need to know about.

"I hate this," Brad said in a soft voice. "I hate that I can't touch you right now."

"Me too."

"You don't know how bad I want to be close to you. I wanted to kiss you the moment I saw you."

"Did you?"

"Yeah, I did." Silence. This wasn't exactly how Brad pictured this meeting going. Not really sure what he thought would've happened with the two of them being in public, but this tension between them damn sure wasn't it. "So, I told her," he said matter-of-factly, eyes trained on the water.

"What?" Jason's head whipped around. Brad could feel the weight of his shocked stare, like heat searing into the side of his head. "What happened?"

"Well, she's not happy about it, obviously."

"Obviously."

"She's going to let me stay at the house. She says we'll figure it out. I think she just wants to understand why I married her and started a family with her if I've always felt this way."

"Did you explain it to her?"

"Yeah, but… I don't know. It's a lot to handle, you know?"

"So now what?"

"I don't know." Brad finally looked over. "I know I want to go somewhere and just… be me for a little while, even if I have to leave eventually. I want… to be close to you for a little while."

"Then why don't you?"

"Honestly, it doesn't feel like the right thing to do right now. Like I would be adding insult to injury."

"She doesn't have to know."

"And something about that feels so damn wrong."

"It's guilt. You don't want to hurt her."

"I really don't."

"Look, we don't have to do anything. We can go back to my apartment and just… hang out or something. I think we both could use a little down time."

"I would like that."

21

"MY PLACE isn't great, okay? It kind of sucks actually," Jason said as soon as Brad climbed out of his big SUV. Jason's little red clunker was parked beside it. He thought he would warn the reporter, though if the guy had actually taken a look around, he would've noticed the entire apartment complex was one big, nearly collapsing shithole with busted shutters and rusted security bars over broken windows. How the hell the thing managed to survive Hurricane Katrina was anyone's guess. Hey, at least the roof didn't leak and the air worked... most of the time.

"I'm sure it's fine."

"You're an optimist," Jason teased.

"How bad could it be?"

Jason chuckled softly as he started up the rusted metal steps. Each one creaked and groaned as soon as his feet planted down on its surface. Soft gusts of early evening air brushed against his arms and face, raising tiny chill bumps on his flesh. Maybe it wasn't just the air. Maybe it was the nervousness of having someone he cared so much about finally seeing the squalor he lived in.

Brad followed behind him until they both reached the front door. Jason wrenched back the screen, and the hinges squealed in protest. It took a good thrust of the hip against the wood before Jason could get the damn door to budge open. He silently cursed his life for not affording him someplace nicer to take someone so out of his league.

As soon as the door sprang open, darkness and cool air spilled from the opening. Jason cringed. He never invited anyone back to his place simply because his meager existence alluded to someone waiting for death. Not a young, vibrant dancer embracing a life of ministardom. In the nearly five years he'd lived there, he hadn't bothered to decorate, hadn't bought any new furniture, hadn't bothered to make the place his home. He'd never intended on spending any real time there, so he never really saw a point. "Sorry, it's not—"

"It's fine. Stop worrying," Brad interrupted.

Brad reached out and, much to Jason's surprise, pulled him into a tight hug. There was no promise of sex, nothing leading or suggestive, just one man needing support during a hard time in his life. Jason could certainly sympathize. Guilt and desire, unrequited love and shameful feelings for a married man, had been kicking his ass for a while now. They both carried such heavy self-imposed burdens, the weight was almost paralyzing. And if Brad only wanted support, comforting, a shoulder he could cry on, then Jason would be the best damn shoulder he could be.

With one hand cupping the nape of Brad's neck, Jason splayed the other over the small of the reporter's back. Brad laid his head on Jason's shoulder, and they just stood there for a long while, silently holding each other, simply being there for each other.

As Jason held him, the forbidden L word tap danced across his brain. It trampled all over his heart and tickled his nerves. He wanted so badly to say those three dangerous words, to let Brad know exactly how he felt and how he'd been feeling since before they'd left the hotel. The words became a cruel joke, teasing and taunting him. He couldn't say them, not yet. Brad had been through too much already and bringing love into the equation would complicate things in a way neither of them was quite ready for. Those three beautiful words had the potential to destroy everything, and that wasn't a gamble Jason wanted to take yet.

BRAD finally lifted his head from Jason's shoulder. Their eyes met and he stared into the dancer's brilliant green gaze. If he were to be completely honest with himself, he could see a long, happy future with the man in his arms. He would admit those scary feelings brewing in the warm, dark depths of his heart. He would own it and be one with it… if he could *somehow* manage to be honest with himself.

Without uttering the first word, his lips planted against Jason's. He gripped his lover's hips, holding their bodies tight against each other as he stroked his tongue back and forth across the seam of Jason's mouth.

God, the taste and the feel, the incredible sweetness, the gentle fullness. Brad could've devoured him. He could've kept him in a kiss until they both had to fight to breathe again, then pulled him into another.

Jason's lips parted.

Brad's tongue dove in and an even sweeter taste exploded against his mouth.

Perfection.

Maybe Jason's mouth tasted like any other mouth. Maybe it was his imagination. Maybe the things he felt made him believe Jason's lips tasted like fresh strawberries on a summer day or a piping cup of hot chocolate on a cold winter night. It didn't matter. To him, Jason's mouth was the only thing sating his cravings. And God help him, he didn't want another set of lips like he wanted his.

The kiss broke and Brad said in a husky voice, "I want you so bad," as his hands tightened on Jason's hips.

"But what about...?"

"I don't care. I can't help it. I want you. I need you."

"I want you too, but—"

"Don't say 'but'." Brad rolled his hips, legs parting enough to press his hardening cock against Jason's thigh. The sensation made him moan. "That's what you do to me. I can't deny it and I sure the hell can't fight it."

"I don't want you to fight it anymore."

"Let me have you, please."

"Have?"

"I want to fuck you."

"I don't bottom."

"Never?"

"No. You know that."

"Would you try for me?"

WHATEVER erection Jason had hit the road and left him with a flaccid waste of unexcited phallus. Oh, he still wanted to have sex. Jason didn't see himself ever being able to turn down Bradley Britt. He just didn't care for the idea of having Brad's huge cock in his ass, not one bit. Nothing had ever been inside his most tender of....

Wait, that wasn't true. What about the finger job Lance had given him? Didn't he kinda, sorta, in some small way enjoy that? Sure the hell did. Who's to say he wouldn't enjoy Brad topping him? After all, he'd never actually been a bottom before and couldn't say he absolutely hated it. He only hated the idea of it. Could he be versatile for the man he loved? Wouldn't it be a small sacrifice for such a huge show of trust?

"I think... I think I can try for you," he said. And the smile curling Brad's soft pink lips lit up the room. "You have to promise to be gentle. Promise me."

"Jason." Brad reached up and cupped either side of Jason's throat. Their foreheads pressed together. "The last thing I ever want to do is hurt you. I want you to trust me, but if it's too soon for this, I understand."

"I want to trust you. I believe I can trust you. I don't think you would hurt me on purpose."

"I wouldn't."

Jason nodded slowly. An uneasy half smile tightened his lips.

Neither of them immediately darted for the bedroom. They only stood in the middle of the den with the cool darkness enveloping them, keeping each other close. Brad cradled Jason's neck in his palms, thumbs stroking the hard line of his jaw. Jason's hands stayed at Brad's hips, gripping tight enough he could feel the reporter's pelvis through his khaki slacks.

22

JASON took Brad's hand, their fingers lacing as he guided his lover to his bedroom. The room was just as dark as the den, just as boring and twice as bland. The walls were the same pale shade of off-white they'd always been. In the middle of the floor, a pair of ratty old mattresses, stacked one on top of the other, sat disguised in designer sheets. Those fancy, Egyptian cotton, zillion-thread-count sheets were probably the most expensive thing he owned, and he only had them because they'd been a gift from someone he'd fucked regularly way back in the day.

At least the room didn't stink of New Orleans' squalor. It actually smelled more like his cologne. He pretty much showered himself in the stuff before stepping foot outdoors. Jansen had bought it for him the first Christmas they'd spent together, right after Jansen had been attacked. It was probably one of the most emotionally intense nights of their lives: the way they held each other, the way Jansen cried. He could almost remember the entire conversation. He could almost hear Jansen begging him not to let anyone hurt him again. And God help him, he tried. Then Dorian Grant came along and everything suddenly changed. Jansen no longer needed him and didn't seem to want him.

Brad gave Jason's hand a slight tug, and Jason lifted his eyes. "You okay?" he asked.

"I'm fine," Jason said with a soft smile. "Sorry this isn't—"

Brad pressed his finger to Jason's lips. "Stop worrying about your place. This is perfectly fine, okay? There's no place I would rather be right now."

"That's good to hear." Jason reached out and started unbuttoning Brad's shirt, silently cursing every one of those stupid little white buttons as his graceless fingers fought to push them through their tiny holes.

As soon as the deep-blue dress shirt fell open and Brad's tanned, muscled chest became exposed, Jason's cock started hardening again. He imagined running his tongue over every ripple and mound, plunging into the warm depths of Brad's body, slowly stroking until they both came. The thought made a purr rumble in his chest.

"I like that sound." Brad reached down and unfastened Jason's jeans. They pooled at his feet and his erection sprang free. "And I love the sight of this," Brad said as he rubbed his hand back and forth across Jason's crotch. "I can't wait to be inside of you."

The words made Jason's throat fist and his ass clench. Holy shit. Maybe he couldn't do this. Maybe he couldn't let someone fuck him, no matter how much he felt for that someone. Maybe he would have to—as gently as possible—take back the offer of sacrificing his derriere for Brad's enjoyment. One thing was certain, if he didn't find some way to relax, neither one of them would be getting too far.

"I'll be right back," he said, stepping out of the mound of denim at his feet.

"Where are you going?"

"To the bathroom. Get undressed. I'll be right back, I promise."

He left the bedroom with Brad standing there and went straight to the door between his room and Jansen's old room.

The bathroom was barely big enough for the shower and toilet, let alone the tiny vanity they'd somehow managed to cram in there. Black-and-white checkerboard tile lined the floor and walls. Half the fixtures worked like they were built to. The other half worked only when they had the inclination. Everything about the room reminded Jason of the many things he sincerely hated about living in that dump and how badly his life royally sucked.

"I gotta get out of this place," he mumbled as he reached into the medicine cabinet and pulled out a pill bottle. He dumped one small yellow pill into his hand. Ecstasy, his drug of choice. Not that he should need it to be with someone he wanted so badly. He hadn't even done it since the first night he'd met Brad. Just didn't need it. But he also had never considered letting someone have their way with his semivirginal ass.

He tossed back the pill, leaned his head down under the water faucet, and sucked it all down. Ten minutes. That's all it would take for the drug to kick in. Then, no matter how and where Brad wanted to touch him, it would feel nothing less than absolutely amazing.

He reached down and gently rubbed his hand over his hard-on. "Oh yeah." The nerve endings had already started coming alive.

Still gripping his cock, he went back to his bedroom and found Brad lying on the bed, legs spread wide, one hand fisting his own erection. Brad's hooded hazel eyes landed on him, wound down his body, and stopped at his crotch. Jason gave it another stroke, hand moving from base to tip then back again.

"You going to play with yourself all night," Brad teased, "or are you going to get your ass over here and join me?" Jason licked his lips and sidled up to the bed. He started to climb on top of Brad, but his lover slid to the side. "Lie down on your chest," he instructed, patting the empty spot beside him.

"What? No foreplay?"

"Do what I tell you. I promise, you won't regret it."

Jason rolled over, eyes closed, breathing steady… for right now. That didn't mean he would have any kind of control of his respiratory function once he felt the tip of Brad's cock pushing against his ass. He tucked his arms under the pillow and rested his head, tried not to think about anything involving any kind of penetration until the X fully kicked in.

But then he felt Brad's lips at the nape of his neck. The mattress dipped around him as his lover's palms pressed against the bed. "You'll enjoy this," Brad whispered before moving his kisses a little lower, lower, lower. Then the firm tip of his tongue replaced the soft press of lips. It licked down the valley between Jason's cheeks, and he could already feel his sac tugging and his cock growing even more rigid.

"Holy shit," Jason rasped. The sensation made his legs spread wider. The ecstasy high made him grind his hardened cock against the bed. He felt Brad's tongue circle his puckered opening, and every synapse in his brain triggered a chain reaction in his body. "Fucking hell. Don't stop."

Brad licked rings around the tight opening, dipped inside, teased and toyed. Every single brush and stroke brought Jason closer to coming. His cock thickened, became almost uncomfortable to lie on. He lifted his hips and the movement opened him wider. Brad's tongue dipped deeper. Jason let out one long, rumbling moan.

Then the soft moistness of Brad's tongue left the tight warmth of Jason's ass. He almost wanted to protest, to beg him to do it again, but before he could even open his mouth, the tongue had been replaced by a finger and the lips went back to the base of his spine.

"How does that feel?" Brad whispered between kisses.

"Good. Incredible actually," Jason breathed.

One more finger eased inside him, and Jason hissed at the sudden change in pressure. "Just breathe," Brad whispered, but Jason already knew the drill. He had said those words to the tight-assed guys he'd been with in the past. Breathe. Relax. Just let it happen. Check.

Those two strong fingers began to open and close, working the ring of muscle and slowly stretching him open. He bit down on his lip and kept his breathing as steady as he could. Eventually, the sting wore down and all he wanted was to feel Brad's cock buried inside of him.

"Do you have condoms?" Brad asked.

"In the bathroom. Medicine cabinet."

"Don't move, okay?"

Jason nodded his head, breathing raggedly into his pillow. Every subtle movement, every brush of the sheets against his erection made his sac tighten against his body. He didn't know how much longer he could hold out.

As if Brad had been inside of his head, hearing the urgency in his silent voice, he reappeared with a little aluminum square between his teeth. Jason looked back as soon as he heard the creaking of floorboards beneath the tattered brown carpet. He caught sight of Brad tossing a spare condom onto the floor next to the stack of mattresses while he rolled the rubber down his shaft. Every fear he had of being topped fell by the wayside. He only wanted relief and wanted it from Brad.

The mattress dipped again, and Jason buried his face into the pillows. He could already feel his heart racing—partly with fear, partly with excitement. *Trust him,* Jason silently reminded himself. *He'd never do anything to hurt you.*

Brad's rock-hard cock brushed against the valley of Jason's cheeks as his head lowered to Jason's shoulder. He stroked back and forth, back and forth, and each little tease and tickle relaxed Jason's body but excited his libido.

"You sure you want this?" Brad asked before pressing another soft kiss to Jason's skin.

Fuck yeah, he wanted it. Now that he was completely turned-on and high as a kite, every little touch or breath or sound from Brad's lips only turned him on more. "Yes. Please, fucking yes. Just… be easy."

"Okay, but don't clench. Breathe, okay?"

Jason nodded with his face still buried in the pillow. The stroking between his cheeks stopped and the tip of Brad's erection pressed through the ring of muscle. Jason growled out a string of curses, ass clenching hard around the head of Brad's shaft. It took a hand lovingly petting his spine and a few softly whispered words before he could even dare to relax.

Letting the breath he'd been holding onto go, Jason willed his tense muscles to release and relax. He calmed himself to the soothing touch of Brad's lips against his neck.

"You okay?" Brad asked.

JASON mumbled something into the pillow's surface. Brad couldn't make out a single word, but as soon as he felt him relax, he knew it was okay to keep going… slowly.

Brad pressed his palms into the mattress on either side of Jason's body. He kept kissing his lover's back, shoulders, and neck as he gently pushed deeper inside. He heard the muffled whimpers and moans, and he hated the fact Jason had to suffer one second of discomfort for this, but damn him, he couldn't help it. He wanted to feel the dancer's body sheathing his cock. He wanted to make love to him and wanted Jason to know, no matter what, he would always be able to trust the fact that Brad would never do anything to hurt him.

Brad gently pulled back, until the ridge of his head met the ring of muscle, then he pushed deep inside again. The friction made his sac tighten and his erection thicken. Every hardened inch throbbed with each slow stroke. Rolling his hips, Brad found their rhythm and fell into a gentle, steady pace.

"I'm going to make you come," Brad whispered, lips fluttering against Jason's skin. He dipped his hips again and his cock dove deeper inside Jason's warm opening, grazing the sensitive nub buried in his lover's body.

"Shit!" Jason cried. The husky sound of his lover's voice crying out in heated passion did something for Brad's ego. It was a man thing. To know what he was doing felt good enough to make a man let go and scream out, it just… it made the animalistic side of him roar to life, made him want to stake his claim so no other man would take him away. "Oh, God!" Jason yelled out. "I'm about to come!" His back curled and his cheeks spread wider.

Brad pulled back and then thrust inside again.

Jason growled out another deep sound, then he collapsed to the bed.

Brad could hear the heavy breathing, and it made a smile part his lips. He kissed the center of Jason's back as he eased himself out of his lover's body. While he'd satisfied one carnal appetite, a very different desire in him had been sated. He'd pleasured Jason's body, proved to the dancer that being a bottom—for the right top—could be rewarding and enjoyable. He'd also proven Jason could trust him, and wasn't that the basis for every strong relationship? Of course it was.

"Good God," Jason rasped, rolling away from the big-ass wet spot he'd left in the bed. "I don't think I've ever come so hard."

"Glad I could please you," Brad said with a teasing smirk.

Jason reached over and rubbed his hand over Brad's erection. "You need to let me take care of you now." His other arm flopped off the edge of the bed and when it came back up, he had the spare condom between his middle and forefingers.

As Jason started to tear into the package, Brad locked his hand around Jason's semiflaccid cock and started to stroke, rousing Jason into another full erection. Jason moaned, thrusting his shaft against Brad's soft palm. As soon as he was hard again, he sat up in the bed and rolled the rubber down his many firm inches. He patted his thigh and Brad just stared.

"Come here," Jason said in a sex-drenched voice. "I want you to sit on my lap with your back to me." Brad's brow quirked. "What? Never done it like that before?"

"Not with a man."

"Trust me, you'll like it."

And Brad did trust him. Infinitely.

When he sat down on Jason's lap, he could feel his lover's erection press between his cheeks. Jason didn't enter him, not immediately, which was both a blessing and a curse. It prolonged the sensual teasing. It heightened the passion.

He felt Jason's lips at the curve of his neck about the same time he felt two fingers slip inside his body. First instinct made him tense. The feel of those strong, slender fingers easing into his tightened opening made him hiss, but the sound faded into a soft moan.

As Jason worked them back and forth, he reached his other hand around and gently gripped Brad's shaft. Brad purred as his lover's hand and fingers and lips toyed with all of his most sensitive places. "Make love to me, Jason," he breathed. "Have sex with me. Make me believe you love me."

"I...." There was a pause, and for a moment, Brad thought he'd said the wrong thing, like he'd struck a raw nerve or something. "I will," Jason said in a hoarse voice.

A thick, firm cock slowly replaced the fingers that had been moving in and out of his body. Brad closed his eyes, sat back and eased himself down Jason's hardened shaft. He felt his lover's lips at the nape of his neck again. Then suddenly, Jason's fingers knotted in his hair and he turned Brad's head until their lips met in a deep, heated kiss.

23

"SHOWER," Brad moaned against the pillow. The sound made Jason laugh softly. They both lay naked in the bed, sweat beading from nearly every inch of their bodies. Both their hearts raced, and neither one could muster much more than a shallow breath. Their heads turned in until they stared at each other. Their voices erupted in laughter. Post-coital bliss at its best.

"My shower is tiny. You might want to go first," Jason offered with a wistful grin.

"You sure?"

"Yeah," Jason mused, eyes hooded, smile wide, the remnants of an incredible orgasm disrupting his brain function. "I'll get this mess cleaned up then I'll take mine."

They both eased off their respective sides of the bed and met where the footboard would've been if he actually had a bedroom suite. For a moment, they only stood there, smiling like dopey-eyed fools. Jason's voice finally broke the silence, but there was no conviction in the sound. "Do you, um… want to stay here tonight?"

Brad took a step closer, their naked bodies meeting in a delicate kiss of firm chests and spent cocks. "Is that what you want me to do?"

"I would like to sleep beside you."

"Then I'll stay," Brad whispered as he leaned in and touched his lips to Jason's. He licked the seam of his lover's mouth, tongue parting Jason's lips. They stayed locked in the kiss, hands caressing the curves of each other's backsides.

When the kiss finally broke, Jason said in a hoarse voice, "Then I'll run downstairs and wash the sheets. You take a shower."

He watched as Brad sauntered by, studying the dimples on the sides of his lover's perfectly delicious ass and the way his thick thigh muscles flexed as he walked. The sight made his mouth water and his cock twitch.

The door closed and Jason's gaze shifted up toward the ceiling. He stared at the cracked and peeling paint for a second before closing his eyes. If there was a God listening, he sure the hell hoped they heard his prayer. "Don't let me screw this one up," he whispered. "I've already fallen too hard for him."

With a sigh, he broke free from his prayer then leaned over and ripped the sheets from the bed and tossed them to the floor. He grabbed his clothes, pulled his wrinkled jeans up and fastened them, yanked his tattered T-shirt over his head, then slipped his feet into some worn-out flip-flops. He wasn't trying to impress anyone. He only wanted his damn sheets washed so he could go to bed with the man he loved on something that didn't smell like it came from an hourly rate motel.

Of course, he had to fight with the front door again just so he could get downstairs and use the shitty, semifunctioning washer and dryer in the makeshift laundry room. Hooker hangout with no security to keep people from stealing shit.

He tossed the sheets in the wash and grabbed a box of powdered detergent from the vending machine, half surprised the damn thing didn't take his money without giving up the goods. He poured in the blue-and-white powder then let the machine go to town. He wouldn't be able to leave until everything was cleaned and dried, which presented a small problem. It kept him away from Brad and left him lonely in that godforsaken shithole.

Pulling out his phone, he stared down at the screen and debated playing a game or something to pass the time, but just as he went to hit the little icon with the big red bird, the damn thing started to ring in his hand. "Jansen," he said as he answered the call. "What's up?"

"Just wanted to call and check on you."

"For what?"

"Because, I worry about you."

"You do?"

"Well, duh. You okay?"

"Yeah, I'm fine."

"You home?"

"Yeah, why?"

"Just asking."

"What gives, Jansen?" Jason leaned against the washer, legs crossed at the ankles to keep it from knocking around and making so much damn noise he couldn't hear the conversation. "Why are you calling me in the middle of the night, asking me a bunch of cryptic questions?" A long, silent pause made him think he'd dropped the call, but when he checked the screen, it said the call was still in progress. "Jansen? What's up?" he asked again with a little more seriousness in his tone.

"It's Dorian. He went out with Angelo tonight."

"So?"

"So, someone is probably getting their head beat in as we speak. He was so pissed off when he left, even took his big pistol with him."

"I fucking told you he was trouble," Jason muttered.

"He's not trouble. I just… I couldn't stand sitting here thinking about it. The house is too quiet, and if I stay here alone much longer, I'm going to lose my mind."

"What do you want me to do, Jansen?"

"Meet me somewhere."

"I can't."

"Why not?"

"I have company."

"Who? The married reporter?"

"Don't say it like that. I'm… in love with him."

"I know. You told me. Doesn't change the fact he's a married man."

"And you're about to be a married man too. So what do you want me to do?" The washer buzzed behind him. "Hold on. I need to switch out the laundry." Jason set the phone down on the dryer, then transferred the linens from one machine to another. He cranked up the heat and got the dryer going before picking up the phone again. "I'm back."

"Why are you doing laundry in the middle of the night if Brad's there with you?"

"What does it matter?"

"Just curious."

"It's none of your business."

"Right. So, I guess I can't come over then."

"I'd rather you not."

"Why? You don't want the old love of your life meeting the new love of your life?"

"That's a shitty thing—" Jason stopped mid-sentence. This wasn't Jansen's personality. He'd never been snarky just because he could be. If nothing else, the kid had better phone etiquette than that. "Have you been drinking?"

"Does it matter?"

"I guess not, but you'd better not get behind the wheel of a car right now."

"I want to see you."

"Look, go climb into bed and get some sleep. I'll talk to you tomorrow, I promise."

"Whatever."

"Don't be like—" Jansen didn't even give him a chance to finish his sentence before the asshole ended the call.

Jason didn't like that a bit. Not only did he not like being hung up on, but he didn't like knowing his drunken, desperate friend might climb into the car and drive away from Grant's mansion. Unfortunately though, there wasn't much Jason could do. He didn't know where Dorian lived, didn't know how to call his best friend's partner, and he knew if he called Jansen back, it would just piss him off more, maybe even start a fight.

"Shit!" he bit out as he grabbed his half-dry sheets out of the dryer. He knew good and damn well he needed to do something about Jansen so the idiot didn't do something stupid and get himself hurt.

He climbed the rusted steps back to his second-floor apartment, and this time, he had enough pissed-off coursing through his veins it didn't take too much fight to get the front door open.

As soon as he burst through it, Brad's head whipped around and his eyes widened. Jason tossed the damp sheets onto the couch beside him. "I have a problem," he said, head shaking, jaw clenching. He let out a sigh as the heel of his hand pressed against his eye socket. "My best friend is sitting at home alone and drunk, and he wants to get out of the house. I'm afraid if I don't at least meet him somewhere, he'll try to drive all the way out here and…."

"It's okay," Brad said as he stood from the couch. "I can go back to my place."

"No, I don't want you to go home. Why don't you go with me?"

"Is that a good idea?"

"He won't tell anyone."

"That's not… I mean…."

"If you don't want to, you don't have to."

"I just don't want to be in the way. Maybe he needs his best friend right now."

"And I need the man I—" Jason closed his eyes and let out a sigh. Thank God he'd managed to stop the word before it left his lips, though honestly, it was probably too late because the implication was already there.

"The man you what, Jason?" Brad asked in a calm voice.

Jason ran his fingers through the fallen tendrils of his chin-length auburn hair. He hadn't meant for this to happen this way. The timing was all wrong. Brad still had a wife and kid. He didn't need some clingy dancer falling in love with him, did he? Jason couldn't even look up when he finally found the courage to say, "The man I love...."

24

"I'M SO sorry." Jason blanched as he sank down on the edge of his ratty couch. His eyes turned a shade darker. Cheeks rosy red with what Brad assumed to be embarrassment. The atmosphere suddenly felt tense, like their emotions had collided midair and the fallout had the potential to be nuclear. "I didn't want it coming out like that. I wanted to wait until things felt more…."

"Comfortable?"

"I guess."

Brad paced to the center of the room, somehow still defying gravity and managing to stay upright though his knees felt weak and his stomach knotted.

Love.

He couldn't believe what he'd heard, couldn't believe Jason had already reached *that* level of feeling for him. And no matter how hard he tried, he couldn't erase the shock from his face. He stood in the middle of the room with his eyes a little wider and his jaw slightly slack. His heart flip-flopped in his chest like a fish out of water. And where the hell did his brain go?

Hello up there. Input please.

"Will you say something?" Jason asked. His voice sounded so desperate it almost felt like a punch to the gut. "I know it's not the right time for you, but I… I can't help how I feel."

Not the right time, what an understatement. It wasn't that he didn't feel something for Jason. He did, but could he call it "love"? It felt too soon, too fast. It felt right and completely wrong all the same. He couldn't deny how much he wanted to be close to Jason, how much he cared about and enjoyed spending time with him. He couldn't deny how much he loved sex with Jason, but did all that make this thing between them equate to love?

God, help him. He didn't want to mess this up, but now it felt like messing up was inevitable.

"Brad?"

"Can you give me a minute to process this?"

"Sure, take all the time you want." Jason bolted up from the couch, grabbed his car keys from the coffee table, and headed for the door.

No. Brad didn't want him overreacting like that. Running out the door, running away from what he felt would never make this any better. It could only rip them apart in the end, right? Nothing could be saved by running away.

He reached out for Jason's arm and clamped his fingers over his wrist. "What are you doing?"

"Giving you time. I have a friend who needs me right now, and obviously, I just made a huge mistake. So I kind of have an urge to run from it, if you don't mind."

"Let me go with you, please."

"That defeats the purpose of running away, Bradley."

"Don't do that, okay? I just need a minute to…." Brad sighed. "You can't spring shit like that on people."

"What?" Jason's brow quirked and he crossed his arms over his chest. There was a whole hell of a lot of attitude in his posture now, and it wasn't lost on Brad. Not in the least. "You've never had someone fall so deeply in love with you they couldn't keep fighting the urge to tell you?"

"That's not what I meant."

"Then what did you mean?"

"Jason, I have a wife and kid at home. I know what love is. I love them." As soon as he said the words, Brad knew he'd screwed up. It didn't take the lowering of Jason's head or the clenching in his lover's jaw to know how badly he'd messed everything up, but seeing the hurt on Jason's face sure did drive that dreadful nail into the proverbial coffin. "Jason."

"Go home, Brad. Go back to your perfect life and I'll stay where I belong. We can forget this ever happened, okay?"

"Is that what you want?" *Please say no. Please say no.*

Everything fell silent. Not a single breath could be heard. Not a single beating heart. Brad couldn't even feel the low drumming of his pulse anymore. It almost felt like all time and life and the world froze. And everything hinged on what Jason wanted.

"Yeah," his lover said in a low voice. Brad's throat tightened. Jason looked up and his cold, empty green stare met Brad's scared eyes. "Yeah, that's what I want."

25

THE red taillights of Brad's SUV reflected in Jason's watery eyes. He hugged himself tight to keep from falling apart, though it didn't stop his heart from crumbling in his chest. It didn't quench the urge to throw himself in front of Brad's car and beg him not to leave. He wouldn't do it, though. Jason was much too dignified, or maybe too stubborn, to pull such a desperate stunt.

How could he have been so stupid? He just let the man he'd fallen in love with walk out of his life, and honestly, he didn't know if there was a chance in hell of getting him back. He didn't know if anyone would ever make him feel the things Brad did, didn't know if he would ever have a chance at being truly happy.

The cell phone in his pocket vibrated. Jansen's ringtone sang words he just couldn't deal with hearing right now. He fished the phone from his denims and answered the call just to shut the damn thing up.

"Hello?" he said in a soft, broken voice as he sniffled back the rest of his tears.

"What's wrong?" Jansen slurred on the other end.

"Nothing. I'm coming your way. You need to give me the address."

"You sure nothing's wrong?"

"Yeah, I'm sure."

"Okay. If you say so. Let me text the address to you."

"Fine. I'm leaving now."

He climbed into his stupid little car and turned the key in the ignition. Nothing happened. The lights came on but the engine didn't crank. He turned the key again. Nothing. "Really?" The palm of his hand slammed down hard on the steering wheel. His head rolled back against the headrest. Tears streamed down his cheeks again.

This was too much. He couldn't deal with any of this shit anymore. Bottling everything up and letting it fester didn't work. Letting go of his emotions pushed someone very, very important to him away. What the fuck was he supposed to do now? "What the hell do you want from me?" he yelled at the exposed metal roof of his car.

The phone in his other hand vibrated again. It was Jansen, giving him Dorian's address. As if things couldn't get any worse, now he couldn't even get to his best friend when he needed him. With shaky fingers, he fidgeted with the phone until he managed to compose a text telling Jansen about his car breaking down and how he wouldn't be able to make it. He said he was sorry then pitched the phone into the passenger seat.

A few minutes later, the damn thing decided to ring.

"What?"

"I really wish you would talk to me," Jansen said.

"What is there to talk about? My car's fucked. My life is fucked. And I'm an idiot."

"What happened?"

"What didn't happen?"

"Will you please stop that?"

"Stop what?"

"Answering my questions with more questions because you don't want to open up and talk to your best goddamn friend!"

Jason pulled the phone from his ear and looked at the screen. Yeah, it said Jansen's name, but when the hell did the kid grow a magnum set of balls? "Maybe I don't feel like talking about it."

"I'm coming over."

"How? You're still just drunk enough to get yourself in trouble."

"I'll get Dorian's driver to bring me over."

"Don't bother."

"Too late. I was already on the Huey P. before I called you."

"You're an asshole."

"I know, but you still love me."

True. Tragic, but very, very true. "Fine. See you in… what, fifteen minutes?"

"Probably."

He hung the phone up and slipped it in his pocket as he climbed out of the car, but he didn't go back up to his apartment. Instead he stood there staring up at the starry night sky, wondering where in the hell he'd gone so horribly wrong. What had he done in his lifetime to deserve being shit on so badly? He'd always been giving and caring, always kept to the moral high road and helped whenever he could. Why the hell did karma insist on screwing him over so badly? Why did everyone he loved have to love someone else?

Leaning against the trunk of his little red beater, he crossed his legs at the ankles and wrapped his arms around his chest. He glared down at the sparkling, broken bits of glass littering the pavement. If someone were to pick up the pieces, would they make a window that once held out the rain? Or would they make a bottle that once held a magic potion to wash away someone's pain? Each piece belonged to something that once had a purpose, but fate decided to shatter whatever it used to be and leave a wasted mess on a dirty stretch of broken concrete and gravel. He sort of felt the same way about his own life, shattered and incomplete, lost without its purpose.

With a groan, he scrubbed his hands over his face just in time to see two bright white headlights pull into the parking lot. Beyond them, he could almost make out the sleek black sedan, the likes of which no one in his neighborhood would ever have the means to own. It had to be Jansen, riding in on the chariot afforded to him by his rich criminal partner.

He sighed.

The window rolled down and Jansen's shining, blissful, drunken smile gleamed from the backseat. "Come on," he called out. "We're going somewhere else for a little while."

Perfect.

Jansen opened the car door and popped up from the seat, keeping the grin on his face wide and enthusiastic. Jason didn't know how much of the bubbly, happy crap his mood would tolerate right now, and he might have been three seconds from meltdown had Jansen not stepped right up to him and thrown his arms around Jason's body.

Jason lowered his head to Jansen's shoulder, burying his face in the curve of his best friend's neck. He felt Jansen's hands against his back, one stroking up and down his spine, the other simply holding him. At least he still felt wanted, even if it wasn't the way one man would want someone he loved.

"I don't like seeing you this way," Jansen whispered against Jason's temple.

"Trust me, I don't like being this way."

"Then let me help you. Please, let me take care of you for a change."

He nodded against Jansen's shoulder then let his friend guide him over to the sedan. They didn't utter two words to each other. Neither of them really needed to say anything. They always had this mutual understanding of each other and knew exactly how to fix it. And right now, they both just needed to be close to the other.

Jason and Jansen, together again, just like the old days.

26

"I'M NOT coming home tonight, okay?" Brad mumbled into the phone. He knew he did a pretty poor job of hiding his emotions from the person who seemed to know him better than anyone else, but as long as she didn't prod, maybe he could get through this mess with a little dignity.

"Yeah, I'm fine. I just… I need to be alone for a little while. I need to think." And Melody couldn't have agreed more. She told him to take whatever time he needed. His family would still be there when he came home. "I love you," he said, and like always, she said those three little words back.

Nothing had changed. He still very much loved her and always would. They were best friends. They had always turned to each other in times of crisis and always would. He just couldn't keep lying to himself and pretending to be straight just to save their marriage. Thankfully, Melody seemed to be understanding. Now, if he could only take away the pain he'd caused her.

He pulled up to the curb in front of the Bourbon Orleans hotel. The concierge greeted him with a smile and a "Welcome." Bradley tried to keep up appearances, tried to play it cool. After all, he still had a public persona he had to maintain. With a crooked grin, he handed over the keys to his vehicle then headed into the hotel, across the marble floors and straight to the check-in desk.

Again, the staff greeted him with warm smiles and courteous professionalism. He asked for the same room number he and Jason had shared before. The woman behind the desk happily obliged, swiped his credit card, then handed him the key card. He quietly rode the elevator back up to the fourth floor, and when he reached the door, something inside him stopped him from going into that room.

He splayed his fingers over the door and pressed his forehead to the cool white wooden surface. His eyes closed and his heart sank as he remembered those beautiful hours he'd spent with the dancer. It wasn't just the sex. It was the tenderness and closeness, the way they'd both seemed to forget about all their problems and simply enjoyed their lives for a change. They were both completely free and completely true to themselves in that room. Or at least, that's how it'd felt to Brad.

Doors opened and closed behind him. People shuffled by, probably watching him like he'd lost his mind, or maybe he needed help. Didn't he? Need help? He'd never been so confused in his life.

He slipped the key card into the door and the light changed from red to green. The knob jiggled and within seconds, he found himself back in *their* room.

The clean white surfaces were just as he remembered them. It was exactly the same, save for the scent of their mingled cologne and the ambrosia of their bodies. The smell of their shared release didn't cling to the air as it had before. And standing there now, with Jason so far away from him and probably brokenhearted, the hours they'd spent there seemed like a lifetime ago.

Brad lay back across the mattress, legs hanging off the edge, eyes trained on the ceiling. He had the urge to call Jason and beg him to meet him there, but what good would that do? It wouldn't fix the problem of Jason's love, nor would it put a label on the emotions Brad felt for him. It wouldn't magically conjure the right words to Band-Aid the situation, and it wouldn't make all the problems go away.

So why did he go to *their* room in the first place?

Maybe he just needed to feel like he still had a chance, like he hadn't screwed up so badly the bridges couldn't be mended.

He closed his eyes and imagined having Jason in his arms, the way they'd made love to each other and how perfect everything had felt. He could almost feel Jason's solid chest against his palms, could almost feel the dancer's fingers knotting in his hair as their lips met in a heated kiss. Then he felt the weight of his heart sinking down into his gut.

"God, I'm such an idiot," he groaned as he rolled onto his side. His body curled into a fetal position, and his arms wrapped around his legs. He had to come up with something so epic, so huge and so profound to say to Jason, the dancer would have no choice but to melt in his arms.

Great. Unless the words were written on a cue card, he was pretty much screwed.

THE alarm on his cell phone screamed an annoying, grating monophonic sound. Brad bolted up from the bed only to find sunlight pouring in from the sheer curtains. The smooth white linens had somehow turned to a crumpled heap. He blindly reached for his phone, only to discover he'd managed to fall asleep and the hours passed by so fast he didn't even feel rested.

"Six in the morning? Already? Shit!"

He didn't have a change of clothes and had two hours to get to work. Hell, he didn't even have the clarity of mind to report the news of the day. Really, he just wanted to spend the next twenty-four hours marinating in his mistakes and trying to find a way to make all the problems go away.

Brad grabbed the phone from the nightstand, scrolled through his contacts until he found his boss's phone number. The boss probably wouldn't be happy about his star reporter calling in sick, but there was no way in hell he'd be of use to anyone today, and he knew he couldn't fake a media-worthy smile even if he tried.

The phone rang and rang, and just as he was about to hang up, the boss's gravelly voice barked out a raspy, "What?"

"This is Britt. I won't be in today."

"Why the fuck not?"

"I think I have some sort of stomach bug. I can't even pry myself away from the toilet."

"Perfect."

"Sorry."

"Yeah, well… maybe it's best you stay away. Don't bring that shit to the office. I don't need my entire staff sick."

"That's why I called."

"Fine. Get better. See you tomorrow?"

"Maybe. We'll see."

"Right."

27

A DOOR slammed, followed by a weighty, bass-heavy voice nearly growling, "What the fuck are you doin' here?" Dorian Grant. Jason sighed as he covered his head with a throw pillow. His brain pounded inside his skull, and the last thing he wanted was an altercation with the smooth criminal. "Did ya hear me, boy? I said—"

"I fucking heard you. Can you take it down a notch, please?"

"You got some—"

"I brought him here," Jansen called from the foot of the stairs. "He's my best friend and he was having a bad night. Calm down."

"Nothin' better not have happened," Dorian grumbled.

"You know, if you're going to marry me or whatever, you need to learn to trust me," Jansen said.

Jason threw the throw pillow to the opposite end of the couch as he swung his legs over the edge. His eyes squinted from the sun spilling in through the windows facing the backside of the house. Every sound, every ounce of light, just made his head pound harder, and at the rate he was going, his shitty mood might end up being the kick in the ass he needed to give Dorian a piece of his mind. "Can you two take your lover's quarrel somewhere else?"

"Boy, this is—"

"Boy?" Jason bolted up from the couch and stomped toward Grant, finger stabbing out ready to plow right into Dorian's sternum. "I've got your boy right—"

"Guys, come on." Jansen jumped between the two of them. "Can we not do this right now?"

Dorian's eyes narrowed. He pointed over Jansen's shoulder, right at Jason's face, and said, "You're messin' with the wrong one."

"No, Jansen's messing with the wrong one."

Jansen sighed and shook his head, turning between them so he faced Dorian. "Why don't you go upstairs? I'll join you for a shower, okay? Maria said she'd make us all a big breakfast."

Dorian leaned his head down and pulled Jansen into a kiss while keeping his stare glued on Jason. Jason rolled his eyes and turned to walk away. He started toward the downstairs bathroom when he heard Jansen say, "Why do you do that?"

"Do what?" he asked, but he kept walking away.

"You know exactly 'what'."

"Because I don't like him." Jason turned back around. "I think you're settling for some lowlife thug. You can do better than him."

"What? Like being with you?"

"Fuck you."

"No, I'm serious. You hate him because he's with me and you can't have me. Admit it."

"I'm not doing it. I hate him because he's an asshole."

"And you're not?"

"Again, fuck you."

That was so not the kind of conversation two emotionally charged men with hangovers needed to have before breakfast. Shit had the potential to get out of hand fast. Jason changed his direction, and now, instead of heading for the bathroom, he headed straight for the front door. He gripped the knob and wrenched the damn thing open. Morning sun smacked him square in the face and he flinched.

"Where the hell are you going?" Jansen called from across the room. His voice echoed, and by the time it hit Jason's ears, it sounded like he'd screamed through a bullhorn.

"Home."

"How?"

That's right, Jason didn't have his car because the damn thing had broken down last night. *Fuck!* "I don't know. I'll walk."

"Now you're being a stubborn asshole."

"Maybe." He shrugged.

"Will you please come back inside? I'll have Dorian's driver take you home."

"I don't want shit from him," Jason barked. "And honestly, I don't want shit from you. I just want to go back to my life and pretend everything is okay, that I don't need anyone to love me and I can be happy alone. Is that too much to fucking ask?"

He felt the sting of tears in the back of his throat as his best friend lowered his head. None of this crap was his fault, but Jason didn't hesitate to take his frustration out on the only person who'd always been there no matter how shitty he acted.

"I'm sorry," Jason said in a low voice. "I didn't mean to snap like that."

"It's okay. I get it. You've been through the wringer here lately, and I imagine your emotions are all over the place." Jason nodded. Jansen closed the distance between them. He wrapped his arms around Jason's body and that's when the tears finally broke free again.

"I just wanted him to love me back," Jason finally confessed.

"I know, baby, and he'd be a fool not to. But you said it yourself, he has a lot going on right now. He's married, for God's sake, and he just admitted to his wife that he's gay. You're going to have to give him some time to process things, to accept things. He's smart enough to know what a good guy you are. He'll be back."

"God, I hope so."

28

EVERY passing day made Jason's hope diminish a little more. Friday came and the only sight or sound from Bradley Britt had been through the television, through local news reports Jason had never bothered watching before that blond-haired, hazel-eyed hunk of superstar had walked into his life. He only turned it on now so he could pretend Brad was still right there, waiting and ready to accept him and the love he had to offer.

What a joke. He'd messed up bad on this one, and really, he needed to start forcing himself to get the hell over it before he turned himself into a lunatic. But he knew good and damn well getting over Brad wouldn't be easy and sure the hell wouldn't happen overnight. When Brad walked out of his life, he took a huge chunk of his heart with him.

Jason's worn-out Converse tennis shoes slapped against the hall floor leading into the backstage area off Sin & Seduction. The sound echoed against the cinderblock wall and made each footfall sound so angered and deliberate. Lance leaned against the opening, arms crossed over his chest. A gentle smile brightened his face.

"Hey, baby," Lance said, pushing up as soon as Jason was close enough for a hug. "You doing okay?"

Though he didn't really want to, Jason gave into the arms reaching out toward him. "I'm fine," he said, pushing away from the hug almost as quickly as he'd succumbed to it.

"You sure?"

Jason staged his most fake, most utterly convincing smile. "Yeah, I'm golden. Just been a really long week. Is everyone here?"

"They're all waiting for the schedule."

"Good."

Jason started to walk off, but Lance grabbed his wrist and pulled him back. His tanned fingers uncurled and in the palm of his hand sat a little yellow pill. Promising. Tempting. Jason looked back up and met Lance's cool blue stare. Lance licked his plump pink lips then smirked. Teasing.

"You're going to have a great night," Lance purred. "And I'm going to help you."

"Really?" Jason arched his brow. The corner of his lips quirked. He leaned in and seductively whispered against Lance's ear, "And how do you plan to do that?"

Lance reached one hand down and gripped Jason's crotch, giving it a gentle squeeze. He held the other hand up to Jason's lips and said, "You'll just have to see for yourself, won't you?"

Fuck it, right? Why not? It wasn't like Brad would be running back to him anytime soon, if ever, and obviously he was way too proud to call the guy and talk things out. Rejection. Damn, it had a way of making him swallow a hard dose of reality.

Better start getting over the reporter now while you still have a bit of sanity left.

And while this might not have been the best decision in the world, it made sense right now. He lowered his head, pressed his lips to Lance's palm, and licked the yellow pill into his mouth. His eyes closed as he swallowed it down.

"That's it, baby," Lance cooed. "Let it wash the bullshit away."

"Give me twenty minutes. Then, I'm all yours."

A lascivious grin stretched across Lance's handsome face. The excitement reached up and filled his eyes, like just the idea of Jason giving him a shot in the back room turned him on. Maybe it did. And maybe, when the time came, Jason would be able to perform without the anxiety of wronging Brad. They weren't together, after all. The love was unrequited anyway, so what did it matter?

Jason headed into the backstage area where all the dancers gathered during the show. As soon as he entered the room, all conversation ceased and the room fell as silent as a church. He frowned. "You girls okay? You're acting like God just walked through the door." He gave each one of them a quick glance. They all kept their lips tightly sealed. "Wait, were you guys talking about me?" No one said a word. "Assholes," he grumbled.

"And he's back!" Lance said excitedly. Laughter erupted. Heat rushed Jason's face.

Maybe he was actually back, or at least getting there. The idea of being his old self again felt great. Despite the ever-present empty hole in his chest where his heart used to be and Bradley Britt making reappearances in his head, things felt like they might have a chance of falling back on track.

"Okay, Davi, you're up first. You have thirty minutes to get ready. I'll be in my office."

He glanced over his shoulder, gave Lance a wink, then started toward his office door. The nagging feeling came back, like what he was about to do with Lance would end up being the biggest mistake of his misguided life, but what did it matter now? Hadn't he fucked up too much to go back? Hadn't he already ruined any chance he had with the reporter? For God's sake, if the man wanted him, wouldn't he have called by now?

Gripping the knob, he pushed the door open and went straight for his desk lamp. He wanted the lights low when Lance came in there. Part of him wanted to pretend it was the man he loved, while the other part wanted to forget Bradley Britt had ever stepped foot into his life. And if fucking someone else unlocked the door to his freedom, then he would take it and hope his conscience didn't raise too much hell over it.

As he reached into the desk drawer, a soft tapping at the door raised his head. Lance's smiling face peeked in through the opening. Jason held the condom he'd just fished from his desk up in the air, and Lance stepped on in and locked the door behind him.

The soft light from the desk lamp glowed against Lance's tanned, muscled body. He had nothing but a black G-string on and with the ecstasy high Jason suddenly became aware of, his cock started hardening instantly.

Lance sauntered toward him, got a handful of the bulge beneath his denims as he pressed his mouth to the side of Jason's throat. But as soon as those soft, supple lips touched his flesh, he cringed. This wasn't right. Those weren't Brad's lips and—

He pressed his palms to Lance's chest. "No kissing," he insisted, and the dancer nodded his head. Kissing was too intimate, something meant for lovers. Lance wasn't his lover and never would be, no matter how bad Lance wanted to have a relationship with him. Sounded shitty, but he couldn't deny the truth, couldn't deny the lack of *those* kinds of feelings.

Lance slipped his hands beneath Jason's black tank top, eased it over his head, and tossed it onto the desk. Then his fingers went straight to Jason's zipper. This slow and sensual shit just wasn't working for him right now. He needed raw and gritty; no feelings, no intimacy. He needed downright, dirty fucking and nothing more.

He fisted Lance's hair and spun the kid around, stretching him out over the surface of the desk. Lance moaned his approval as he thrust his ass in the air. "Damn, baby. Doing it rough tonight?"

"I want to fuck. That's all. Can you handle that?"

"Mmm… hell yeah," Lance purred.

Jason bit down on the corner of the condom wrapper, ripped the package open, and then rolled the rubber down his hardened shaft. The ecstasy high made every nerve ending beg for attention. Even the sensation of the rubber ring rolling down his cock made his sac tighten against his body.

Then Jason reached into his desk drawer and blindly searched for a bottle of lube that had been kept there for more reasons than Jason cared to go into. He squeezed a blob onto his palm, then wrapped his hand around his dick, thoroughly coating his shaft.

"Fuck me now," Lance begged.

Right. That's all Jason needed to hear. He reached an arm around Lance's torso, holding him right where Jason wanted him, and in one quick stab, he plunged every firm inch of his cock deep inside Lance's body.

Lance reached back with one hand and fisted as much of Jason's ass cheek as he could grab, the other hand white-knuckled the edge of the desk. Jason pumped fast and furious. In and out, so hard, in fact, the metal legs of the desk scraped against the linoleum.

Shit started falling off the edges of the desk, but that didn't stop him. In fact, the more noise the furniture and the man beneath him made, the more excited Jason became. Each moan and whimper made him drive faster. His rhythm became almost animalistic. And despite being high as a freaking kite, he realized he was attempting to fuck all his frustration with Brad away and poor Lance's ass would bear the brunt of it.

"You okay?" he rasped.

Lance nodded. "Don't stop. Fuck. Don't stop," he begged.

Apparently, Lance didn't have an innocent bone in his body, and sex was no big thing for him. Scary thought. At least Jason always played it safe.

The arm around Lance's torso moved down until Jason found his hand on Lance's shaft. He gripped the firm length of it and every time he plunged his cock into Lance's ass, the dancer's erection was met with the same urgent stroking.

Lance raised his knee to the edge of the desk, opening his body wider, giving Jason more access for the hand job, and within minutes, they both came. Jason belted out a gravelly roaring sound. Lance screamed out his name. The desk whined in protest as its legs scraped the linoleum one last time. And when Jason finally pulled his spent cock out of the dancer's ass, he could barely stand.

He flopped down in his office chair, panting as he tried to resume normal breathing, pulse racing, sweat beading from every pore. Lance rolled over on the desk. His flaccid shaft glistened against his thigh. Neither one of them said a word. Neither one of them would look in the other's eyes. Lance was a rebound fuck, nothing more, and they both knew it.

29

JASON wouldn't lie and say he didn't feel like shit for using Lance the way he did, but hey, Lance offered. Lance got him high. And Lance didn't seem to mind being grudge fucked in the dirty office of a New Orleans nightclub by someone who'd been pining over his lost love for God only knew how long. Lance knew damn well what he was getting himself into.

No harm, no foul, right?

Then why the hell did Jason feel so guilty for that little tryst?

Because, no matter how many times he tried to deny it, no matter how many times he tried to convince himself otherwise, he still loved Brad. And because of that seemingly undying love for someone else, what he'd just done with Lance was wrong. Damn wrong.

He stood there with his arms crossed over his chest, clipboard buried in the fold, watching all the dancers laugh and have a good time. No one really spoke to him anymore, not since Jansen left to go play houseboy to his rich lover. The only other person he knew well enough to confide in was Lance, and that sure the hell wasn't happening, not after the stick and go he'd pulled in his office.

God, he had to get out of there before he went insane.

"I'm going up to VIP to chill for a bit," he whispered to Lance. "Can you make sure the dancers get on stage?"

"Yeah. Sure." Lance frowned. "You okay?"

"No, but I will be."

"You wanna talk about it?"

"No." Jason brushed his hand across his brow as he gave everything one last look. "Just… handle this, okay?"

"Okay."

Shoulders rounded with defeat, Jason left the backstage area, bypassed the crowd, and headed straight for the VIP balcony. He passed Dorian's booth first, thankful the asshole hadn't come out tonight. He sure the hell didn't need an altercation with that guy, not right now. And he damn sure didn't want Jansen seeing the brooding mess he'd turned into.

Christ, he couldn't even enjoy the damn buzz he had off the X right now because the only person he really wanted to touch, kiss, fuck, be near, whatever... was still MIA.

He continued to make his way down to the last booth in the row, the one he'd taken Britt to the first night they'd met. Though it felt like a lifetime ago, he could still picture the reporter gripping the back of the booth with his ass proudly pressed to the air. He could almost remember the scintillating conversation leading up to that unexpected yet precious moment in their brief history together.

And the only thing that had changed since the night they left the VIP booth was the two of them. The leather was still dark and well cared for, tabletop clean. Honestly, it almost looked like no one had been there since. Really made it feel like *their* booth.

He sat down on the same edge of the seat where he'd nervously kept his distance from the captivating reporter, occasionally glancing over to see if somehow, Brad had magically appeared. He never did of course, and knowing Brad would never be near him again made his heart break a little more. No amount of rebound fucking or fighting to forget would take that pain away.

With a hard sigh, he let his head rest against the dark leather and closed his eyes. His imagination went back to their swanky hotel room at the Bourbon Orleans, back to a time when everything was lighthearted and fun despite the guilt of sneaking around. Back then, he'd thought he would always have Brad in his life and nothing would come between them. He never imagined he would wake up and find himself without the only person who really made him feel wanted. He thought his days of being alone had ended the moment he realized he'd fallen in love.

Obviously not.

The music changed from the driving, tribal Latino rhythm of Davi's number into something a little more melodic, but still appropriately upbeat. The house lights lowered. Smoke whirled through the air. Then only the yellow stage lights came back on, and the MC announced the next dancer. It was Golden Boy's turn in the spotlight. Great.

Lance swished and twirled his way to the edge of the stage. His body moved like golden fluid, curling and rolling in all the right places. His hair flowed like blond silk down the center of his back and his eyes, holy shit those piercing blue eyes of his were almost as devastating as Brad's. Fucking Golden Boy made sense. Everything about him screamed of sex. Wasn't it understandable to give in to temptation when it came in a package like that? Sure. Absolutely.

Then why in the hell did he feel so damn guilty for giving in?

"Enjoying the show?" a smooth, velvety voice said from the edge of the booth. Jason's heart stopped. His breath hitched in his throat and his body froze. Every feeling he'd had and tried to forget—the love, the loss, the emptiness—trampled over everything he'd been thinking about. He opened his mouth to speak, but couldn't find his voice.

"Will you talk to me, please?" The voice was suddenly lower beside him. He turned his head and saw Brad's beautiful hazel eyes looking up at him. Every instinct screamed for Jason to throw his arms around Brad's body and never let go. Every inch of his being begged to be as close as he could be to the man he loved.

"Brad," he finally somehow managed to choke out. Tears burned the back of his throat and made his voice sound hoarse. "I...."

"No. Not you. Me." Brad reached up and took his hand, their fingers lacing together like two flawed ribbons coming together to make the most beautiful, flawless bow. "It wasn't you."

"I'm so sorry."

"You have nothing to be sorry for. You don't owe me any apologies." Brad pulled their joined hands up to his lips and kissed

Jason's knuckles. He gave Jason the softest, most genuine smile. And Jason all but turned to mush. "I've missed you so much."

The smile warmed Jason's heart, but the words poked at his conscience like a kid poking a stick at a rabid animal. If he didn't force himself to look away from those beautiful, endearing eyes, he knew he would fall into an uncontrollable fit of sobbing right there.

"We need to talk," Jason finally said.

"I agree, but can we talk later? Right now I just want—"

"No. I really need to do this now."

"I understand."

"Can you meet me out back, in the employee parking area?"

"Sure." Brad frowned. "Is everything okay?"

"Yeah. No. I um…." Jason swallowed hard. "I don't know."

"I don't like the sound of that."

"Just… meet me out back, okay?"

"Okay."

Their fingers unlocked and Brad stood from where he'd been kneeling next to the booth. He gave Jason one last worried look before heading toward the VIP entrance. Jason watched every step he took, pulse racing as fear ate away the edges of his consciousness. He still loved Brad with every ounce of his being, that hadn't changed. And somehow, he would come up with the bravery to be completely honest with him, even about what happened in his office not even an hour ago. He could only pray the news of his infidelity wouldn't turn Brad off the idea of being with him.

30

AT BEST, the back parking lot of Sin & Seduction was a spooky place for the dancers to hide and do God only knew what while the bosses and security guards weren't watching. At worst, a criminal's heaven to break whatever laws their hearts desired and, most likely, prance away with no threat of prosecution because no one saw them or cared enough to narc them out.

Darkness filled almost every inch of space. The few street lamps didn't put off a whole lot of light and the chain link fencing... well, it left a lot to be desired and didn't look like it really served its purpose at all.

Brad took a deep breath as his eyes scoured the lot over and over again. They occasionally landed on the employee entrance, but didn't stay there long. He worried for his safety a little more than he worried about Jason taking too much time walking through that door.

Every little noise, from the scurrying of rats in the darkness to the sounds of voices in the distance, made him twitchy. If Jason didn't hurry the hell up, Brad might just have to abandon ship and send him a message from inside the club.

The bottom edge of the metal door scraped against the concrete, and Brad nearly leapt out of his body. His pulse jolted up into his throat and his eyes widened.

Jason's handsome, auburn-haloed face appeared first. The copper-colored light made his green eyes almost ethereal. He looked like an enchanting porcelain-skinned angel. Brad's pulse began to slow and a smile curled the edges of his lips. Maybe it was the time they'd spent apart from each other, but he'd never seen Jason look so amazing.

Brad took a step forward and held out his arms, ready to embrace Jason entirely. He only wanted to feel the warmth of being close to his lover again, wanted to feel their bodies touching. He didn't care about being naked beside him or making love to him. He just wanted to be close to him again. He wanted to feel like nothing had changed and nothing ever would change.

Only, as soon as Jason stepped into the hug, Brad felt his body stiffen, like he really didn't want to be there or things had changed so drastically he didn't feel the same about their relationship anymore. God, he hoped he was wrong. After everything Brad had done, after the changes he'd made in his life, it would be a hell of a notion to lose Jason now, before they ever had a chance to be happy together.

Brad pulled away with a frown. "Okay, what's wrong with you?"

At first, Jason didn't say anything. He only kicked at the loose pavement or fidgeted with his fingers. Brad could tell he needed to confess something but couldn't figure out anything beyond that. He'd never dealt with dating a man before, so this new territory threw him for a loop. He almost wanted to tell Jason to say whatever he needed to say. They would get through it no matter what. But that wasn't a promise he could make. Not with the way Jason had been acting since he'd shown up at the club.

"I never thought I would see you again," Jason finally murmured, eyes casting away.

Is that all? "I'm right here." Brad curled his hand around Jason's chin and gently lifted his head until they had no choice but to look at each other. "I came back."

"I thought I'd messed up too bad and you didn't want me anymore. I thought I'd scared you away."

"No. Not at all. I wanted to be here. I just wasn't ready to face the feelings you felt, nor the ones I felt. I needed time to—"

"I fucked someone," Jason blurted.

"Oh," Brad said, only because he couldn't think of anything else to say.

His hand dropped from Jason's face, and he slowly backed away. It felt like his soul was being ripped from his body, like his heart had stopped and the life had been drained away. Everything ceased: the lights, the sounds of the rats, the people in the distance. The world froze, just like his heart.

He slowly turned around, back to Jason, hand clamped over his mouth. He took a few careful steps to put some needed space between them. The ache in his chest made it hard to breathe. The shaking in his legs made it hard to keep standing. Spontaneous combustion. He could feel it coming.

How the hell could Jason do that? He couldn't believe it. He couldn't believe how much those three words hurt, how they could make everything solid and believable in the world crumble into a pile of nothing.

But didn't he deserve it? Hadn't he done the same thing to his wife?

"I'm sorry," Jason finally said in a quiet voice. "I thought we were through and you'd gone back home to your wife and—"

"You can get over someone you love that easily?"

"No. I wasn't over you. I'm still not over you."

"When?"

"What?"

"When did you fuck someone else?"

"Tonight," Jason admitted, head lowering again.

"Did you use protection?"

"God, yes! What do you take me for?"

"I don't know, Jason." Brad shrugged his shoulders and shook his head. "I don't know what I thought." He paced a small circle, steadily shaking his head like he still couldn't believe Jason would screw around like that. Not that he considered it cheating, but how the hell could he just go off and fuck someone when he loved someone else?

"Please don't think I'm a whore or whatever. It wasn't some random guy. I've been with him before. We just.... It was a thing. He gave me a hit of ecstasy and—"

"How the hell does that justify anything?" He spun on his heels, face curled into a frown. "You took drugs then fucked someone just for the hell of it?" He shook his head. "How does that make any sense to you?"

"You bailed on me!"

"You told me to leave!"

"I fucking loved you!" Jason cried. "I still love you, but you won't let yourself feel a damn thing for me!"

"I won't?" Brad's brow quirked. "You think I don't care about you? You think I would throw away everything I've built in my life because I don't care about you?" He closed the distance between them. "Why the fuck do you think I came back here? Why do you think I came looking for you?"

"I don't know, Brad. Why did you come back?

"Because I miss being with you and goddamn you, Jason, I love you too!"

31

"YOU... you love me?" Jason asked, shock filling his voice and gripping his heart in a way that made him wonder if it would ever beat right again. "I thought—"

"You assumed I didn't and couldn't. I told you I loved my family and that's true. It will *always* be true. I would hope you can understand that."

"Of course I understand. Why wouldn't I?" He took two careful steps forward, not really invading Brad's space, but close enough to touch. He reached out and gently laid his hand on Brad's forearm, and the reporter lifted his head. Jason swallowed so hard he could hear the sound ringing in his ears. He softly said, "I never wanted to lose you. If I thought for one second you were going to come back to me and tell me you loved me, I would've never messed with Lance. Brad, you're the only person I ever wanted. You're the one I still want. I think we can be happy together if you'll give us a chance."

"I want to be happy with you. I really do."

"But?"

"No... no 'but'. Not this time." Brad laid his hand over Jason's, their fingers intertwining. "I'm ready to be myself. I went back to the hotel room we shared the night you and I parted ways, and as I lay there staring at the ceiling, I realized with you, I could be completely true to myself. I'm completely at peace when I'm with you. So then I went home and I spent time with my wife and daughter, but I couldn't stop thinking about you and she knew it. She told me I didn't look like myself, that I didn't look happy, and I wasn't. I mean, I was happy to be with them, but I felt so incomplete, like I'd lost a very fundamental piece of myself. She told me to come find you and make things right."

Jason's eyes widened. "She did?"

"Yeah." Brad nodded. "She did."

"I don't know what to say."

"Neither did I." They both laughed. "So I didn't say anything. I kissed her cheek, hugged my daughter, then left to come find you. You're the one I want, Jason. You're the one who makes me happy."

"You make me happy too."

They pulled each other into a tight hug, silently held each other as the feelings and revelations processed and the sadness of being apart for the last week slowly diminished. It wasn't a perfect ending and damn sure wasn't a perfect situation, but nothing in life was ever truly perfect. They had their rocky road paved out in spades, but together, they would navigate it and conquer it, then drive on home to their happy ending. That was a promise Jason made to himself the moment he felt Brad's arms around him again. And if he didn't manage to keep any other promise in his life, he would keep that one.

Brad touched the side of his face, thumb stroking over his cheek. "Why are you crying?"

"I didn't realize I was," Jason said with a hint of laughter as he brushed his hands over his eyes. "It's been a pretty emotional week."

"Who are you telling?"

"The man I love." He smiled as he leaned in to steal a taste of his lover's lips.

Had he been any more lost in the kiss, he wouldn't have seen the flash go off at the end of the alley. He really didn't think anything of it, but then the second, and the third, and the fourth flash went off, and they both raised their heads. The light flashed again and by the time they'd regained their sight, all they could see was a dark figure running back out to the street.

"What was that?" Jason asked.

Brad sighed, jaw clenched as he shook his head. "A really bad feeling."

"What do you mean?"

"Someone took a picture of me kissing you. What do you think?"

"You're fucking kidding me."

"I wish I was."

"How much trouble can you get into? Honestly?"

"I don't want them embarrassing my family."

"Maybe it was nothing."

"Maybe."

"Why don't we get out of this alley? You can hang out in my office. There's a couch in there. You can relax then maybe we can go back to my place or back to the hotel or—"

"I think that's a good idea."

Taking Brad's hand, Jason guided him into the employee entrance and down the long, dark hall into the backstage area. Luckily, they wouldn't have to pass by the group of curious, gossiping dancers to get to his office door. He could hide Brad away without any of them seeing him come in.

He led the reporter straight to his office and closed the door behind them. Thank God it didn't smell like sex or Lance's cologne. Talk about adding insult to injury.

"I'm going to make a few phone calls," Brad said. "How much longer do you have to be here?"

"A few more hours. I can bolt early if the stage is on time."

"That would be great, if you can manage."

"I'll do my best."

Jason stole one last kiss before leaving his office to return to the gaggle of dancers hanging out in the dressing area, but before he made it to the group, Lance snuck up beside him and whispered in his ear, "Who's in your office?" It gave Jason a start and he jumped. "Didn't mean to scare ya, boss."

"Jesus Christ! Why do you want to know who's in my office?"

"It's the reporter, isn't it?"

That stopped Jason dead in his tracks. His head whipped to the side and he glared right at Lance. "That's none of your business."

"Does he know you fucked me in that room?"

Jason slammed his palm down on Lance's shoulder, and he backed the kid against the wall. Inches from Lance's face, he growled in a voice so low no one else would hear them. "You're going to keep that shit to yourself. Got it? Anyone finds out about it and I didn't tell them, it's your ass. You won't dance in another New Orleans club again. Clear?"

"Crystal."

"Good." Jason released his grip and Lance's muscles relaxed so much his shoulders rounded. Jason let out a breath, softened his expression, and said, "Look, I know what we did, but... I didn't know he would come back. I thought he and I were over, okay? I don't want anything messing this up. So, please keep it to yourself. I'm asking as a friend."

"Don't worry, Jason." Lance gave him a half smile as he brushed the top of his forefinger over Jason's sternum. "I would never do anything to hurt you, okay? We're friends."

32

BRAD clenched his cell phone between his palms as he weighed the pros and cons of calling his wife and telling her about the mystery photographer. If he let her blindly walk into a mess his libido had caused, God, she'd be so pissed at him, and who knew what she would do then. Pretending he didn't know about it would be just another lie, something he promised he wouldn't do to her ever again. But what if it turned out to be nothing and he was panicking for no reason. Wouldn't it be better not to make her worry?

"Shit!"

Brad sighed, eyes closing as his brain teeter-tottered on the edge of absolute insanity. Why did this crap have to be so damn complicated? Why couldn't he just be with who he wanted without fear of retribution? Screw it. He had to tell Melody about the photographer. He couldn't let her get ambushed over his mess.

Hesitantly, his thumb punched in the number to her cell phone instead of the house phone, hoping not to wake the baby. The phone rang and rang, and for a moment, he wondered if maybe she was sleeping and maybe a call this late would actually upset her even worse. He started to hang up the phone when he heard her winded voice saying a punchy, "Hello?"

"Everything okay?" he asked. His pulse jumped a little. He began worrying with the tiny hairs at the nape of his neck.

"Yeah, I didn't have the phone with me. It was on the coffee table and I had to run from the kitchen to catch it."

"Oh, I'm sorry."

"No, it's okay." She paused a moment. "Are you alright? I thought you were going out tonight."

"I did. I'm at Sin & Seduction, but I'm hiding out in Jason's office."

"Oh." She sounded surprised. "I thought it sounded pretty quiet for a nightclub."

"Look, I need to talk to you about something, okay?"

Melody didn't immediately say anything, and for a moment, he worried maybe telling her wasn't the greatest idea. Hadn't he sprung enough bullshit on her already? Didn't she deserve a break from his madness?

"What?" she finally asked, but she didn't sound agitated at all. In fact, she sounded rather preoccupied, which was really odd for her.

Whatever. Just spill the beans already.

"I think someone got pictures of Jason and me hugging in the alley behind Sin & Seduction."

"You think?"

"Well, I know they got pictures, but I don't know… what might come of them."

"You were just hugging, right?"

"Well, not exactly. We kissed and Jason was…. He had tears in his eyes and I know how it looked. I'm just worried what might happen if those pictures hit the media. I don't want any trouble for you."

"Why weren't you more careful?"

"Melody, I didn't think—"

"That's your problem, Brad. You don't think." He could hear her sighing even through the phone. Suddenly, she didn't sound preoccupied at all. In fact, her attention had never been more focused. "What do we do now?"

"I didn't mean for this to happen, Mels." He propped his elbow up on his knee, forehead pressed to his palm. "If it comes out, then I'll be honest about it. If they chase me out of town, then I guess I go."

"Why don't we not jump to conclusions and wish for the best."

"I don't want them attacking you and Hope in church, Melody. Just be careful, okay?"

"I will."

"Promise me."

"I promise."

"I love you," he breathed.

"Bradley, I love you too. Everything will be okay."

"I hope so."

He hung up the phone and leaned back against the couch. His eyes closed as the whole scene in the alley played on infinite loop in his head. From the fight with Jason, to the photographer capturing a harmless, semi-intimate moment between them, the whole mess had his temples pounding and his blood pressure reaching explosive.

This shit could very easily cost him his career. It sounded ridiculous, even in this day and age, that people could be so damn judgmental, especially in a city like New Orleans, where a seedy lifestyle and an element of danger spurred the city's major source of income. But there were still those fundamentalists who plastered their beliefs to their foreheads, and being an out gay man in the public eye didn't fit into their doctrine. Boy, heads would definitely roll over a scandal like that.

The door to the office opened and he popped up from the couch, eyes wide. When he saw Jason standing there, he calmed down and held out his arms. "Come here," he said in a low voice. Jason approached the couch, eyes trained on Brad. "I just need you close for a second," he said as he wrapped his arms around Jason's body and buried his face against Jason's chest.

"Are you still worried about the pictures?" Jason asked as he ran his hand through Brad's hair. The gentle touch comforted him, if only a little. For a split second, he could've forgotten everything but his lover's tender caress.

"Yeah, I really am."

"I'm so sorry about that."

"No." Brad raised his head and looked up into Jason's loving green eyes. "Don't apologize. It wasn't your fault. I should've known better than to stay in that alley. Like I told you before, I'm always in the public eye. I'm always under scrutiny."

"Would it be so bad if you came out?"

Brad half laughed, shook his head, and said, "I would most likely lose my job, probably wouldn't be allowed on television anymore."

"Seriously? Isn't that illegal?"

"Yeah, probably. I don't know. I signed an agreement not to be involved in any scandals that might look bad on the station. Being at this club alone is scandalous."

"True."

"I'm more worried about Hope and Melody than I am myself. I can't let this hurt them. I—"

"Hey, stop worrying about it. If...." Jason sighed. "If it comes down to it, I know someone to call who will keep them safe."

33

ANOTHER week passed, then another and another. It might've actually been a month, but who was really counting anymore? Save for the breaks for work, the days all seemed to blur together.

The photos had yet to surface, which was good in one sense, but it kept Brad and Jason on edge. Jason started getting tired of the "careful" routine they had to go through when they were in the public eye, which seemed to be almost never. If they went to the hotel, Jason always booked the room and paid with cash. Brad would show up an hour or two later. It always varied so no one would figure out their pattern, and they never, ever, left together. Brad didn't go to Sin & Seduction anymore. He even went back to making regular appearances in public with the family.

At first, Jason didn't mind being the dirty little secret. He knew they had no choice if Brad wanted to keep his job and his family safe. He knew he had to sacrifice a lot, and that didn't bother him, but he started feeling like they were being forced to miss out on some of the important facets of being in a relationship. Just once he wanted to walk down Bourbon Street or through the park while he held his partner's hand. He wanted to be able to spend hours dancing beneath neon club lights with Brad pressed tight against him. He wanted to show off the human version of Adonis and be proud of the fact Brad belonged to him.

"How long have you been awake?" Brad asked in a husky voice as he rolled over in the bed.

The fine white linens twisted around his torso as he laid his head on Jason's chest. Jason's arm wrapped around Brad's shoulders, fingers lightly grazing his lover's upper arm. "A while, I guess."

"Christ, do you ever sleep?" Brad teased.

"Once upon a time." Jason laughed as he pressed his lips to the crown of Brad's head. He closed his eyes and took a deep breath, smelling nothing but the remnants of the reporter's high-dollar cologne. He'd fallen in love with that scent the very first night they'd met, and to this day, it still didn't disappoint. "You need to get going soon. You have to work today."

"Maybe I should call in. I really don't want to leave this bed."

"Yeah, I don't want you to either, but that's not very responsible, Mr. Britt."

"I know."

"Hey um…." He probably didn't need to bring this up again, because last time he did, they'd gotten into a huge argument over it, but what the hell. "Did you ever decide if you were going to Dorian and Jansen's commitment ceremony with me? You know it's tomorrow, right?"

Brad sighed. "I told you, it's not a good idea."

"I know what you told me. And I told you it's safe there. It's not going to be a big party. Dorian is still pretty much in the closet as far as everyone outside his house and the club is concerned. He doesn't let anything spill out into the public eye. It'll be dancers from the club and a few of Dorian's closest friends. It'll be safe."

"What if someone sees me going to Dorian Grant's mansion? How the hell would I explain that?"

"Say you're doing a story."

"Why would I do a story on him? He's a criminal."

"He's also one New Orleans' richest residents. He's a premier businessman. As much as I hate his ass, he does return some of his wealth to the community."

"I don't know, Jason," Brad said as he shook his head. Jason rubbed his thumb and forefinger against his own eye sockets. "We'll talk about it after I get off work, okay?"

"It's tomorrow. We don't have a lot of time to talk about it, and I would really love to have my partner with me. I know it seems like I'm asking a lot, but I want to be able to go to at least one place with you, hold your hand and—"

"And show me off to everyone?"

"No. God." Jason sighed. "Just go to work, okay? I'll check out of the room, and after I get off tonight, I'll go straight home. Call me if you... I don't know."

"Please don't be frustrated with me. I know this situation sucks, but I am doing the best I can. I want to make you happy, but right now, I just need you to understand."

"I swear, I do, and I'm trying my best to be patient with you. I just... I thought the commitment ceremony would be the *one* place where we could be together without having to worry about who's watching us."

"Let me think about it, okay?" Brad leaned up and gave Jason a quick kiss.

As he pulled away and climbed out of bed, Jason watched his glorious naked form move across the room like it was any old day and he'd found comfort in this stupid routine. If it wasn't for Brad having a daughter he wanted to be close to, Jason would've suggested they move away to a place where the reporter didn't have a past and didn't feel the need to keep up false pretenses just to save face.

Brad disappeared into the bathroom and Jason curled around his lover's pillow. He could smell Brad's shampoo and his cologne, could smell his body as if the man were still in bed beside him.

Where feelings and romance were concerned, they had the perfect relationship. Honestly. They never really got into it over anything, and Jason never once doubted how much Brad loved him. Had it not been for that, they might not have lasted this long. The strain of being so secretive seriously tore at the thread holding them together. He could only pray they remained strong enough to keep fighting for each other.

The sound of water running in the bathroom finally died down. The door opened and Brad's glistening body returned in nothing but a towel. Damp, tousled blond hair haloed his handsome face. He shot Jason a gleaming, dimpled grin and Jason's heart all but melted.

Jason drank in the sight of his muscled lover's incredible tanned form and let it refresh him. He wished they could both stay in the room and make love, and sleep together, only to wake up and make love again. His cock gave a tug and he reached down to adjust, only to find his morning wood getting harder by the second.

He moaned and shifted in the bed, legs spreading enough his erection pitched a subtle tent in the sheets. He smiled as soon as Brad's stare landed on the general direction of his crotch.

"You're making it hard not to call in sick."

"You're making *it* hard."

"I see."

"Come back to bed."

"I have to go to work."

"Call in sick."

"You're a bad influence."

"I know."

34

ON ALL fours, Brad climbed back into the bed. His boss wasn't too happy about him missing work, but at least they had a backup they could call in at a moment's notice. Who knew, once Brad got outed for his indiscretions, the backup could quite possibly become the station's new full-time reporter, but right now, he didn't really care about the station, or the news, or his boss and the mysterious backup. He only cared about pleasing the man beneath his body.

"Are you happy now?" he asked as he lowered his lips to Jason's shoulder. He trailed kisses along the curve of his lover's neck until he reached the sensitive spot right behind Jason's ear. Jason shuddered against him as soon as Brad's mouth fluttered over his flesh. "You have me all to yourself for the rest of the day."

"That makes me incredibly happy, Mr. Britt," Jason half purred, half moaned as he shifted his hips, brushing the bulge hidden beneath the sheets against Brad's thigh.

"You're an easy one to please, huh?" Brad slid his hand down, working his fingers beneath the soft white linens, down farther until they tickled the patch of coarse hairs at the base of his lover's shaft. Lips teasing Jason's jawline and throat, Brad wrapped his hand around Jason's shaft. The warm flesh of his palm caressed the dancer's thickening cock. "I want to keep pleasing you. Will you let me?"

Jason pulled his bottom lip between his teeth and bit down hard, head rolling back as he moaned out a ragged "mhm." His legs spread a bit wider.

Brad slowly pulled the sheets away, exposing his lover's porcelain-skinned body, the copper-colored curls surrounding his thick erection, the muscled thighs and sculptured calves. Then he lowered his head and devoured every firm inch of Jason's cock.

Tracing the tender, throbbing vein under Jason's shaft with his tongue, Brad felt the tightening of his lover's sac against his palm. The feel of it all, the reactions Jason's body had to his touching, and licking, and teasing, made his own cock begin to throb, and a satisfied moan rumbled through his chest.

AS SOON as Jason felt the vibration against his sensitive flesh, his shaft began throbbing harder. His back arched and his hips shifted, giving Brad all the space he needed to get as close as possible.

"Holy shit," he breathed, reaching down to fist Brad's soft blond hair as his lover's mouth fully sheathed his erection. He felt Brad's lips at the base of his cock, felt the tip dipping down into Brad's throat. "Fuck. Oh, fuck me!"

Brad had always been amazing at giving head, but Christ, this was probably the best it had ever felt. The reporter wasn't holding back. He wasn't being gentle and wasn't trying to stave off Jason's orgasm like he normally did. Brad acted like he truly wanted to taste the warm bitterness of release against his tongue, like he wanted to swallow it down and wouldn't stop until he tasted Jason's orgasm.

"Fuck, Brad, I'm about to—"

Before Jason could get the sentence out, Brad flicked his tongue across his slit then around the tender ridge of his head. His sac tightened. The throbbing shot down his shaft. Damn, he came so fucking hard, and Brad was completely unrelenting, milking and sucking every single drop.

His spent cock fell out of Brad's mouth. The reporter lifted his head and licked his lips as he smiled down at the quivering pile of goo he'd turned Jason into. Brad rose onto his knees. His hands smoothed down Jason's thighs, down the backs of his knees, down to his calves. He hooked Jason's legs around his waist and rolled his hips. His shaft brushed against the valley of Jason's cheeks, teasing his opening.

Skin on skin, every single sensation uninhibited by tight, constricting rubber. It was nice, not worrying with condoms anymore.

Since they were tested together almost a month ago and decided to be completely monogamous, they'd stopped using the rubbers, and the sex reached a level of epic Jason had never dreamt of.

"Do you want me to make love to you?" Brad asked, gently pushing the tip of his erection against Jason's ass.

Jason swallowed hard, let out a ragged breath, and nodded his head. His arm flopped over to the nightstand and he blindly fumbled to reach the bottle of lube they'd left out from last night. Somehow, he managed to hook it between his middle and forefinger, managed to drag it over the bed without dropping it on the floor.

He squeezed a few drops into his palm then reached down between their bodies and wrapped his hand around Brad's cock. His grip tightened, slathering every rock-hard inch while Brad rolled his hips and thrust his erection against Jason's palm.

"You're the only person I could ever imagine fucking me," Jason rasped.

"That's good"—Brad gave him a lazy-eyed grin—"because I refuse to share you."

"My first and last."

"Absolutely."

As if Jason lying beneath him, waiting and ready, wasn't enough to turn him on, having the kid vow his body in such a way damn sure did it. Brad had always been the relationship type anyway. He never did understand the draw to casual sex, and maybe that was part of the reason he didn't get why Jason had fucked that other guy from the club, but it didn't matter anymore. That was the past and this was the now, and right now, he wanted to feel his lover's body sheathing his cock. He wanted stroke his way to bliss then pass out in Jason's arms until they woke up and did the routine all over again.

With Jason's leg still wrapped around his waist, he rolled his hips again and the tip of his erection began to slip inside Jason's body. He lowered his head and pressed his lips to his lover's, tongue slipping inside his mouth with the same gentle tenderness he used to push his sex deeper inside all that glorious, tight warmth.

Jason's arms hooked under his, hands caressing his shoulders. He loved the way Jason held him to a kiss like that, the way their bodies always seem to meld together when they made love. The connection he felt when he was with the dancer made his heart soar and always managed to let that warm, loving emotion spill into their sex.

Brad licked at the roof of Jason's mouth as he slowly rocked back and forth, pulling his erection out until the sensitive ridge of his head met the ring of muscle inside his lover's body, then easing it back in as deep as he could go, all the way in until the small patch of coarse hairs haloing the base of his shaft kissed the tender skin between Jason's thighs.

He kept that perfect, gentle rhythm until he felt the pulsing down his sex and the tightening in his sac. He pulled back again, and this time, when he dipped back inside, the friction brought a release so intense it broke the kiss, and he threw his head back to let the sounds of his pleasure fill the air, while the seminal gift of his orgasm filled his lover's warmth.

35

FIRST assumption when waking up: this would end up being an absolutely disastrous day. Jason knew as soon as he brought up the subject of Jansen and Dorian's commitment ceremony, an argument would start and Brad would get mad. Then Jason would get mad, they would go their separate ways for the day, and then maybe, after family and church time on Sunday, they might figure out a way to make up. He would spend the entire ceremony brooding and worrying, and would miss the most important day of his best friend's life. He couldn't do that. He couldn't be that kind of friend.

So what did he do? He didn't say shit about it, and he damn sure wouldn't if he could help it. The subject would be avoided. He would go and have a good time, and try not to be upset about Brad missing it.

He climbed out of the bed, padded across the room, and started packing his duffel bag, cramming his three days' worth of clothes back into the tiny black bag without folding them. He gathered his toiletries and shoved them into the side pocket. Then he sat down at the desk, grabbed a piece of paper and a pen, and started to write a note.

He would say something simple, something sweet and to the point, not biting or scathing. Just a simple explanation of where he went and when he would be home if Brad wanted to come by later. Then he would sign it with love and tuck it under the coffeemaker so when his lover finally woke up, he would find it. The plan sounded so perfect.

But as soon as he scribbled out Brad's name on the off-white page, his sleeping lover shifted beneath the sheets. He made a grumbling sound, like the slightest little noise bothered him. Like he'd discovered Jason's absence and probably knew he was planning to bail. Jason turned his head to find Brad's eyes fluttering open and a sleepy smile curling the edges of his pouty pink lips.

"Hey," he said, keeping his voice low and nonabrasive enough for early morning greetings. "Sleep okay?"

Brad groaned, rubbed his hand over his chest, and met Jason's gaze. "What are you doing?"

"I was… I'm getting ready to go home."

"Why?"

"I have to get ready for the commitment ceremony."

"Oh yeah. That."

"Yeah." Jason crumpled the piece of paper in his fist then tossed it into the wastebasket beneath the desk. There was really no point in leaving a note now. *Choose your words carefully.*

He stood from the chair and went straight to the bed. Brad watched his every step. "You don't have to get up," he said as he brushed his finger through the reporter's sleep-tousled hair. "We don't have to check out for a few more hours. I just need to get going because I'm part of the ceremony."

"When do you have to be there?"

"Not for a few more hours, but I need to get home so I can shower and change into the suit. Jansen said Dorian is sending his driver to come get me."

"You going alone?"

"I guess."

Jason pulled his hand away, disappointed because Brad still didn't offer to go with him. He wouldn't cause a scene, wouldn't make a stink. He would let this one go because there were too many more important things to deal with. Brad had a family to think about and being out with his lover would cause problems. As long as he kept reminding himself of the wife and child, he could deal with the way things were for them. Jason wasn't such a brat he couldn't forget and forgive and let go of something so trivial for the sake of the man's family.

He went back to packing his crap. His duffel bag lay open on the floor, and when he bent down to close it, he felt Brad's crotch pressing against his ass. The morning stiffness caught him in just the right spot and he had to take a deep breath, focus on being disappointed, or heartbroken, or anything else so he wouldn't end up getting tangled in the sheets with his lover before he had a chance to escape.

Then he felt Brad's palm at the small of his back, fingers curling enough for his manicured nails to rake against the flesh as he pushed his hand up Jason's spine. Brad leaned forward and said in that beautiful, husky, velvety voice of his, "You don't have to go alone."

Jason's jaw clenched, teeth grinding together. He didn't want to fucking go alone in the first place. He wanted Brad there and that shit was just cruel. He took another deep breath, let it go slowly, and in the calmest voice he could fake, he said, "I'll be fine going alone."

"You don't want me to go now?"

"Of course I do." Jason bolted straight up and the sudden movement forced Brad to jump back. Jason spun on his heels, arms over his chest as he glared at Brad. "But you're being a big—"

Brad's lips covered his mouth before he had a chance to say something so epically stupid he couldn't take it back. And the longer Brad devoured his lips with heated kisses, the more his anger and frustration faded away. By the time the kiss broke, Jason forgot what monumentally ridiculous thing he'd wanted to call Brad in the first place.

"Is it *that* important to you?"

"It is. I don't mean to sound like a spoiled brat, but it's... I want to be able to hold your hand and show people how proud I am to be with you. I know that's a lot to ask for right now, but it's what I want. And I swear to God, if it's something you can't do, then I'll be as understanding as I can be. I just—"

"Stop," Brad interrupted. "I can do it. I want to. I know how much you've sacrificed by being with me and I feel like I've been selfish." His head lowered as he reached for Jason's hand again. "I don't want to be the guy who holds you back. I don't want to be the person you end up resenting."

"I would never—"

"You can say that for certain?"

"I guess not," Jason said quietly as he intertwined his fingers with Brad's.

He looked down at the knot of their hands and wondered how much it would take to pull them apart. Right now, there wasn't anything Jason wouldn't endure for him. Nothing would make him hate Brad, not even sharing the man's time with a completely separate life, a family he would never be a part of. Right now, love was a pretty strong bond, but could that love always endure the strain they both put themselves through just to be together?

"I never want to resent you," Jason finally said.

"And I can only promise to do my best to make sure that never happens."

36

"YOU look incredibly handsome." Brad's head rested on Jason's shoulder as he stared at the reflection of his lover in the mirror. The black Brooks Brothers suit, perfectly tailored to fit only him, hugged his body in all the right places. The grooms had picked a vest-and-tie set nearly the same color of a sparkling chardonnay. It made the green in Jason's eyes appear almost crystalline, lighter and brighter than their natural mossy hue. And his auburn hair resembled the flames of a fire.

Brad reached around Jason's waist and began fastening all the buttons of the double-breasted suit. Everything about the moment, about them dressing together and being so close to each other, felt so incredibly natural, like they were always meant to be like this and always had been.

"Thank you for helping me get ready," Jason said. "I don't know why I'm such a nervous wreck. You would think I was the one getting married." Brad's fingers stopped moving and their eyes locked on each other's reflections. "Um... not that I want to get...." Jason sighed.

"Stop. It's okay. You don't have to watch your every word around me."

"I just don't want to say something incredibly stupid and regret it later."

"You know, you're really cute when you get flustered like that."

Jason's brow arched and his lips pursed. "Cute? Really?"

Brad shrugged and gave him his award-winning, made-for-TV smile.

"Jesus, you're such a cornball sometimes."

"And that's what makes me great for television, my love."

He gripped Jason's shoulders and spun him around, took another nice long look, and his "cornball" smile only widened. "You really do look very handsome in that suit."

"Eh. Maybe, but it's not me."

"I know. If you could go in your jeans you would be a happy man."

"Exactly."

"So, are you ready to see your best friend marry a man you hate?"

Jason rolled his eyes. "Not particularly, but I can pretend to be supportive."

"And I'm sure that's all Jansen expects of you."

Silence. They stared at each other for a long moment, subtle smiles on each of their faces. The tiny bathroom didn't give them much room to move and didn't allow much distance to come between them.

Fine by Brad. The closer, the better.

He touched the side of Jason's face, stroking small circles over his lover's cheek with his thumb. He leaned in and stole a quick kiss, nothing too heated or passionate. Or maybe the lack of heat made it more passionate. And when he raised his head again, he said in a breathy voice, "I love you so very, very much."

"I LOVE you too," Jason breathed. Heat flushed his face and filled his cheeks. He never was one to blush, but Christ, Brad had a way of bringing the lovesick romantic out in him. And every time they found themselves in perfect moments like these, that goofy little nerd liked to peek his head right on in.

He threaded his arms around Brad's waist and even through their matching black suits, Jason could feel the bulge tucked away in Brad's boxer briefs. It was enough to make him consider being late for the ceremony despite Jansen's threats of torture.

"We should probably get going," Jason said in soft voice as he spread his hand over Brad's heart. "We keep this up, it'll take a crowbar to pry us off of each other."

They both laughed, and about that time, a car horn blared from outside the apartment. Jason took Brad's hand and they headed down to the sleek black sedan. The driver stood waiting, with the back door open like he was waiting on royalty or some insanity like that.

Jason really hated taking Dorian's offerings: the suit, the chauffeured sedan. And he probably wouldn't have, had Jansen not insisted. After all, this was all for his best friend anyway. He could behave himself and enjoy the day for Jansen, especially with Brad by his side.

The drive to Dorian's mansion lasted about thirty minutes. Jason's nerves were about as raw as they could be. The only thing that kept him from tugging at the suit or fidgeting with all the little knobs and handles and switches on the door was having Brad's fingers tightly laced with his. As soon as the sedan pulled down onto the long, winding road leading to Dorian's place, Jason saw a parade of champagne-colored balloons littering the edge of the pavement. They led the newcomers straight back to Dorian's multimillion dollar house hidden behind the trees.

Jason tightened his hand around Brad's. He turned toward the window, gaze fixed on the landscape. No, he wasn't happy about this ceremony. And though it had a lot to do with his absolute hatred for Dorian Grant, most of it had to do with the feelings he had for Jansen. It might not be the kind of love that made fairytales come true. It might not be the kind of love people abandoned themselves for, but he still loved Jansen, nearly as much as he loved the man beside him.

"I have a confession to make," he said in a low, uncertain voice without turning his head.

"I don't like the sound of that." Brad's fingers squeezed tighter around Jason's hand.

"I don't want there to be any secrets between us. I never want *anything* to come between us." Jason finally turned his head and their eyes met. He could see the trepidation in his lover's hazel gaze. It made a little flutter of pain brush over the surface of his heart. "I love Jansen.

I've loved him for five years, almost. But I'm not in love with him anymore."

"You were in love with him? Like romantically 'in love' with him?"

Jason nodded slowly. "At one point, I was. I convinced myself I would never have him once he and Dorian hooked up, but I never stopped loving him."

"But you don't love him the way you love me, right?"

"No. Not anymore."

"Something is still bothering you though?"

"Yeah." Jason lowered his head and stared down at the clenched hands. Everything felt safe, unbreakable, and infinite while they held hands. The knot of their fingers became his strength when the tough stuff started to resurface. "I don't want him to commit himself to Dorian. I don't like them being together. I don't know if it's because I'm being selfish and I don't want to lose my best friend, or if it's because I sincerely believe Dorian will hurt him one day. I don't know. I just... I know I don't agree with this and wish one of them would come to their senses and put a stop to it."

Brad sighed. His brows furrowed but his eyes never left Jason's face. "You can't say what is wrong or right for them. Obviously, they love each other very much. Who are you to say it's wrong?"

"I'm no one."

"In their relationship, no, you're not. You have to let Jansen go and let him find his way on his own."

"How are you so calm about this?"

"Because I know who you're with and who you would choose to be with. At least, I believe I know. I have faith in you and your love for me. If I didn't, I wouldn't have left my wife."

"I do love you, and yeah, if I had to choose, you would be the person I wanted."

A soft smile tugged at the corner of Brad's lips. He leaned over and gave Jason a chaste kiss then said, "It's good to hear you say it."

THE sedan pulled to a stop right at the front of the sprawling white mansion. Champagne-colored toile was draped between the large white pillars and down the brick walkway. Everything looked perfectly manicured, from the big green bushes lining the front of the house to the tiniest group of colorful flowers.

Brad's heart sank down into his stomach and it wasn't from intimidation or the sheer perfection and attention in every single detail. It was the people with their microphones and the cameras flashing from the edge of the yard. Dorian Grant, celebrity and criminal, and everyone wanted a glimpse into his life. Or maybe they were waiting to find out which crooked lawmakers and businessmen would come to such an event. Regardless, Brad wouldn't be getting out of that vehicle anytime soon.

"I had no idea it would be like this," Jason offered.

"It's okay. It's not your fault. I just can't... I can't go in there."

"Driver," Jason said as he leaned forward, "is there a more private entrance? Somewhere we could take him so they won't see?"

"Not one that Mr. Grant likes for his guests to use."

"Well, you tell Mr. Grant—"

"It's okay," Brad said, pulling Jason back against the seat. "No need to start any trouble. You go on in. I'll... figure something out."

"No. You wait right here. I'll go inside and talk to Jansen. We'll get you in under the radar." Jason didn't even give him a chance to argue. He bolted out of the car, slammed the door so hard behind him it made Brad flinch, and charged right up to the door like he owned the damn place.

Brad sat back in the sedan and tried to relax. At least the windows were tinted so dark no one would be able to see his face. No one would be able to identify him and share his dirty little secret with the fine viewers of the greater New Orleans broadcast area.

He scrubbed his hand over his brow as he thought about the unexpected turn his life had taken, how he'd finally listened to his heart, and obviously his cock, and gone after reality and truth, but yet couldn't accept reality and truth enough to be honest about any of it. Jason was strong enough to admit loving someone he couldn't have. He was strong enough to own up to screwing around, yet Brad remained a coward, hiding in the back of a sedan while his lover made arrangements to sneak him into a gay wedding.

"Jesus Christ, what am I doing?"

He reached for the handle, and a split second before he decided to walk into his own death sentence, he thought about his wife and daughter, his Melody and his Hope. Coming out would make things… bad for them, wouldn't it? Or would it give Melody the freedom to find someone she deserved? Would it give her a means to walk away from their marriage and find someone to keep her warm at night? She already knew what he'd done and accepted it. If he finally admitted what he was, wouldn't it give everyone a little peace?

The front door of Dorian Grant's mansion opened just as Brad gave the handle a tug. It clicked and the latch sprung free. Light spilled in through the crack. His leather-loafer-covered foot stepped down onto the driveway of its own volition. Cameras began to flash again. Jason's eyes met his and the frown on his lover's face stopped him before he made an incredibly stupid mistake.

"What are you doing?" Jason asked as his hand locked over the edge of the door.

"I don't know," Brad admitted. "I… I have no clue what I'm doing."

"Just…." Jason shook his head. "Get back in the car. We're going somewhere else."

37

THE driver drove back down the driveway and pulled onto the winding road. He made a right, then another right, and another right. The very next right turned into a driveway veiled on both sides by tall, thick green bushes. It led down to a giant garage with four automatic doors. The car stopped as one lifted; then it continued to pull down into the darkness. They all waited until the door fully dropped before getting out of the car.

"I feel like I'm meeting a mafia boss," Brad joked.

"Not far from true," Jason responded flatly.

"He's not that bad, right? I mean, shady, but not that...."

"He has a fulltime security guard who goes everywhere with him."

"Oh."

"Yeah."

They met at the front of the car, stopped, and stared at each other for a moment. There was a new brand of tension in the air, unsure and completely unwavering. Did they walk in holding hands, Brad wondered? Did they share a quick kiss in private because showing any kind of intimacy in public would be way too taboo? Would the guests recognize Brad and immediately run to tell their friends he was at a gay wedding with his gay lover, even though he pretended to be straight in the public eye?

"Ready?" Jason asked in a soft voice.

"Almost." Brad took a step closer and laid his hand on his lover's hip. "I just need a moment. I have to admit, I'm a bit nervous about this."

"I understand. We can hide. Once the ceremony is over, we can find a room far away from the festivities and hide away until the place clears out."

A soft laugh slipped through Brad's smiling lips. He pressed his forehead to Jason's as he brushed his thumb back and forth over the hard ridge of Jason's hip bone. "Everything will be okay," he said, and while he might've been referring to the party for the sake of the conversation, part of him knew everything—their lives together and the sneaking around, the hiding from the truth and denying themselves what every good relationship needed—would get better one day. He could only hope Jason would endure the bullshit for now and stay with him for the long haul.

"Relax, Brad." Jason gripped his shoulder and gave a solid squeeze. "You're too tense."

"I'm trying." Brad moved his hand from Jason's hip to his wrist. He brought his lover's palm to his lips and pressed a kiss to his skin. "Let's go before your friend gets worried."

When they walked through the service entrance door, it opened into a back room resembling an oversized pantry, then through another door and into a kitchen filled with dark wood cabinets and cream-colored marble countertops, high-end fixtures and elaborate lighting. The kitchen alone was nearly as big as two rooms in Brad's suburban cookie-cutter. He had to remind himself to keep his mouth closed and not gape at everything he saw.

Brad stayed close behind as Jason led him into the living room. People stood around, sipping glasses of wine, talking in their tight-knit circles: straight couples and gay couples, women and men, people Brad recognized from the club and some who would never darken the door of such a place. The diversity of the crowd was comforting enough for Brad to relax, until heads rose and eyes landed on him. The room quieted and the only sound was their varied whispers. He suddenly felt like a man standing naked on a stage in front of the world's judging eyes.

He could feel his throat start to tighten and his pulse start to race. He didn't want to be noticed, didn't want people talking about him after they left the party.

"You okay?" Jason whispered. Brad nodded. "Maybe I should get you a glass of wine." He nodded again.

A big, burly man with a long dark ponytail entered the room. Brad could only describe him as a freight train. He had wide shoulders and arms so thick the sleeves of his suit looked like they were about to burst. "I need everyone involved in the ceremony to come with me," he announced, voice so filled with bass it rumbled. "We'll be startin' shortly."

"I have to go," Jason said. "Will you be okay down here?"

"I'm fine. I'll be fine," Brad offered, though the words didn't convince him and he doubted they convinced Jason. "Go. I'll see you shortly."

Jason gave him a tight-lipped smile before disappearing with the huge, intimidating man. Brad stood there alone, trying not to look at anyone directly. He thought if he didn't make eye contact, he could escape unscathed. Maybe they would forget, or maybe they didn't know him and this was all his imagination.

A servant walked by with a silver tray in his hand. "Wine?" the man asked. Brad took the glass and lifted it to his lips. When he turned back to face the group, he stood face-to-face with the man he recognized as "Golden Boy," one of the dancers from the club.

"Well, hello, Mr. Britt," the guy purred as he took a sip from his own glass. "Fancy meeting you here." He offered his hand. "I'm Lance."

"Lance," Brad gritted, taking the man's hand. So he's the guy Jason screwed? He could certainly understand. The dancer was beautiful, the type most would fall for. He had amazingly bronze skin and golden-blond hair. Brad could imagine anyone drowning in those bright blue eyes. How could anyone not want him? "Nice to meet you."

"Look, I just want to let you know, you got lucky with Jason. He's a great catch. Take care of him, okay?"

"I plan to." Brad took a sip of wine. It quenched the dryness in his throat, but didn't settle his nerves. Between Jason's former lover and the crowd staring at him, he could almost feel the walls closing in around him. "You care about him, don't you?"

"Of course, I do. How could anyone not? He's an amazing person."

"He is."

"Do you love him?"

"I do. Very much actually."

"Take care of him. He puts up a strong front, but he's very sensitive beneath that façade."

"I know. I intend to take care of him. I just… have things to fix first."

"Whatever you have to do, he's worth it, remember that," Lance said before walking away. Brad took a deep breath and turned his back to the crowd. He sucked down the last of his wine then grabbed another as the server passed by again.

38

"YOU'RE a nervous wreck." Jason laughed, watching Jansen pace back forth as he wrung his shaking hands. The groom cracked his neck. He rubbed the nape of his neck, paced a few more steps, and then let out a deep breath. "Are you going to calm down?"

"Does everything look okay down there?"

"Everything is fine, I promise."

"Where's Dorian?"

"I haven't seen him."

"What?" Jansen's head shot straight up, eyes wide. "What do you mean?"

"Jansen," Jason grabbed his shoulders, forcing Jansen to look him in the eyes. When he spoke, his words came out slow and measured, calm and even. "Everything is going to be okay. Now, calm down before you break."

There was a loud, meaty banging at the door. Both of them nearly jumped out of their skin. "It's time, kiddo," a deep voice said.

"Thanks, Angelo," Jansen responded. He looked back at Jason. "It's time."

"I heard." Jason grabbed the groom's suit jacket and held it out so Jansen could slip his arms into the sleeves. "Want me to adjust your package for old time's sake?"

They both laughed as Jason reached over and grabbed a boutonnière made from a single white calla lily and slender green leaf from the dresser. He affixed it to Jansen's lapel with a pearl-tipped stickpin, then adjusted his friend's champagne-colored tie and vest. He brushed his fingers through the pasted sprigs of Jansen's spiky chocolate-brown hair. "You look very handsome," he said in a low voice. His throat fisted around the sound. The whole situation had him more choked up than he'd expected to be.

"Thank you. You look very handsome as well. I really like you in a suit—makes you look debonair." Jansen paused. He turned to the mirror to check his suit one more time. Then he looked over his shoulder and Jason knew he'd caught him staring. "You still love me, don't you?"

"I always will. You've been the best friend I've ever had."

"I love you too, you know?"

Jason's eyes narrowed. He would never admit being shocked, would try like hell to hide his surprise, even though he knew his face gave it all away. "But you're completely in love with Dorian, right?"

"Of course, just like you're completely in love with Brad."

"Exactly."

"We're both making the right decision here. We make better friends than lovers."

"We make great friends."

"You hate Dorian."

Jason sighed. "I think he makes selfish decisions. And you don't care for me being with Brad, do you?"

"I think he needs to *make* decisions."

"But we're both happy."

"Incredibly."

The meaty fist pounded at the door again. "Guys, 'nuff screwin' 'round in there. It's time to go."

WHEN they finally made it downstairs, Jansen seemed to have calmed a little. Jason stood beside him, holding his hand, fingers intertwined as they waited in front of the French doors. Beyond the patio furniture and hot tub, out in the center of the massive garden, people sat waiting in white folding chairs. A white aisle runner parted the rows. Arrangements of white flowers led to an altar cloaked in champagne-colored silk. A man with snow-white hair, dressed in an off-white suit, stood waiting to unite Jansen and the man he'd chosen to spend his life with.

Jason opened the door and a choir of violins and cellos sang a soft song. The big man he assumed to be Angelo stepped down the aisle first. Dorian Grant followed shortly behind. Angelo stepped to the right of the altar and Dorian took the spot beside him, right in front of the officiator.

"Do you have the ring?" Jansen asked. His voice trembled.

"Yeah," Jason said as he reached in his pocket. The platinum ring slipped over his thumb and he held it out for Jason to see. "We're all set, baby. You ready?"

"Let's do this."

Jason started down the aisle first. He scoured the small crowd of people, looking for Brad. He saw the dancers from the club all scattered about, even the owner and his partner. A few of the bartenders he recognized, but he saw no sign of Brad. His heart sank, but he kept smiling, kept walking down the aisle like he didn't have a care in the world. As soon as he turned to the left to take his spot, he found his lover standing in the corner, arms crossed over his chest, with a soft smile on his face. Everything felt right again.

Shortly after he took his spot, Jansen appeared beside him and the music quieted. Jansen and Dorian took hands. They exchange a dreamy-eyed glance, and Jason saw the love between them reflected in the way they looked at each other. For the first time, he didn't see Dorian Grant as a criminal and a homicidal maniac. He saw Grant as someone who would take care of his best friend, someone who would love him and keep him happy. And he knew then, he could let go of his worries, let go of his fear, and wish Jansen a long life full of happy years.

"We are gathered here today," the officiator began, "to join Dorian and Jansen in a union of hearts and lives. They have invited you here to witness this celebration of their love because you are special to them and they hope you'll support them as they venture into their new lives together."

The sound of the officiator's voice faded away, drowned out by Jason's thoughts. He imagined Brad standing beside him, holding his hand as a minister or judge or whatever began their own ceremony. He could hear Brad's velvety voice vowing to love him forever, cherish and honor him. It was a ridiculous notion, considering they hadn't been together long. Not to mention Brad having a wife. But that didn't stop him from envisioning them growing old together, being happy in their own place, with their own family.

God, where the hell was this coming from? Jason had never wanted to be Johnny Homemaker before. He'd never had any inclination to be one of those men who picked just one special guy to settle down with, bought a house with a white picket fence, and somehow managed to have two-point-five kids to care for.

But he'd also never been with anyone like Brad. The reporter made him appreciate nights snuggled in someone's arms. He made Jason appreciate waking up next to someone with imperfect hair and sleep-filled eyes. Brad made him realize the answer to his loneliness wasn't in sleeping with the first person to pay him attention while pining over losing someone he loved to someone unworthy.

"The ring," the officiator said. Jansen looked over his shoulder and held out his hand.

Jason removed the ring from his thumb and set it on Jansen's palm with a smile. He listened to every single word Jansen spoke to Dorian as he held the ring just above his partner's knuckle. Jansen promised to be faithful, to respect, love, honor, and cherish Dorian Grant, to be with him and care for him in sickness and in health. Dorian took an identical band of platinum from Angelo and repeated the same words.

Then came the kiss.

Dorian cradled Jansen's face in his massive hands. Jansen's arms wrapped around Dorian's waist. Their lips pressed together and there was nothing quick or chaste about the kiss. Their bodies seemed to meld together, like the union had been about much more than just their lives. It was passionate enough to make the crowd blush and hot enough to turn on the voyeurs. And with their mouths still firmly connected, the officiator announced the nuptials to the crowd.

Everyone jumped to their feet and cheered. It was a truly beautiful moment, seeing everyone being so supportive of two men sharing their love for each other so openly. Jason wondered if Brad gained anything from the experience, if it made him think again about coming out. Chances were it didn't, because the hundred or so people there represented a very small portion of the populous. But he could hope, right?

39

"AREN'T you the reporter? Bradley Britt?" a soft, feminine voice asked from beside him. The question knotted his stomach. Not that he didn't expect to be recognized. Not that he wanted to be recognized.

He calmed himself as much as he could, took a short breath, and donned the best smile in his arsenal, then turned to face the tiny woman beside him. "Yes," he offered his hand, "I am."

Her light-brown eyes sparkled through executive-type designer eyewear and her bright-red lips curled. She brushed a fallen brown curl from her face, but the wind kept blowing it back. She didn't get flustered. No, this one probably didn't aggravate easily. She seemed too refined for such a thing.

"Do you know Dorian?" she asked.

"Actually, no, I'm a friend of a friend." She frowned. "Jansen is my… friend's friend."

He simply couldn't explain it any better than that, and she'd probably already formed her own opinions anyway, so there wasn't much point in going into the fine details of the matter. She rolled the stem of her wine glass between her fingertips. That's when he saw a single gold band on her left ring finger. No oversized diamond, just the band. "Are you a friend of Dorian's?"

"Dorian doesn't have 'friends'." She air-quoted the word. "I'm his attorney."

"I see."

"Well, anyway, I enjoy your broadcasts. You have a great television personality."

"Thank you," he said nervously. "Thank you for viewing. Is your husband—"

"Wife, sweetie."

"Oh. I'm so sorry for assuming."

"No. It's okay. It's natural to assume a woman is married to a man when she has a band on her finger. I'm used to it." She gave him a warm, genuine smile, considered him for a long moment, long enough it made him squirm. Then she said, "I think it's great, someone with so much presence in our community supporting same-sex marriage the way you are."

Brad took another gulp of his wine. "I—"

"We need more open-minded people willing to speak out."

"Well, I—"

"Would you be willing to do an interview for our newsletter?"

"Our?"

"Oh, I'm so sorry. Where are my manners? I'm Rebecca Chambers, local president of the Equality Fighters."

"Equality Fighters?"

"Yes, we're pushing lawmakers to legalize same-sex marriage in Louisiana. It would be great to have you on board as a spokesperson."

"I—"

She reached in her purse and pulled out a little silver card holder as she continued on about their mission and her vision for the group, and how great it would be to have him speak up for their cause. He felt like such an ass, silently standing there while she went on about things that could never, ever happen.

Between her middle and forefinger, she held a little white business card with a giant rainbow heart on the front. "Please, call me so we can get together on this."

Nodding, he took the card and deposited it in his suit pocket just as Jason popped up beside him. "They're done taking pictures. I'm free to do whatever now." Brad's eyes darted between Jason and Rebecca. She smiled at Jason then shot a knowing glance at Brad. His heart sank down into his toes. Jason's eyes bobbled back and forth between them. "Did I miss something?"

The woman gave Jason her dissertation about the group and what they did. Brad quietly listened to her little speech again, not really paying too much attention to her and focusing more on Jason's smile and the way he politely placated her. She patted him on his arm, then gave Brad one last grin before dismissing herself.

"Do you think she knows?" Brad asked softly so no one else would hear him.

"Probably. Does it really matter? Do you think she would go back and tell a bunch of people that Bradley Britt is gay, especially if you never affirmed it?"

"I don't know." He rubbed his hand over his upper arm as his eyes scoured the crowd.

"You're not enjoying yourself, are you?"

"I'm trying, Jason. I swear I am," he said in a terse, tense voice.

"Why don't we go inside? We'll go somewhere private where we can relax."

How could he ask Jason to do that? This was his best friend's wedding. Jason already gave so much to ensure his comfort and what had he done to give back? "No. Enjoy the party. I'll be okay."

GOD, Jason wished he could make this better somehow. Brad looked so incredibly uncomfortable, and that's the last thing he ever wanted. "How about this? How about we stay for the toast, since I have to make a speech, then we'll go back to my place and relax in front of the television or something? Does that sound like a good plan to you?"

"I think that sounds wonderful."

Jason fought the urge to reach for Brad's hand. In the time they'd spent together, it had become instinct, whenever one of them needed comforting, the other always wanted to hold hands. Which in most cases was no big deal, but in situations like this, in public, they had to be more careful. One day, hopefully, things would change. Right now, though, they both dealt with it the best way they could.

He looked out through the crowd and found Dorian with Jansen nestled against him. They sat at the head table, smiling and greeting the guests. To Jansen's right was an empty chair where Jason should've been sitting, but he didn't want to leave Brad's side.

"If you want to join them, you can. I don't need a babysitter, you know?" Brad offered.

"What?" Jason looked back at him, surprised to hear Brad so in tune with his thoughts. "I wasn't—"

"Yes you were. I can tell you want to be over there in your rightful spot. Go. I'll be okay."

"Are you sure?"

"Of course. Go. I'll be around. I might explore the house a little. Dorian's home is impressive."

Jason leaned in and whispered, "I love you so much. Thank you."

"I love you too," Brad said in a voice quiet enough for church.

They exchanged a quick smile before Jason headed over to the main table. He took his seat next to Jansen, and immediately, one of the servers brought him a fresh glass of wine. He sat back in the chair, brought the glass to his lips, and kept his eyes trained on his lover.

"It'll get easier," Jansen said in a whisper. Jason hadn't even noticed him leaning over. He turned his head toward his best friend. Jansen gave him a tight smile and said, "He just needs to figure things out."

"Everything is fine. We're fine."

"I know how badly you want him to acknowledge you. I can tell."

"He can't, right now. We're still working through… things."

Jansen sat back in his chair. Dorian reached down and grabbed his hand. For a moment, a brief, fleeting moment, Jason felt the green, nagging thrust of envy. He was trying damn hard to put on a happy face for his best friend, and for the most part, it'd been working well, at least on the outside. As far as everyone else knew, everyone save his best friend, Jason was the same, happy, fun-loving guy he'd always been.

"The photographer is ready for you to cut the cake," a man in a black semisuit leaned across the table and said to the couple. "Are your guests of honor ready for their speeches?"

Jansen looked over at Jason and Jason gave him a curt nod. He could do this. He was ready. Feelings aside, he could stand up in front of their closest friends and say something sweet and monumental without letting his jealousy get in the way.

Jason cleared his throat as he stood from the table. His wine was replaced with a glass of champagne. Servers made their way through the crowd, passing out glasses of bubbly to the guests. He said, "Can I have your attention for a moment?" Everyone stilled. Their eyes all settled on Jason. He looked down and gave Jansen a quick grin. Jansen's face turned red.

"I'll be the first to admit, I never expected Dorian and Jansen to last. I never expected them to go as far as committing themselves to each other. But I'll also be the first to admit I was wrong." His eyes shifted to Dorian. "I have to say I'm sorry for underestimating you." Dorian nodded and Jason looked back out to the crowd. "Jansen is like a little brother to me. He always needed someone to look after him, and I always needed to keep him safe. I've watched him grow from a lost, scared boy into a successful man, and I know he wouldn't have pushed so hard had it not been for Dorian's love. Now, I can honestly say I don't think there has ever been or will ever be anyone more perfect for Jansen." He turned back to the couple and held up his glass. "I wish you both many, many years of love, happiness, and good fortune. Cheers!"

The crowd roared a unified, "Cheers," and then they all tilted their glasses back to their lips.

Jansen's eyes turned a little glassy, and as soon as Jason sat back down, his best friend leaned over and kissed his cheek. "Thank you," he whispered. Jason smiled and nodded his head, a silent "you're welcome" in understanding.

40

BRAD stood back in his distant, quiet corner of the patio, watching and listening as his lover gave his speech. He knew how hard it had to be for Jason to say those words, especially with the feelings he'd admitted to having for the groom. Nonetheless, Jason pulled it off flawlessly, and Brad admired him for being so damn strong. Even in their relationship, Jason had all the strength and courage where Brad remained cowardly and secretive. He envied Jason.

Vibrating in his pocket pulled his attention away. His wife's name appeared on the caller ID. Weird, he thought. She knew he would be at the wedding and said she wouldn't call unless it was an emergency.

"Melody?"

"Bradley, Hope's sick. She's not holding her food down, she won't stop crying, and she's burning up. I'm taking her to the emergency room."

Brad's heart stopped. His baby. His sweet little girl. He should've been there with them. "I'll meet you there. I'm leaving now."

"You don't have to—"

"Yes," he barked. "I do. I'm leaving. I'll be there as fast as I can."

He hung up the phone and slipped it back into his pocket as he pushed his way through the crowd to get to the head table where Jason sat alone while Dorian and Jansen cut their cake. Whatever was written on his face, Jason read it perfectly and bolted to his feet. He darted around the table and met Brad in the middle of the crowd.

"I have to go," Brad choked out. "My daughter is being taken to the emergency room."

"Okay. I'll get the driver," Jason said as he reached out and grabbed both of Brad's trembling hands. "Do you want me to go with you?"

"Please."

"Okay. I'll be right back. Meet me in the garage."

And they parted ways, Brad tearing back through the house, Jason heading over to Jansen.

"I HATE to interrupt," Jason said to Dorian, "but I have an emergency. I need your driver to take me and Brad to the hospital."

"Is everything okay?" Jansen asked.

"Yeah," Jason nodded, closing his eyes for a split second as he tried to calm himself down. "Brad's daughter is sick and he needs to go. So I'm going to go with him."

Dorian whispered something to Angelo. Jansen gave Jason a tight hug. "If you need us—"

"We'll be fine. We just need to get there."

"Angelo's gonna take ya," Dorian said, "He'll getcha there faster than anyone."

"Thanks," Jason said to Dorian as he pulled out of the hug. "I appreciate it."

He followed Angelo's massive body as the big man tore through the house and into the garage. He found Brad pacing a small circle while he wrung his hands. As soon as the door slammed, Brad's head shot up and his eyes locked on Jason. The fear and worry nearly took his breath away.

Angelo held out his big arm, aiming a remote at the sedan, and the lights flashed. The doors unlocked and the car cranked. "Get in," he barked in his thick, rumbling voice. Like he'd spoken some magical command, they both jumped in the back of the car.

The door to the garage didn't open fast enough for anyone's taste. Angelo muttered curses. Brad chewed down his nails. Jason wrung his hands in his lap. He wanted to comfort the man he loved. He wanted to promise everything would be okay, but this was unfamiliar territory. Would everything be okay? Did his kid just have a little cold, or something worse?

Setting sunlight filled the dark garage and Angelo floored the pedal so hard it nearly pinned them both to the backseat.

Angelo drove like a maniac, and had it not been such an emergency, Jason might've asked him to slow down. Brad's cheek pressed against the window. He hadn't uttered two words in a long while. Jason carefully reached over and laid his hand over the reporter's. That's when Brad finally raised his head and looked back at him. He turned his palm up, fingers clasping around Jason's hand. They exchanged a glance. Jason saw the tears Brad had been trying to hide.

"I'm sure she'll be okay," he said in a soft, comforting voice. "I'm sure they're taking care of her."

Brad didn't say anything. He only leaned over and put his head on Jason's shoulder and started to sob. This had to be about more than just a sick kid, unless there was more to her illness than Brad had said. Either way, the pain in his eyes and his cries broke Jason's heart. He wrapped his arms around Brad's trembling shoulders and held him as tight as he could.

WHAT Jason didn't know was all Brad's sobbing and pain and fear didn't end with his daughter being sick in the hospital; rather it was the culmination of everything he'd been going through and kept going through. Granted, most of it was self-induced, but stressful all the same. Something had to give. He had to come to a conclusion to fix all of it before someone had a breakdown.

The sedan skidded to a stop right outside the emergency room entrance. They both bolted straight out of the car and met somewhere on the walkway leading up to the glass double doors. Without really putting much thought into it, Brad reached down and grabbed Jason's hand, nearly dragging him by the arm. The doors ground open and Brad only waited until he had enough space to squeeze them both through before he charged down the corridor until they reached the information desk.

"My daughter," Brad panted. "Hope Britt. She was brought in tonight."

The woman behind the counter clanked her nails against the keyboard and Brad clenched Jason's hand tighter. Whatever she was looking at, it wasn't feeding her information fast enough. Every passing second made Brad's blood pressure and temper rise. His foot beat against the linoleum. Why wouldn't she hurry? Why didn't she know where they'd taken his kid?

"Ma'am, can you—"

"I'm hurrying," she barked. "These damn computers only go as fast as they want to."

"Calm down," Jason breathed against his ear. "She's doing the best she can."

Brad clenched his jaw and closed his eyes. He took a deep breath then slowly let it go. He was now gripping Jason's hand so tight, his nails were biting into his own palm, but the slight pain of it seemed to anchor him almost as much as his lover's voice.

"She's in ER-4, Mr. Britt," the woman finally said. "Just go down this hall." She hefted her rotund ass from her seat and pointed around the edge of the desk. "It'll be on the right."

AS BRAD took off, dragging Jason behind him, Jason managed a quick, "Thank you," and quickly beat feet to keep up. His heart thumped ninety to nothing, banging against his chest cavity and pounding in his head. They charged down the off-white corridor, each footfall hitting the linoleum hard and echoing against the sterile walls.

Then suddenly, Brad stopped and standing in front of him was a tall, slender, incredibly beautiful woman with long blonde hair and bright blue eyes. She looked so prim, so proper and elegant, even in yoga pants and a sweatshirt. Her cheeks were rosy and the rims of her eyes were red. She held a crumpled tissue up to her pouty lips. And as soon as she saw Brad, her tears erupted again.

"Where is she?" Brad asked.

"The doctors are with her right now," she said as her eyes darted over to Jason. "They told me to go to the waiting room until they called my name."

Brad let go of Jason's hand and he went to the woman. His arms wrapped around her shoulders and he pulled her into a tight hug. Jason swallowed the knot in his throat as his eyes cast away from them. It was rude to watch, but more gut-wrenching to go through. He didn't want to watch Brad holding his wife. Selfish, maybe, especially considering the circumstances, but it didn't change the way Jason felt. And what made it worse, Brad seemed to completely calm down the moment he had her in his arms. Why hadn't Jason given him that comfort?

"I'll be in the waiting room," he said, thumbing over his shoulders toward the double doors they'd just stormed through. Neither of them acknowledged him, and for a second, he wondered if he'd even said the words aloud or if they'd only filtered around in his brain, desperately hoping to leave his lips.

He turned and started down the hall, head hanging a little lower, shoulders a little more slumped. Maybe this was wrong, loving a man who had a family of his own already. Maybe he should've let it go. No matter, now wasn't the time. He would quietly hang in there for now, then do the right thing when this was over. He would do his best to let go of Brad. He would do his damnedest to let the reporter go without a fight. That was the right thing to do, right?

In the waiting room, televisions all buzzed with contradicting stations. One played cartoons for a little girl spread out on a bright pink blanket in the floor. A group of people surrounded a TV playing one of those awful talk shows where people yelled and fought and no one could really understand a word of it.

Jason sighed as he padded over to a lonely corner, far away from the grieving, worried, and sickly. He sat down and laid his head back against the wall, arms crossed over his chest. He had a nagging feeling he should've just stayed at the wedding. Maybe then he wouldn't feel so devastated and helpless. He wouldn't feel so selfish.

41

"THEY'RE saying it might be some sort of infection in her intestines. I... I don't know," Melody managed to say before the tears choked her voice again. "They want more tests."

"I'm sure everything will be okay," Brad offered, smoothing his hand up and down her back as she laid her head on his shoulder. His cheek pressed to the crown of her head. The scent of her coconut shampoo made the sterile stench of the hospital a little less nauseating.

"Was that him?" she asked softly without raising her head.

Brad's body tensed. He'd all but forgotten about dragging Jason through the hospital. He turned his head, hoping to find his lover waiting behind him, but Jason wasn't there and he had no clue where he'd gone. His stomach knotted.

"Yeah, it was," he whispered, voice wavering with fear and uncertainty. "I didn't mean for you to meet him like this. I'd hoped...."

"It's not your fault." She finally raised her head and their eyes met. Hers were cracked and watery, tired and full of pain. "I... would like to meet him, if that's... okay."

Brad frowned, swallowed again and slowly nodded his head. "Then you'll meet him. Do you mind if I talk to him first? I'm sure this has been hard for him, being dragged into this situation."

"By all means, please. I... I don't want him thinking I hate him or... whatever." She gave him a tight-lipped half smile as she let her arms fall away from his waist. She took a step back. "I'll wait here for the doctors if you want to go check on him."

"Thank you," he said softly, stepping away from her. His gaze lingered on his wife, taking in the changes she'd gone through in these few months. The pain he'd caused her was now written in wrinkle lines and dark rings around her soft blue eyes. He'd caused it all. He'd sucked the life and youth out of her beautiful face, and he knew no matter how hard he tried, he would never be able to make it right again.

With a sigh, he made an about face, then pressed on through the double doors and into the waiting room. As his eyes scoured the populated side of the room, he reached both arms behind his head and both hands fisted in his hair, pulling the thick locks tight into his fingers because the pressure somehow made his head stop pounding. He didn't see Jason and worried he'd given up and gone home. He turned toward the coffee maker, and that's when he spotted his handsome lover.

For the first time since he'd left the wedding, Brad had a reason to smile. Jason looked relaxed. His eyes were closed and his arms crossed over his chest. He'd loosened his tie and unfastened the first few buttons of his shirt.

Brad's arms dropped to his sides as he made his way to the quiet end of the waiting room. He stood there for a long moment and Jason didn't so much as open his eyes. "Resting?" he said softly so he wouldn't startle him.

"No. Just thinking." Jason lifted his head and looked up at Brad. "How is everything?"

"No word yet." Brad took the spot beside him. He laid his arm on the rest, palm up, fingers curled. Yes, he knew what he was doing. And no, he didn't give a shit who saw them. He had more important things to worry about right now.

Jason looked down at his hand, then up at his eyes and frowned. "What's this?"

"I want to hold your hand."

"Why?" Brad's eyebrow quirked, rising to a high arch and wrinkling his brow. "I mean, aren't you worried about...?"

"Not really. I'm more worried about my daughter and my wife... and you." Jason laid his palm against Brad's, their fingers lacing together, renewing the bond they'd had since the moment they'd realized they had feelings for each other. "Melody wants to meet you. She wants to be properly introduced to you."

AND those were the last words Jason had ever expected to hear. "What? Why?" he said as he bolted upright in the uncomfortable plastic chair. His eyes widened, shifting back and forth from the double doors to his lover, then back again. "Why does she want to meet me?"

"She just does. I told you, she's accepted what I am and... I don't know why. I guess it's what she needs for closure, or maybe she still wants to make sure I'll be a part of her life and since you're a major part of mine.... Will you meet her, please? For me?"

"Yeah, that's fine, but is this the right time? Is this the best place?"

"Let's wait to see what the doctors say. Right now, she's a little on edge. We both are and Hope is—" His voice abruptly cut off, eyes turning glassy. His fingers tightened around Jason's hand. "I need to know my daughter is going to be okay. I can't even think straight at the moment."

"Of course, she should be your first concern."

And though they both agreed to wait on awkward, formal introductions, the person walking through the waiting room doors apparently had something else in mind. Brad's wife looked over at them and gave them a soft smile. She gracefully glided toward them. Her tennis shoes didn't even squeak, she took such light, dainty steps. She sat down next to Brad, legs crossed, hands clasped together in her lap and her back straight as a board, like she'd been sent to one of those snobby, formal etiquette schools.

"Any news?" Brad asked as his free hand reached for hers. Jason couldn't have felt more out of place, and he would've pulled away if Brad hadn't had such a firm grip on his hand.

"No. She's sleeping. They're keeping her hydrated through an IV. Her temperature is slowly coming down now."

"That's good. We'll be able to see her when she wakes up, right?" The woman nodded. "Um, Melody, I would like you to um...." Brad swallowed, squeezing Jason's hand a bit harder. Jason could see the faint beginnings of a fine sheen of sweat on the reporter's brow. Maybe it had been there the entire time. Maybe it was from the running. "This is Jason."

She immediately offered her hand, keeping her polite smile nice and believable. Jason truly wanted to like her. He wanted this to go well for all of them, mainly so Brad wouldn't have any problems seeing his daughter whenever he wanted, and honestly, Melody looked like the kind of suburban bitch housewife who would try to keep him away from his kid out of spite.

He took her hand and gave it a gentle shake. She said in a soft petite voice, "It is a pleasure to finally meet you. I only wish we'd met under better circumstances."

Jason didn't know what to say. He never really expected this day to come, even though Brad had mentioned them meeting several times before. "It's nice to meet you too," he finally managed to say. So there they were, all holding hands in an awkward semicircle, Brad—the shared love—between them. How much more uncomfortable could one situation get?

"You should come to dinner one night," Melody said.

And that little invitation gave new meaning to the word "awkward."

"I would be honored," Jason blurted.

"We'll do that once Hope is well," Brad interjected. "I would like Jason to meet her when she isn't under the weather."

"I agree," Melody said.

Jason silently sat there with his lips pressed tight together. He felt like he'd entered the freaking Twilight Zone or something. How could she not be completely outraged? How could she be so calm about meeting the man her husband cheated on her with? Christ, if Jason had been the one on the screwed side of this scenario, it would've taken everyone in the room to keep him from clawing the screwer's eyeballs out. Yet there she sat, completely at peace and almost angelic. Maybe that's what made Brad love her.

Shit.

"You okay?" Brad leaned in and whispered.

"I'm fine," Jason mumbled.

And before things could get any weirder, the silver-haired doctor popped in through the door and called Brad and Melody's names.

They both popped up from their seats, Brad still holding everyone's hands. Jason tried to let go, but his lover's fingers had taken control of the situation and his mind had yet to send the release order down his arm.

"Brad," Jason said. The reporter looked back and Jason nodded at his hand.

"Oh, sorry. I'll be right back."

"I'll be right here."

He watched as Brad and his wife followed the doctor down the hall. As soon as the doors blocked his sight, he leaned his head back against the wall and closed his eyes. In a way, he was glad they were both gone again. He just needed a second to wrap his head around what had just happened. He needed a moment to make sure he hadn't really stepped off into the Twilight Zone. Sure, he'd heard stories about wives accepting shit like this, but he'd never seen it in real life. He figured it was all Hollywood bullshit, made up to make things this fucked up look at lot easier than they really were.

"Excuse me," a soft, almost nervous, voice said. "I hate to bother you, but was that Bradley Britt?"

Jason peeled back an eyelid and what he saw made him raise his head. He'd seen that pixielike face before, though he couldn't quite place it. If it wasn't for the Adam's apple bobbing in the kid's slender neck, he would've sworn the dude was a chick. He had the tiny waist and the curves, had the long legs and dainty arms. He even had black hair down to his ass and plump, pouty lips. Now, why the hell wasn't he working at Sin & Seduction?

"I'm sorry," the kid mumbled. "I'm being a pain in the ass."

"No. You're fine." Jason raised his head and sat back up in the chair again. "Where do I know you from?"

"I don't... um...."

"I know your face."

The kid shrugged. "I'm trying to be a dancer."

"At Sin & Seduction, maybe?" His little dark eyes grew wide and his pink lips curled. "That's what I thought. What's your name, kid?"

"Jordon."

"Did you have a stage name?"

"No."

"Right. They never do."

"You didn't answer me."

"About what?"

"Was that Bradley Britt?"

"Why?"

"I thought he was straight."

"He is."

"No, he isn't."

Jason arched his brow and tilted his head. The kid had some major cojones, thinking he could just walk up and randomly bust someone out like that. "What makes you think he's not?"

"Are you?"

"That's not the question here."

"I saw him at Sin & Seduction, watching the dancers."

"He was doing a story."

"I saw him with you in the alley."

"He's a friend. He was having a bad night."

"I saw you holding his hand just now."

"What are you, a stalker or something?"

"No. Not really." The kid lowered his head and all that long black hair fell around his face. "I'm a photographer, amateur. Just like I'm an amateur dancer and amateur writer and—"

"I get the point."

"So is he…?"

"What? Gay?" Jordon nodded his head. "You have to ask him, kid. We're just friends." God, he hated having to lie like that. Jason sighed, propped his elbows against his knees, steepled his arms, and clamped his hands together under his chin. "His kid is sick. He's stressing out right now, so do me a favor and leave him alone. And those pics you have of him, get rid of them, please. A very dangerous man was about to come looking for you. Got it?"

"Yeah. I got it." The kid didn't bother looking back at Jason, but he didn't move from his seat either. Jason just wanted him to go the hell away. He wanted to sit alone, enjoying his solitude while his thoughts chipped away at his sanity. Was that too much to ask?

42

"THEY'RE letting her go home." The sound of Brad's voice made Jason's head shoot up from the wall. His eyes widened instantly, but he couldn't really focus on one single person or object. Shit. He'd dozed off. And what happened to the stalker? "You okay?"

"Yeah." Jason let out a long yawn, mouth stretching as wide as it could. He rubbed his palms over his eyes. "What time is it?"

"Just after one in the morning. Sorry you've been here so long."

"No," Jason said as he stood from the uncomfortable plastic seat. He twisted his spine right, then left. All the vertebrae snapped right back into place and he groaned. "It's okay. How is your daughter?"

"She's fine now. Bacterial infection. They're sending her home with a prescription."

"That's good. I mean, going home and all." Brad reached down to touch his hand and Jason immediately pulled it back. "You might not want to do that. You have a stalker."

"A what?"

"Curious George, the one who took the pictures, he was here tonight."

"How do you know? Did you talk to him?"

Jason nodded. "Yeah, he asked if you were gay."

"What did you tell him?"

"That you're not." Jason frowned. "That's what you wanted me to do, right?"

"Yeah. You did fine," Brad said, but he suddenly looked flustered, distracted even, like that wasn't what he wanted at all. God, he sure did have a way of confusing the shit out of Jason sometimes.

His hand clamped down on Jason's shoulder. "I'm going to go home with them tonight, help Melody take care of Hope. Thanks for taking care of that mess. We'll… figure it out, okay?"

"Okay," Jason nodded, faking a smile though he was really falling apart inside. God, how could he be so selfish? Of course Brad would choose his family over a fuck. "Call me tomorrow, okay? I'll be home. The deli is closed this weekend for renovations."

"I promise to." Brad's eyes shifted around the room, like he needed to know no one was listening in and no one cared what they had to say. Then his gaze settled on Jason again. "I love you. I'll call you tomorrow."

"I love you too," Jason managed to get out before Melody called her husband's name. She had their daughter in her arms, and despite the bundle of pink and baby, she took time to give him a courteous wave and a genuine smile. Christ, the woman really was a freaking saint.

As they left the hospital with their bundle of joy, happy and almost healthy in their arms, Jason's gut felt like it had been ripped apart, shredded, and discarded like yesterday's hot fad. He felt like a novelty that had finally lost its appeal. And there he was, being selfish and whiny and overly emotional again.

He stepped out of the hospital and into the New Orleans night. The Brooks Brothers suit he'd been in all day had finally started to wrinkle. He didn't even want to venture a guess at his hair. Fuck it. He wasn't going home, not now. Not alone. He didn't give a shit how late—or rather, early—it was. Home wouldn't work. Not right now.

Waving one hand in the air to catch a cab, he shoved the other down into his pocket to fish out his phone. He scrolled through his contacts until he found Lance's number. For a second, one split second, he debated on not calling him, on just going home and getting some damn sleep so he would be nice and rested when he saw Brad again. But the little red devil on his shoulder demanded something else. It didn't want to be alone, especially when Bradley Britt had someone he could curl up with and cuddle with and love on. Why should he have to suffer alone?

The phone rang as a cab pulled to the curb. He climbed inside to the sound of club music and Lance screaming over the mix. "Where are you?"

"Sin & Seduction," Lance yelled back. "Where are you?"

"Leaving the hospital."

The club mix gradually quieted. He heard a door slam. Then Lance said, "Did you say hospital? Oh my God, are you okay? Is everything okay?"

"Yeah, I'm fine. It wasn't me. It was... never mind. You gonna be around for a while? I thought about going out for a bit."

"Sure. I can wait for you. You headed this way now?"

"Yeah. As soon as the cab can get me there."

43

SEVEN hours passed and Brad never left his little girl's bedside. Her breathing had remained nice and steady, soft cooing sounds came every few minutes. The rhythm had become a calming lullaby, and eventually, it'd put him to sleep in the glider beside her.

Melody parted the pink curtains. Sunlight spilling in and interrupting the darkness finally woke him. He sat up and twisted his body until the kink popped out of his back. His baby girl's eyes were still closed. Her tiny hands balled into fists. He stood from the chair to peek over into her crib. His little angel. The one perfect thing in his world.

"Sleep well?" Melody asked in a low voice.

"Not really, but it was worth it to be so close to her."

His wife brushed her hand over his back as she stood beside him. For a moment, things felt real, like they had the day the young couple brought their newborn home from the hospital. They felt like a family again. But even as he stood there enjoying the little life they'd created together, he couldn't stop thinking about Jason, the man he'd met by accident and fallen in love with through chance. A surreal, magical sort of bond he'd never really felt with anyone else before had formed between them, a bond he would never again try to deny.

"If you wanted to shower and change…," she offered.

The black suit he'd worn to the wedding yesterday still had most of its finely pressed creases. He'd hung the jacket on the back of the bedroom door and lost the tie as soon as they'd gotten home, but putting little Hope to bed and staying by her side had been far more important than his personal comfort. So the rest of the suit stayed on.

"I might do that. I should probably try to call Jason. I know it's early, but I know him and he probably didn't sleep at all last night."

"Go. Call him. Then get a shower and get comfortable. I'll make some breakfast."

"Thank you," he said as he leaned down and kissed her cheek.

Brad went straight to their bedroom, right over to the dresser. He pulled out one of the drawers and gathered a fresh change of clothes, something comfortable to lounge around in. He'd planned on spending the day with Hope then meeting up with Jason later that night.

When he raised his head again, he caught a glimpse of himself in the mirror and he didn't like what he saw: the dark circles and tired eyes, the wrinkles that had never been there before, the sickly hue of his skin. All the worrying, the stressing over his lover, his wife, his child, and his secret, it had a price and his body paid the toll.

He sat down on the edge of the bed, fished his phone from his pocket, and punched in Jason's number. The phone rang and rang, but his lover never answered. Just as well. If Jason had managed to sleep, Brad sure didn't want to bother him. Maybe he would try again after his shower.

He padded over to the bathroom and stood there silently debating the giant Jacuzzi tub, a hot soak to ease his achy muscles, or a shower to waken his tired soul. Honestly, neither of them sounded as appealing as crawling into bed with Jason and curling around his lover's body while they slept the day away.

And with that, he chose the shower. He would be no good to his family if he walked around like a zombie all day.

Hot watered rained down from the showerhead. He pitched his suit into the corner, wrinkles be damned, then stepped into the tiled, confined space and closed the thick glass door behind him.

As soon as the heat hit his tense muscles, they started to loosen, and he felt like he could actually take a full, deep breath again. With his palms pressed to the tiles, he let his head hang loose under the spray. Water trickled down the nape of his neck, down his spine, and between his cheeks. The winding warmth tickled his ass in passing and only made him wish for Jason more.

God, to have his lover right there, naked beside him. To feel the toned, tight muscles against his palms. To feel the hard length of his lover's aroused cock in his hand. To have Jason's soft lips kissing his throat as their bodies pressed together. Heavenly. And the thought tightened his sac, made his shaft start to thicken. He wished he had Jason there, wet from head to toe, ready to please him in a way only he could. Physically. Emotionally.

Brad groaned as he wrapped his hand around his shaft. As he tightened his fingers at the base, every synapse in his brain fired up, sending pleasant little jolts of sensation through his body. Every nerve ending came to life, begging to be stimulated as his hand rode down the veiny length of his aroused cock.

Did he lock the door?

Would Melody walk in and find him jerking off in their shower?

Did he care?

Actually, the threat of exposure didn't make his phallus retreat. It actually hardened more. He felt like a pubescent teenager again, hiding in the bathroom and beating his stiff willy into submission over the toilet before his parents found him. Only the older, more refined Brad could appreciate the excitement of the situation.

His fingers waved, tightening and loosening as they rode up and down the length of his shaft. Tip to base, then back again. He could almost feel Jason's body, the ring of muscle and the warmth, gripping his cock. He could almost hear Jason's voice, begging and moaning as they came closer to release.

How the hell he ever thought he could deny that man was a mystery. Everything about Jason turned him on. Hell, just thinking about his lover had him jerking his shit in the shower.

His sac pulled tighter to his body. The throbbing became so intense it made his thighs quiver. The pulsing spilled into his shaft, making it grow thicker and thicker. Pressure built in the base of his spine and heat shot down his back. A growl rumbled in his chest and a thick, pearly explosion erupted from the head of his cock.

"Fuck. Me!" he cried out as his fingers gripped the tiles and his neck turned to Jell-O.

He took a few short, ragged breaths as he let himself collapse against the wall. The cool tiles felt so damn good against his hot cheek. He released his spent sex with a smile.

Brad finished his shower with a newfound zeal. He soaped his arms and legs, cleaned every inch, head to toe. Then he climbed out of the shower and dried his body enough so he wouldn't track wet spots through the bedroom and across the off-white, high-end carpet.

He grabbed his phone from the dresser, sat back down on the edge of the bed again, and hit redial, hoping this time Jason would answer the call.

Oh, someone answered, but that wasn't his lover's voice on the other end. "Who the hell is this?" he growled, gripping the phone tighter.

"Lance. Who the hell is this?"

Brad's heart sank. What the fuck had happened overnight? Why was Jason with Lance? Did he somehow screw up? Was Jason mad at him about something?

"It's Brad," he bit out, jaw clenching.

"Hang on. I'll try to wake him up."

The silence was deafening, or maybe more maddening. It gave him time to build a collection of what-ifs and self-doubt. Maybe he hadn't been the kind of lover Jason needed. Maybe he'd been kidding himself this whole time. Why would Jason look for someone else if his needs were being met? Obviously, they weren't.

"Hello?" Jason said in a gravelly, sleep-filled voice.

"I...." He didn't know what to say at first. Handle the situation with kid gloves or come out with both barrels blazing. All he could manage was a quiet, "Why?"

"Why what?"

"I thought we were okay now?"

"Okay, I'm awake enough to know you're not making any sense. Please don't make the hung-over man think too much."

Hung over, huh? That explained so much and not enough all the same. Now Brad was mad, mad as hell even, and he let that rage fill his voice as he barked, "Did you fuck him again?"

THE lights in Jason's noggin all came on at once in a blinding epiphany. He bolted straight up on the couch. "No! God, no!" Though he knew why Brad would think that. "I didn't want to go home alone so I went back to Sin & Seduction. We drank until the place closed, and I couldn't get a cab back to the house. Lance's apartment is right behind the club so I went to his place and crashed on his couch." Silence. Jason sighed. "Nothing happened, I swear. I'm only with you and I only want to be with you."

He scrubbed a shaky hand over his face as he listened to the sound of Brad's labored breathing on the other end of the phone. He couldn't tell if his lover's anger had started to subside or if his explanation of last night only pissed off the reporter more, and he wouldn't dare say another word until he heard Brad's voice.

"I'm sorry," Brad finally said. "I assumed—"

"Don't assume anything. You have to trust me. I love you and wouldn't do anything to hurt you."

"I know. I just.... If it was anyone other than Lance, I wouldn't have freaked."

And Jason could certainly understand why. He deserved that. He really did. "I'm about to leave. I slept in my suit last night, and I really need a shower and a change of clothes. What are your plans for today?"

"Spend the day with the family, but I want see you. I need to see you."

Damn, that was good to hear. Jason needed him too, more than he'd ever admit to in front of anyone else. "Then later, we can...." Go out for dinner was his first thought, but wouldn't that be a no-go?

Wasn't going out in public still off limits? "I guess you can go to my place and we'll order take-out or something."

"Sounds good. How about I call you before I leave?"

"Right. Perfect." Or not.

"You okay?"

"Yeah, I'm fine. I just want to go home and get a shower, maybe sleep in my own bed for a few hours. Hey, how is Hope doing?"

"She's going to be okay. She slept through the night with no problems. Fever's gone. We're going to see if she'll eat something."

"Good. I'm glad she's okay."

"Me too. So, I'll see you later, then?"

"Yeah."

"I love you."

"I love you too."

The call ended and Jason's phone slipped from his hand and landed between his legs. He propped his elbows against his knees, arms steepled under his chin. His head pounded and he felt like a wrung-out rag that had been soaked in vodka and beer and God only knew what else.

The cushion dipped down beside him. The smell of fresh-brewed coffee replaced the stench of day-old booze. He raised his head and smiled as Lance offered him a mug of hot java. "Thanks," he muttered before taking a sip. It tasted so fucking good and felt even better rolling down his throat.

"Everything okay?" Lance asked sincerely.

Jason nodded. "Everything's fine."

"I was worried."

"Me too."

"He wasn't pissed?"

"At first, yeah. He thought we'd fucked again, but I told him we didn't."

Lance laughed. "While I would've given anything for that, I don't mess with married men."

"Married?" Jason gave him a droll stare. "I'm not married. Wait, was that a stab at my moral fortitude?"

"Not at all. And yeah, you might as well be married, sweetheart. You two stay up each other's asses... literally." Jason glared. Lance pressed his palm to the air. "Not saying it's a bad thing, just an observation."

"I just wish we could be... I don't know... like a real couple. We can't go out on dates, can't hold hands in public. He's constantly checking over his shoulder. It's hard. It's fucking exhausting, honestly."

"So the honeymoon's over, huh?"

"Not even close," Jason drawled as he hefted himself up from the couch. He sat his mug of coffee down on the table then padded across the room to grab his jacket and shoes. "Look, I'm going home. I'll see you later, okay?"

"Be careful. You know I worry about you."

"Because you're a damn fool."

"Maybe, but that won't stop me from caring."

44

DINNERTIME came and went. Brad still hadn't called, hadn't shown up. Jason sat all alone on his lumpy old sofa, staring at a bare wall and an empty television screen. Honestly, he doubted he would see his lover tonight. Disappointing, but not surprising. Juggling two separate and completely different lives kept the guy busy, so Jason could at the very least be sympathetic. He could try not to be upset about it.

Brad loves me.

He'll be here as soon as he can.

I mean, c'mon, he has a sick kid to deal with and....

Damn, this internal dialogue was starting to get old. Jason sighed, cranked his head from side to side to loosen the tension in his neck as he stood from the couch, and started toward the kitchen for a beer. If he kept arguing with himself over the issue of his love life, he'd turn into a crazy person. He just knew it.

And just as he gave up on seeing Brad, he heard a solid knock at his door. "Come in," he yelled without asking who was there because he knew the sound of his lover's knuckles rapping against the wood.

"Sorry I'm so late," Brad offered as he stepped inside. The soft light of the room made Brad's tanned face look almost bronze, his lips a deeper shade of pink. It made his eyes look darker than normal, or maybe his lover just needed a break. He looked tired and worn down, but still handsome as ever.

Brad met him with a chaste kiss and a brief hug. "Melody and I were having a discussion about things and... well, it carried on a lot longer than I'd expected it to."

"Things?" Jason's brow quirked. "God, that was so nosey. I'm sorry."

"No. It involves you."

"Me?" He frowned. "Why would you two talk about me?"

"Because," Brad said as he took both of Jason's hands in his. He looked his lover straight in the eyes. "Today I made a decision that could easily cost me my career, and I need to know you'll support me. Melody is completely behind me and I just… I need to know you'll be there too, okay?"

"Okay."

"I'm going to do it. I'm going to come out."

Jason's eyes widened. "What? What made you decide that?"

"It's been coming. I just decided not to fight it anymore. I can't lie, Jason, having Lance answer your phone scared the shit out of me. I thought… I thought you'd given up on me, and honestly, I wouldn't blame you if you did. But I can't have that. So, that was the final straw, I guess." Brad guided him over to the couch and they both sat down. He didn't let go of Jason's hands. "Melody and I talked about it, since anything I do will affect her and Hope, and we both decided it was time. She's worried about me. I'm worried about me. You're not getting anything you deserve out of this deal. It's time for us all to be happy."

"That's commendable and all, but what if the station fires you? Do you have any legal recourse?"

"No, unfortunately not. I talked to that lawyer, Rebecca Chambers, the one I met at Jansen and Dorian's wedding. She said I could try to fight them, but in Louisiana, sexual orientation isn't protected under any antidiscrimination laws, and with the contract I signed with the station, they would be well within their legal right to fire me."

"Fuck."

"I know."

"So what will you do?"

"Rebecca says if they fire me, I need to make a big stink about it, get it out in the public eye. I say we quietly move away. Melody is prepared to relocate with Hope if that happens. I just need to know you're prepared to do the same."

"Yeah. Sure. I mean, I'll go wherever you want me to. I don't have anything tying me down here."

"Good. It's settled then."

"Brad, are you sure? I mean, it's a big step. Is this something you really want to do?"

"I'm absolutely positive. And Monday morning, I'm going to go into my station manager's office and have a word with him about this. I hope he understands, but I'm not going to let that job hold me back anymore. I need to be with you, and I need to know I'm giving you everything you need in a relationship. Right now, I'm not and I know I'm not. You deserve better."

Jason certainly agreed. "Okay." He nodded his head. "Then, I'll stand behind whatever you think is right."

"I think this the only *right* solution."

They exchanged a look of relief, like their fight had finally ended, though really, Jason knew it had just begun. At least this was a step to bring them closer together rather than continue to drive them away from each other.

Brad reached up and touched the side of Jason's throat, and instinct made him lean in until their mouths pressed together. He licked across the seam of Brad's lips, sampling the exquisite taste.

In that moment, everything felt right again. The future—their future—wasn't just some unimaginable abstract with no definition and no place to begin. Their future began right there—with a promise, with a difficult decision, with a kiss. The road would be hard traveled, but every bump, every twist and turn would make them stronger. And Jason couldn't be more ready for the journey.

WITH a dopy-eyed grin, Brad pulled back from the kiss but kept his hands on either side of Jason's neck. He pressed his forehead to Jason's and gave him a hint of a smile. It felt like the weight of the world had finally been lifted from his shoulders, like he could finally move on, be truthful with himself and everyone else. It felt like he could finally have the happiness and freedom he'd been chasing for so long but could never get his hands on. And he could rest assured he would have Jason by his side through it all.

"I love you so much," he said. He stroked his thumb over the hard line of Jason's jaw.

"I love you too. I'm glad you've finally found peace with everything."

"Me too." Brad dropped his hands then sat back on the couch, eyes closed as he brushed his fingers through his hair. "I'm glad the hiding will be over soon, even if it does end with me having to uproot my life. I'm just... tired of having to lie all the time." He turned back toward Jason, giving him a crooked half grin. "I'm just glad I won't have to do this alone, you know?"

"You never have to do anything alone, I promise."

"You don't know how good it is to hear that."

Jason climbed over to Brad's side of the couch, straddled his legs, and leaned down until their lips almost touched. A rush of excitement made Brad's heart flutter. The feel of his lover being so close, the warmth of Jason's body against his, made his cock jump in his pants. A soft purring sound rumbled up through his throat as he reached around to grip Jason's ass.

"You want me, don't you?" he teased.

"When do I not want you?"

"Mmm... I can't think of a time you didn't."

"I can't help myself," Jason said. "You're so damn sexy, every time I see you I think about stripping your clothes and bending you over."

"Why bend me over?" Brad smirked as he pushed their bodies up from the couch. Jason's back landed on the surface of the coffee table. Brad's knees hit the floor. The table had the perfect height to put Jason in the best possible position. "I think this will work just fine."

"Then why are you still talking?"

He reached up and hooked his fingers around the waistband of Jason's pants, pulling them down until his lover had nothing on but the tank top covering his chest, but as soon as Brad started undressing himself, Jason lost the top. He tore it over his head and tossed it to the side with Brad's immaculately starched dress shirt. With little effort, Brad had his slacks unzipped and pooling at his knees. His semierect cock sprang free, aching more and more the harder it became.

"Damn, it feels like forever since we've been able to do this," he said in a breathy rush as he wrapped his hand around his shaft and started to tug.

"It really hasn't been that—" Brad lowered his lips down over Jason's erection. His lover moaned, and if Brad hadn't had a mouthful, the sound might've made him smile.

His head bobbed up and down, up and down as he lavished the sensitive flesh of Jason's cock with his tongue. He kept the exact same rhythm with his hand, meeting stroke for stroke, making his shaft harder and thicker, ready for his lover's warmth. And God help him, every satisfied sound Jason made only excited him more. It took every bit of his resolve not to dive right in.

He tongued the firm ridge, licked down the underside of Jason's erection, swiping back and forth across the thick pulsing vein until he brushed the ginger-colored patch of coarse curls sprinkled around the base of Jason's hard-on. But he didn't stop licking. He continued downward over his lover's jewels, further down, laving the fine landing of soft flesh between Jason's sac and his warm opening.

Jason whimpered as his thighs spread wider. His legs hooked over Brad's shoulder. He lifted his ass enough for Brad's tongue to find the puckered skin it'd been aiming for. "Fucking hell," Jason rasped as Brad licked back and forth.

Brad teased him only because he knew how much Jason enjoyed the carnal game of their relationship. If Brad had his druthers, he would already be thrusting every inch of his cock into Jason's body. He was hard as rock and ready to take his lover, but Jason was still fairly new to playing bottom, and all this careful attention made the ring of muscles relax. It made the sex twice as intense and ten times more satisfying.

And just as Brad dipped his tongue inside his body again, Jason growled out a hoarse, "Fuck me!"

The power in Jason's demand made Brad's head bolt straight up. He'd never heard such rawness in his lover's voice, and holy shit, if it wasn't the hottest thing he'd ever heard. He brushed the drop of precum over his head, pulled it down until his fingers were wrapped around the base of his shaft, and aimed right for Jason's puckered bull's-eye.

Pushing his hips forward, Brad pressed the tip of his cock to Jason's ass. He eased into the ring of muscle as soon as Jason exhaled, and he watched as his lover's head rolled back and his tongue swept across his lips. The sight of it, the utter beauty of the moment of penetration, made the pulsing in his erection speed. It throbbed harder and harder as Jason's warmth sheathed his flesh.

He pulled back, the hard, sensitive ridge of his sex hanging at the ring of muscle for a moment. Jason moaned. His body tightened around Brad's shaft as his hands white-knuckled the edge of the coffee table. Jason raised his head, and the moment their eyes met, Brad thrust every solid inch deep into Jason's opening.

Jason let out another rumbling growl, eyes clenching tight as his head lay against the table. That's when Brad found his rhythm, pulling back and thrusting forward. In and out, stroking the tender nub in his lover's body as his sac slapped against Jason's perfectly rounded ass. The more his pace quickened, the louder Jason moaned and the closer Brad came to orgasming. He loved that sound almost as much as he loved the feel of Jason's warmth sheathing his cock.

"That's it, baby," he rasped, locking his hands around Jason's thighs. "Louder."

"Fuck! Faster!" Jason demanded.

The table squeaked and creaked as Brad pushed and pumped his thickened erection in and out of his lover's body. And on the last solid thrust, Jason roared out one hell of a satisfied sound as his hand locked over his own cock.

Pearly bursts of cum exploded from the head, painting streams of glistening heat on Brad's chest. The undulating pressure as Jason released waved over his shaft and made every nerve ending tingle. His sac drew tight against his body as he continued thrusting and plunging and prodding. Then suddenly, all the pressure that had built in his jewels rumbled down through his erection and exploded inside Jason.

45

THE weekend ended with a bang... or four. The coffee table. The shower. The kitchen. The bed. Nothing in Jason's apartment had been off limits once their libidos got involved. Fine with Brad. He hadn't been able to do anything like that in a very long time. In fact, the booth at Sin & Seduction had been the first risqué place he'd had sex since before he'd gotten married.

But the weekend came to an end and that meant facing the world, the life he had outside of his relationship with Jason, and this Monday was a very special day. This Monday would make or break life as he knew it.

That morning, he left Jason's place early and went home to shower and grab a suit. He wore one of the nicer ones, deep gray with a nice blue button-down and a tie that matched the suit perfectly. He slipped his feet into a pair of stylish leather loafers, combed back his thick blond hair, and hit his neck with a shot of cologne. He looked good, confident, ready.

As he stood in front of his boss's door, waiting to throw himself at the old man's mercy, he rocked back and forth on the balls of his feet and wrung his sweaty palms. And occasionally, when his nerves got the better of him, he would pace in a tight circle.

"Britt," his boss barked from behind the closed door. "Get in here."

Brad took a deep breath and brushed his shaky hands over his suit one last time. Unfortunately, all his nervous preparations—running his speech over and over in his head, smoothing out the few unnoticeable wrinkles in his suit, fixing his hair for the millionth time—wouldn't make the constricted feeling in his chest or the tightness around his neck any better. He reached for the doorknob and considered not saying anything, just letting the chips fall where they may. But wouldn't that make him a coward? Wouldn't doing something so stupid prolong everyone's misery?

One last deep breath then he stepped into his boss's office. The surly old man sat on the far side of the desk, closest to the window. His solid-white hair looked almost luminous with the early morning sun pouring in from behind him.

"Sit," he said, and Britt ass-planted in the first seat he could get to. "What did you need to see me about?" the old man asked without looking up from the stack of papers he'd been shuffling around.

At first, Brad couldn't even find his voice. His mouth moved, but nothing came out, not the first damn sound. He couldn't even hear himself breathing. Oh, but he heard the sound of his pulse pounding in his ears. It was almost nauseating.

"Britt!"

Brad nearly jumped out of his seat, and that didn't do a damn thing for his pounding heart. "Sorry," he somehow choked out. "I...."

"Well, get on with it. I have a station to run here."

"I...." He swallowed hard and took another deep breath. He could do this. He could do this. He met his boss's steely glare. He so couldn't do this. "I have a small problem."

"We all have problems. What's your point?"

"Well, I... Jack, I'm gay," he finally blurted, and something about saying the words, even without knowing the consequence, made breathing a hell of a lot easier. It made his pulse slow, and suddenly, his hands stopped shaking. He felt like freaking Superman now. "I've been seeing someone, and I wanted you to know about it from my mouth, not the rumor mill."

"What about Melody and the baby?" his boss asked. He actually looked up from what he'd been doing, though seeing his face didn't really help. He was pretty expressionless, emotionless, as though he didn't really give a shit about Brad's sexuality.

"She knows. We're working things out. She's not really okay with it, but she accepted it and she's standing by me while I work through this mess."

Jack leaned back in his chair, elbows pressed to the thick leather rests, arms steepled in such a way his fingers intertwined and his forefingers pointed to his pursed lips. Brad hated the way his boss seemed to be sizing him up. It made him want to look away, like he had something to be ashamed of, even if he didn't.

"So, who else knows?" Jack finally asked.

"I haven't come out to anyone, but there's a photographer lurking around...."

"A photographer!"

"Yeah."

"Well, what kind of snaps did they get?"

"I don't know." Brad hung his head a little lower. He stared down at his fidgeting fingers. "A hug. Maybe a kiss. I'm not sure."

"Alright." Jack's lips pinched tight and he nodded his head, just like he did every time he either had something huge to process or his brain had hopped aboard a thought train to some scary, out-of-the-way place. "Tell you what we'll do here, Britt. You keep doing the news. People like you. If pictures surface and the public goes nuts, if the ratings drop, I'll have no choice but to let you go. So I suggest you be on your best behavior at all times."

Brad's head rose and his brow curled. "You're not firing me?"

"No, but I suggest you keep your relationship on the down-low, you know?"

"Excuse me?"

"Keep it out of the public eye."

Now, that didn't set well with Brad, not one bit. The whole point of coming out was so he wouldn't have to hide from people. He wanted to be able to proudly hold his partner's hand as they walked through Jackson Square. He wanted to take Jason out to dinner and the movies, or whatever corny bullshit they wanted to do together, without having to be careful and watch for prying eyes.

What kind of integrity, what kind of backbone, would he have if he let Jack dictate what he could do in his private life?

"I'm sorry, Jack. That doesn't work for me." Brad stood up from the chair and said, "Consider this my official resignation."

"You're quitting on me?"

"Yeah." Brad nodded. "I think I am. My family and my partner are more important to me than this place is. We'll go somewhere else, somewhere that doesn't give a shit what I do in my bedroom."

"Good luck, kid. You'll need it."

"Maybe," Brad said, and he left, closing the door behind him, closing that chapter of his life.

46

"AND I'm Bradley Britt, reporting live from Jackson Square." Brad flashed his award-winning smile for the camera and the people of the greater New Orleans viewing area. The smile was completely genuine because those people—the ones who sat down and watched his broadcasts every night and every day—cared enough to voice their complaints after Brad hadn't appeared on-air. It took exactly one week for the calls and e-mails to flood the station. It took one additional day after for Jack to beg him to come back.

The lights died and the cameraman gave him a thumbs-up. It was the week before Mardi Gras, and the local businesses were gearing up for the insanity. He loved the pre-madness festivities, loved covering it and was damn glad he hadn't moved off.

Eventually, the pictures of him making out with Jason behind Sin & Seduction all those months ago had come out. Brad thought for sure nothing would save his ass then, but Jack surprised him. The way the station handled the scandal was priceless. His boss did this amazing editorial about a man's right to his private life and how the station didn't condone the violation perpetrated against Brad and Jason and even Melody. The kid who'd taken the pictures had dropped the story and abruptly disappeared from the scene. Everything was moving along perfectly.

"I think Hope wants her beignets, Daddy," Jason called from the van.

Brad's daughter had her arms around Jason's neck as she watched every move her daddy made. Melody stood beside him, grinning from ear to ear as she held her boyfriend's hand. Brad loosened his tie as he made his way toward them.

"It's the sugar," he said. "She's an addict just like me."

"And next, she'll be sucking down a pot of coffee a day," Melody teased.

"Maybe we should find a place to sit down and have a real meal," Jason said. "None of us have eaten. We've been shopping for hours, and frankly, my arms are hurting. Not that I'm complaining."

"Here." Brad held out his arms. "Let me have her."

Jason passed the toddler over to her daddy. "We could walk down to the French Market. There are places to get food there."

"Or we could go to Muriel's," Melody offered.

"That place is a little too nice for a kid," Brad said.

"How about you and I go to Muriel's," Melody's date finally spoke. "They can take Hope somewhere a little more kid friendly. How does that sound?"

"I like it," Brad said and Jason agreed.

"Okay." Melody smiled. "That's the plan. Do you want to keep her tonight or bring her back home?"

"Well, we finally got moved in and her room is all set up," Brad responded. "How about we keep her tonight and you two can have an evening to yourselves?"

"I like that plan." Melody leaned up and kissed Brad's cheek, then did the same for Hope. "I'll come get her sometime tomorrow."

"Sounds good."

As he held his daughter in his arms, with his partner by his side, Brad watched his soon-to-be ex-wife walk away with a man who seemed to make her completely happy, and he couldn't be more thankful for the way things turned out. There had to be a guardian angel out there watching over him. This was the kind of luck that won lotteries, the kind of luck Hollywood movies were made of. And never once did he dream things would work out this way.

"You okay?" Jason asked, and the sound of his partner's voice pulled him back from his daze. "You're awfully quiet."

"I'm perfect. Things couldn't be better."

Jason smiled. Brad wrapped one hand around Jason's while he held his daughter against his side with the other. They started walking away from Jackson Square, across Decatur toward Café du Monde. Even late on a Saturday night, the scent of chicory coffee and powdered sugar wafted up through the air. He looked over at Jason and said, "I don't think we can pass on beignets. What do you think?"

"I don't know." Jason twirled one of Hope's blonde curls between his fingers. "Does Hope want beignets?"

She bounced and squirmed in her daddy's arm. "Be-yay!" she declared and they both burst into laughter.

"Beignets it is," Brad said.

As they stepped onto the patio of Café du Monde, Brad couldn't help but think of how incredibly happy he'd found himself. Things started really rocky, but the journey led him right to where he needed to be. Everything seemed to be going well with every aspect of his life. He had the man he loved, and they had a nice place of their own. He had his daughter. He still had his job, and Melody had found her own happiness with a man who seemed really good for her.

Things were finally perfect.

How the story started

ALLISON CASSATTA

Sin &
Seduction

Bourbon Street
Blues Company

http://www.dreamspinnerpress.com

It all started with a dream that made her heart wrench and set of mesmerizing eyes that begged to be seen, and ALLISON CASSATTA the writer was born. A techie by trade, the daydreamer in her wanted to sail away from the mundane, while the hopeless romantic in her searched for the perfect love story. Many poems and short stories were written before her first attempt at a novel, and once that piece of her soul spilled onto paper, there was no stopping it.

She has an eye for the visually stunning and a mind that screams to bring that beauty to life. She gives her readers something they can feel in the depth of their hearts, creates worlds they can touch, and characters who become your best friend or worst enemy.

Born and raised in Memphis, Tennessee, big-city life was a rat race that kept her busy in her career. It took moving with her new husband to a sleepy Mississippi town to make her realize that dreams can come true, and did they ever. She found herself a published author. She found her perfect romance.

Visit Allison at

http://www.allisoncassatta.com

http://www.facebook.com/pages/Author-Allison-Cassatta/158938557051

http://www.goodreads.com/author/show/4417507.Allison_Cassatta.

Also from ALLISON CASSATTA

http://www.dreamspinnerpress.com

Also from DREAMSPINNER PRESS

Irreversible eRROR

Wolf Phoenix

http://www.dreamspinnerpress.com

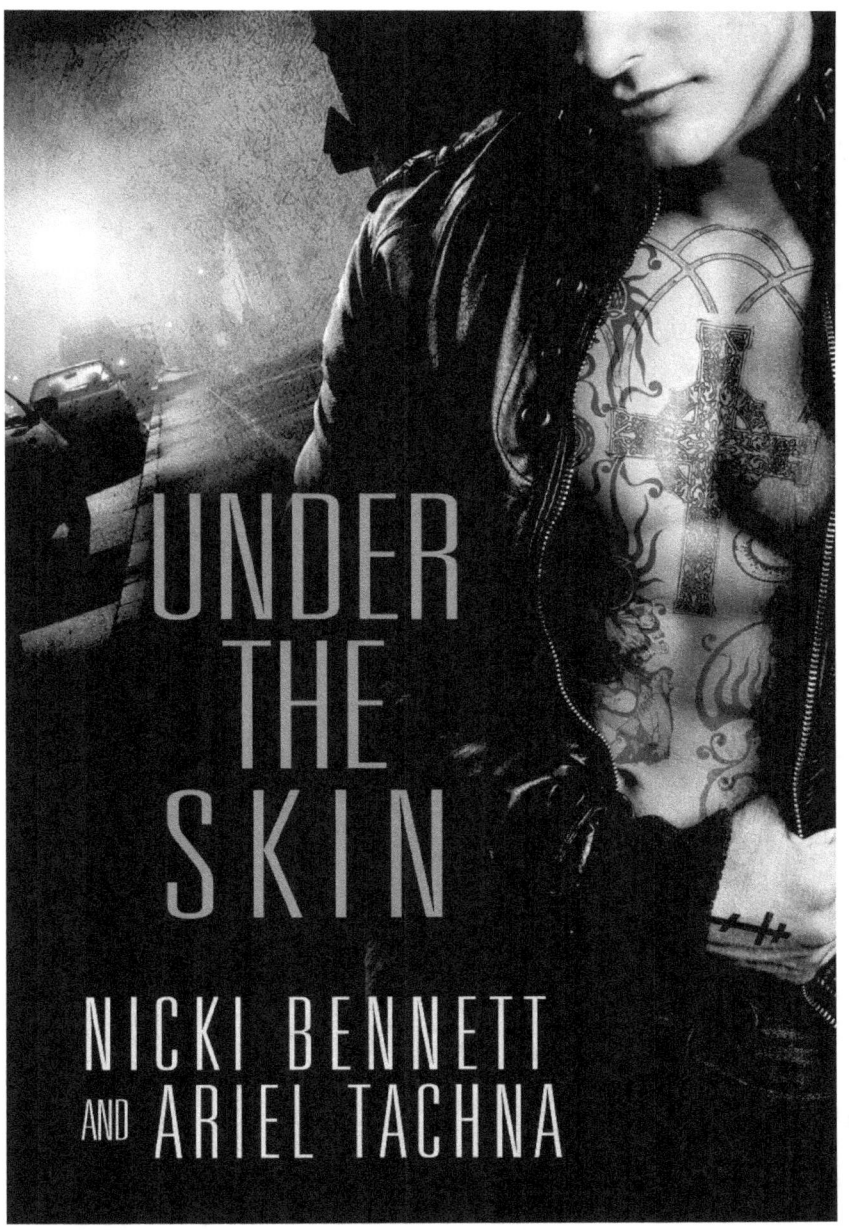